< Dirty Deeds>

<A Meg Malloy Mystery>

< by>

<Mark Terry>

High Country Publishers, Ltd
Boone, NC
2004

High Country Publishers, Ltd
197 New Market Center, #135
Boone, North Carolina 28607
<http://www.highcountrypublishers.com>

e-mail: editor@highcountrypublishers.com

This novel is a work of fiction. No character in this work is intended to represent any real person, living or dead, human or otherwise. Any similarity to any actual person or event is purely coincidental.

Library of congress Cataloguing-in-Publication data

Terry, Mark , 1964-
   Dirty Deeds: a Meg Malloy mystery / by Mark Terry
       p. cm
   ISBN1-932158-52-9 (trade pbk.)
1. Women computer scientists--Fiction. 2. Children of clerty--fiction. 3. Missing persons--Fiction. 4. Detroit (Mich)--Fiction. 5. Ojibwa Indians--Fiction. 1. Title
   PS3620.E769D57 2004
   813'.6--dc22

2003025931

First Printing May 2004
10 9 8 7 6 5 4 3 2 1

To My Wife Leanne . . .

As Always

Other Work by Mark Terry:

Theo Macgreggor Mysteries

Catfish Guru

Visit Mark Terry's WebSite

<http://www.mark-terry.com>

\<Dirty Deeds>

by

\<Mark Terry>

1

"Meg? Meg! Hellooooo! Meg! Earth to Meg!"

I punched off my CD player, Joan Jett's raspy voice dying in my earphones. Controlling a growl, I glared up at Steph from the glowing lines of code that marched across the monitor. "We're already behind schedule," I snapped. "You wanted this fixed by tomorrow. You've got to stop interrupting—"

"The Reverend wants to speak to you."

I turned my attention back to the computer screen, scowling. I closed my eyes and willed this entire mess away. When I opened my eyes the code still resembled alphabet soup and Stephanie Jones, erstwhile website designer and ISP co-owner, was still lurking expectantly over my right shoulder.

"What," I said quietly, "does he want?"

"I don't know. But he's the boss," Stephanie said.

Your boss, I thought. Not mine. I was merely subcontracting on this deal, helping a friend. Stephanie, in this case. Head of WebSpinners, Inc., a website design company. Co-owner of Chavez Technologies, Inc., a small Internet Service Provider. When Chavez Tech's servers crashed and burned I was the one asked to resurrect the corpse from the ashes. Of primary concern was the data that had been lost from the Missionary Church of Jesus Christ Evangelical's website. Almost everything else had been on disk backup, ready for Henry Chavez to restore. But not the database of contributions that had been made between Saturday's backup and Sunday afternoon's crash.

"Where is he?" I checked to make sure I was semi-presentable. Semi was about it. Faded jeans and a Mickey Mouse T-shirt, running shoes. My hair was washed and combed, I wore no makeup—rarely did—but I wasn't dressed for client contact. I told Stephanie this and she, acting like her panties were on fire, told me that I had to go in and talk to him right now, right now, *RIGHT NOW!*—he was her biggest client.

Stephanie, who was wearing navy blue slacks and a cream silk blouse, said, "Oh, thank you. He's in my office."

Glancing around the server room, no bigger than an average mausoleum, I went through a mental checklist to see if I could leave at this moment.

The keyboard and monitor were on top of a large desk similar to a drafting table, beneath which were half-a-dozen Dell servers, each one in matte black about the size of an overstuffed gym bag. More important, off to one side, were six APC power protectors that would kick in if we had a brownout, or God forbid, a blackout. Along the side wall was a stack of shelves containing the routers that looked like small VCRs except for the telephone lines that came in, literally hundreds of them, looking like tangles of long gray earthworms. The room was quiet and industrial-looking, the walls unadorned, the temperature kept at a nearly chilly 65 degrees. Henry had panic attacks if the temp approached 72.

I left the room, past Henry's office. Henry, short and stocky with dark hair shorn nearly to the scalp, looked up and rolled his eyes as I went by. This was Steph's seventh visit to me today, mostly to "Just see how you're doing." I wanted to kill her. I don't know how he did business with Steph.

With Stephanie right behind me, I left the small quarters that were Chavez Technologies—really an office, a bathroom, a kitchenette and the server room—passed through the entryway overlooking the stairs to the main floor, and pushed through the glass doors of WebSpinners, Inc. WebSpinners was a cubicle farm, a large open space with bright fluorescent lights, thick tan plush carpeting, walls of windows and pens made up of gray panel-board dividers. Whenever I saw a cubicle farm I thought: *veal*. Stephanie's office was in the back, and it wasn't a cubicle, it was a large corner office. She was the head veal chop.

The Reverend James Walker was pacing around Steph's office, looking far more agitated than he did during his televised church services. After Stephanie introduced us he politely steered her out the door and shut it behind her, but not before I could see anger and dismay twist her face. I wasn't quite sure how he managed to do that as smoothly as he did, but he was just as gracious as could be as he assured her he'd only be in here for a while.

This was the first time I had met him face-to-face. He was much taller than my five-four, probably six-one or two. Broad-shouldered, he had a profile that belonged on a coin and thick, luxuriously white hair that looked natural. His dark suit fit him so well it had to be tailored, as was his snowy-white shirt; the blue and white silk tie was off-the-rack, but if he picked it out himself he had taste. He turned to face me and I saw his blazing blue eyes were red-lined and puffy, with dark smudges beneath the lids.

"Megan Malloy," he said, his voice deep and carefully modulated. A professional public speaker, a preacher, a persuader, an expert at conversion and verbal manipulation.

I nodded.

He proffered a soft, well-manicured hand. Hesitantly I took it. "Stephanie said you wanted to see me," I said.

"Yes, yes." He hesitated, then sat in Steph's chair. "Please, have a seat."

I sat across from Steph's big cherry wood desk in a comfortable leather chair. A client chair, no high back, but it definitely was comfortable and definitely sent a message to the person sitting in front of the desk. It was a power desk, no doubt about it. Steph had gone from home office to the big time. Dressing for success with an office and attitude to match.

The Reverend Walker closed his eyes momentarily, as if in prayer. I tried to wait patiently, but it's not my strong suit. Finally he opened his gas flame eyes and said, "I understand your ex-husband is a private investigator."

My left eye twitched like it usually does when my ex comes up in conversation. To my credit I didn't burst out laughing or rip out my tongue. "Did Stephanie tell you that?"

"Yes, she did. She told me quite a bit about your background when she informed me she was going with an outside contractor. I wanted assurances about your discretion; if news of our crash got out, the congregation might lose faith in our fund-raising. I was very pleased that your ex—"

I snorted. "Reverend, my *ex*-husband is an *ex*-private investigator. He's an *ex*-computer programmer, an *ex*-teacher, an *ex*-systems analyst ..." I sighed. "An *ex*-computer salesman, an *ex*-website designer, an *ex*-efficiency expert. My *ex*-husband—the only *ex* he's ever been good at—had his mid-life crisis at the age of twenty-three and followed the big bang with ten careers in about seven years. Last I heard he's in Hollywood trying to be an actor. Before that he was trying to be a scriptwriter. Mitch has a short attention span."

Reverend Walker looked devastated, as if I'd just delivered the diagnosis of some terminal disease. Perhaps I had just answered his prayer, only the answer was *This number has been disconnected.* I took a deep breath and found myself feeling sorry for the man.

"Reverend, let me assure you, I'm very good at what I do, and I not only will be able to complete the forensic data recover quickly, I'll be totally discreet—"

When he looked up from his crossed hands I flinched and stopped talking. The look in his eyes was tormented. The look of a man who has seen hell firsthand. I paused, then said, "This isn't about the website, is it?"

He shook his head.

Hmmm. I took a deep breath, ready to plunge off the high board. "Maybe I can help you. During the period Mitch was a P.I. I acted as his partner—" Meaning I did all the work and Mitch slouched around his office pretending to be Bogart, sipping from a bottle of whiskey the walking cliche kept in his desk drawer. "—and I certainly know my way around information and computers."

Don't follow up, my little voice said. *Let it go. He's doubting you because you have ovaries. Screw him. Don't get involved. You do not need this.*

"Truly, Reverend," I heard myself say. "I can help. What's the problem?"

I made sure the door to Stephanie's office was locked, opened the polished cherry cabinet where Steph hid a Sony TV, VCR and DVD, and popped in the tape the Reverend handed me. No explanation. Just handing me a tape he pulled from a briefcase and, "You'd better watch this," in a flat, inflectionless voice, as if computer generated.

I pushed PLAY and sat down on the maroon leather couch to watch. After a few seconds of blank tape it started. There was a queen-sized brass bed with white silk sheets. Tied with lengths of rope so she was splayed to the four corners was a young woman. She had long dark hair, large eyes and high cheekbones. Beautiful, really. She wore only black panties.

I shot a glance at Reverend Walker. I have never seen such a look of horror on any man's face before. He was looking away from the TV screen, staring at a bookcase jammed full of manuals and textbooks on programming languages. Without looking at me or the TV he said, "My daughter Barbara."

I turned my attention back to the television. A man entered the room. He wore tight jeans and a white T-shirt and a ski mask. In one hand he carried a knife. He slowly approached Barbara Walker on the bed, every move filled with purpose and menace.

"No," she said. "No! Don't hurt me!"

The man in the ski mask laughed. His laugh was oily, low and dirty. Goosebumps crawled across my arms and I hugged myself, forcing myself to continue watching. He pressed the knife to her leg, slowly drawing it upward, not cutting her.

She sobbed. "No! Don't hurt me! I'll do anything! Anything you want!"

"Yes," the man said. "You will." He slid the knife under her panties and sliced them off her body. With one gloved hand he tore away the nylon, leaving Barbara completely naked.

She screamed, writhing against her bonds.

The man threw the knife aside, dropped his jeans and climbed on Barbara. While she yelled and tried to arch away from him, he raped her.

Abruptly the tape ended.

It took a moment for my stomach to stop churning. Something ... something in the back of my mind was calling out to me, but I didn't quite hear it. I stared at the blank screen thoughtfully.

Silence. The air felt electric, charged. The tape clicked, and kept on playing. I could hear the murmur of voices outside Stephanie's office. I wasn't sure what to say. Then my tongue began to wag, my brain moving through the shock to the heart of the problem.

"When did you get this?"

"This morning. Tuesday. It was in my mailbox. At the church. Rochester Hills"

"Could it have been left Sunday night?"

"No, I checked the mailbox last evening before I left. Monday." He licked his lips, his voice trembling like earthquake aftershocks.

"Do you still have the envelope it came in?"

"It was ... wrapped in brown paper. The label was ... computer printed."

"Do you still have it?"

He nodded and plucked it from his briefcase. There was no postage on it. I put it aside.

"How old's your daughter?"

"She just turned eighteen. August 18th."

"She in school?"

He shook his head. "She wanted a year off. She graduated from Rochester-Adams in June. She probably should have gone to Cranbrook. But I thought it would be better for her to go to public schools. We were hoping she would go to Harvard ... she has the grades and we can afford it, but she ... she wanted to take time off." I thought he might break down in tears, but he didn't. Instead he focused his gaze on me and I noticed again how blue his eyes were, like the sky on a hot, hazy summer day.

"Will you help me?"

"You should take this to the police if you think she's been kidnaped and ... and raped."

"But the publicity ... the risk to Barbara ..."

"The publicity might help. Has there been any type of ransom demand, any contact at all?"

"No! Not at all. What does that mean?"

Something was niggling at the back of my brain, something about the tape, but I couldn't quite snag it. It kept moving away like a nervous sunfish, nibbling at the bait but afraid to bite. "I'd like to keep the tape and the wrapping," I said, realizing I was making a commitment that I should probably avoid.

"You have to keep this quiet! No publicity. This kind of thing would destroy the church!"

I had no response to that. What was more important? The church or his daughter? It seemed odd, but then again, he was an odd man with an odd profession. "I'll have to show it to some people, but I won't tell who it is and the people I'll be dealing with can keep this to themselves."

"That means you'll help me. It means you ... *can* help me?"

Shit. "I guess that's what it means," I said. "I'll try."

"How much do you want for this? Do you have a fee?"

A good question. When Mitch ran Freeman Investigations he had charged three hundred a day. When I started CyberConduits, Inc. I had charged by the job, though it had become something like a thousand bucks a day until I sold the company for several million in cash and even more in stock over a year ago. I was working for Steph for a hundred an hour—she was getting a bargain.

I said, "Reverend, I prefer to work by the job. If I can find your daughter, you can pay me ten thousand dollars."

He momentarily blanched at the price. But I knew how much he was worth, and he only paused for a moment. His long-fingered hands pressed down on the cherry desk, his shoulders tensing. Lines etched into his forehead, then disappeared. He spun in Stephanie's high-backed maroon leather chair, a beautiful piece of furniture that went well with the rich cherry desk. He stared out the window. In the distance was a gray and blue-glass office building silhouetted against an azure sky only slightly marred by white wisps of cottony clouds. He spun back to me, his face and square jaw set in resolution. It felt vaguely like a performance, as if he were so used to being observed that he was always conscious of his reactions. After another moment's silence, almost a theatrical beat, he said, "You can really help?"

"I can try," I said. "I'll need more information, but if I can't find anything in twenty-four hours, I'll be able to recommend somebody to you. Possibly the police."

He closed his eyes a moment, probably praying on it. I tried not to make a face. He looked up. "Perhaps you're the answer to prayers."

I tried not to look skeptical. I'd grown up hearing that God worked in mysterious ways. If God worked at all, I'd observed, she definitely wasn't sharing the plan.

2

Having made a handshake deal, I followed the Reverend out the door of Stephanie's office. Steph was sitting in the nearest cubicle pretending to go over a site design with one of her employees. Very unconvincing, her body language all wrong. Steph jumped to her feet and spun so quickly toward us when we came out I thought she might be practicing for Stars On Ice!

Before she could say anything, Reverend Walker, voice in perfect control, stepped forward and grasped Steph's right hand while he rested his left on her shoulder. "Stephanie, Ms. Malloy will be helping me out with a few things. She assures me she'll have her job for you done without any trouble. I'm so glad you recommended her to me. Hope this won't be a problem?"

With a smile as stiff and brittle as year-old American cheese Stephanie said that would be just fine. With a nod to me and a, "Keep me updated," to Steph (and probably to me, as well), he made his exit. We politely followed him out. As soon as the glass door was shut behind him she turned to me, an arctic expression on her face. "In my office. Now."

No sooner had her office door closed behind me than Steph went Chernobyl. "What does he mean you need to do some *things* for him?! You're working for me, damnit. You can't just walk off the job without finishing it!"

"You're the one that said he was the boss," I said.

Steph's green eyes flashed. She stood behind her power desk, the better to intimidate me. "Don't do this to me, Megan. Do *not* screw me over on a deadline. Do not abandon me and take off to Maui like you don't have responsibilities. You promised me!"

That lit my fuse and it was a short one with a lot of charge at the end. "Who needs who here?" I mimicked her: "'*Do me a favor, Megan. Please, Megan, just a favor. It'll only take a few days. No one can do this as fast as you can—*"

"You're not finished!"

"'*Hundred an hour, in and out. Just a favor. We don't even need a contract.*' A simple forensic data recovery, you said. Then you started *tweaking* things, now was the perfect time what with the system being down anyway—"

"Stop it! Stop doing that! I trusted you!"

I was almost shouting back at her. "You can trust—"

"What computer work does Walker want done that only *you* can do? Huh? He's my biggest client!"

Was that what all this was about? Fear I'd take over her work?

"Steph, stop being so insecure. This has nothing to do—"

"I'm not insecure! I have responsibilities. People who depend on me. I can't just drop everything and do whatever I want—"

If she mentioned Maui again I was going to punch her. The pressure behind my eyes made me think lightning bolts were going to come shooting out of my pupils.

"—I can't trust anybody! This is my biggest account. It's bad enough the entire system crashed, but now you're running out on me, too!"

A red warning light flashed in my brain. "*Too?*"

But Steph wasn't about to get derailed from a really good rant. She slammed her fist down on the desk. "You're only here a couple days and you're already horning in on my clients. I can't believe you! You're my friend! I trusted you!"

I leaned toward her and snarled, "Sit down and shut up!"

Steph's eyes went wide. "You can't talk to me—"

"I said sit down! Do it before you say something you can't take back. *Now*, damnit!"

Stephanie plopped into her maroon leather executive's chair, looking shotgunned.

I stood over her, the big cherry desk between us. "One," I said, ticking off my index finger. "I am *not* doing computer work for Reverend Walker. I'm acting as an unofficial private investigator. Two, I'm two to four hours from a full retrieval of the church data. I can finish your other accounts by the end of the week—you said they weren't high priority. Any more improvements you can do by yourself. You're a perfectly capable programmer and you've got fifteen perfectly capable programmers on your payroll. Assign somebody to it as a priority."

"Fourteen," she said.

I ignored her. "Three," I said. "Point three. I want to know why in hell you told the Reverend about Mitch being a private investigator."

Stephanie suddenly looked uncomfortable. "I ..."

"Spit it out." I glared at her. "And don't you dare talk about me in the context of Mitchell Freeman to anybody ever again. He is out of my life. I am not an extension of his neuroses. Do you understand me?"

Tears flowed down Stephanie's cheeks.

"Oh for heaven sakes," I said. "Stop it."

She sniffled, reaching for a Kleenex. "I wanted you to take over because you're so good at forensic work. It was an infrastructure problem.

You're the best person for that. And none of us are good at data recovery. I told the Reverend—" She blew her nose and discarded the tissue, plucking another from the box. "I-I told him you were the best. But he's paranoid about image. He was worried if it got out the website crashed big time his parish ... parishioners wouldn't feel it was safe to use it. And it's making him a ton of money. He's syndicated to ninety-nine TV stations across the country. When his show is televised the lines just hum afterwards.I had to ... to con-convince him you were discreet. So I told him about the security work you did, and how you and Mitch worked the P.I. firm."

I sat down in the client chair and rubbed my forehead. Closing my eyes I pressed my fingers against the lids. I took a deep breath and stared at Stephanie. "I haven't wanted to ask. Where's Danny? Danny could have done this just as well as I could. I haven't seen him."

The dam burst. Tears spurted from her eyes and she wailed, "He's go-o-n-n-ne! Oh God, Megan. Danny's gone!" She put her head down on her desk and wept.

I shoved the Kleenex box closer to her, contemplating my next move. Danny Chen had been her partner, lover and best friend. Where Stephanie's real talent was website design, Danny's was programming. Steph could design a website that not only made customers feel it was safe to turn over their credit card numbers, she designed them so they were *eager* to turn over their credit card numbers. It had less to do with understanding computers than it had to do with understanding people's qualms about Internet business, and designing the site to allay those fears.

Danny, on the other hand, had been her first employee, a gifted programmer. He could take Steph's designs and program a rock solid foundation for them. And do it quickly. I had assumed he was out of town with clients. Steph had been more high-strung than usual, and the pressure to finish up was heavy, so all our time together had been in solving the problem, not going over our personal lives, such as they were.

"Why'd he leave?" I asked.

Steph looked up, wiping her eyes. "He-he just left."

Just left. Uh-huh. "Did you argue about something?"

"Well ..."

I waved a hand. "It's none of my business. When did he leave, though?"

"About two weeks ago."

I frowned. Steph and I had not discussed everything I had found while bringing the network back up. Not yet. "Steph ... maybe I do need to know what you two argued about."

"I don't remember ... not ... exactly. He wanted to ... to audit all our old websites ..."

Hmmm. "Audit?"

"He wanted to return to all the commercial websites we've ever designed and go over the programming."

A disquieting feeling ran down my spine like an electric eel. "Did he say why?"

"No. He just said he wanted to ..." She frowned, thinking. "I don't remember. I told him we didn't have time for that sort of thing. It blew up into a fight and he stomped out."

"Weren't you two living together?"

She shook her head, but didn't elaborate. I didn't know if they had ever lived together. Or if they were still lovers. I had been out of touch for a while.

Most—but not all—of my anger had cooled. "Steph, as far as I know, what the Reverend wants from me has nothing to do with computers. It's about his daughter. Look, I've got to do some things for him for the next couple hours, then I can finish up the database recovery from home later this evening. It'll be up and running for you tomorrow and if everything goes okay you'll be all set by Sunday."

"Okay." She hiccuped and sniffled.

"I've got a few questions, though. Why do you think the system crashed?"

Stephanie looked suspiciously at me. "It wasn't just a routine crash?"

I shook my head. "No. I haven't been able to prove this yet, but it looked to me like it was deliberately sabotaged."

"A virus?"

I frowned. "More like manually. A virus is too simple. Every server's hard drive was wiped. Deliberately. Whoever did it knew a fair amount about Henry's system." Like Danny, I thought.

"Could it have been done from ... outside?" Stephanie asked.

I shrugged. "I've been concentrating on the church's database, not the cause of the crash. I'm trying to track the bits and pieces I'm finding, but we're under a deadline, like you said. It's not my top priority to figure out what happened so much as to fix it."

She nodded. "I'm sorry ... I'm sorry about what I said to you. Will you ... will you finish up tonight?"

I nodded and got to my feet, headed for the door. I turned before I slipped through. "Steph?"

She looked up, her expression bleak. "What?"

"One more thing."

"What?"

"If you ever throw Maui in my face again our friendship'll be over. Understand? You don't know shit about Maui."

3

Henry Chavez waved me into his office as I stomped by. Unlike Steph's office, Henry's was bare-bones: three mismatched chairs, two that looked like they came from a card table, one a battered green director's chair that I think he'd kept from college. The desk was a folding table that supported a phone, laptop, laser printer and assorted Star Trek paraphernalia. There was a dusty spider plant dangling in one corner, a small bookcase containing computer texts and an ugly gray four-drawer filing cabinet. A cut-out life-sized poster of Mr. Spock gesturing to "Live long and prosper," was in another corner. Sunlight angled in through the single window and obliterated Spock's face with reflective glare.

"Going back to the warp core?"

Warp core was Henry's name for the server room. "Just to shut it down," I said. "Something came up. I'll finish later tonight from home."

Henry cocked his left eyebrow. "Steph happy about that?"

"Steph is having a meltdown," I said "If I had balls, she'd be threatening to cut them off."

Henry stared at me. Then he suddenly shut down the laptop. He stood up and buckled it into its case. "I think I'm through here for the day." He slung the strap over his shoulder. "I'll walk you out."

"You'd rather spend time with your wife and five kiddies than risk Steph's rage?"

"Damn right. I'm out of here. You coming or not?"

"Let me shut down."

"Hurry up."

I headed for the warp core.

Henry accompanied me out the front door of the three-story office building—gray concrete, horizontal rows of windows, a small parking lot lined with maple, birch and sycamore trees. Chavez Technologies and WebSpinners took up the second floor. The first floor was occupied by a small law firm, and the third floor was dominated by a media research company.

"How you like the Hummer?" he said.

"Handles like a tank," I pointed my remote in its direction and clicked. It came to life with a roar.

"It *is* a tank. What do you need that thing for, anyway?" He pointed to his ten-year-old Dodge. "My piece of shit gets me back and forth just as well."

"It's style, Henry," I said. "It's all a matter of style."

"I think it's a woman thing. Gotta prove you've got the biggest dicks." He winked at me. "You gonna finish up tonight?"

"The church's stuff, yeah."

"Good. Steph's losing it. Get that done, maybe she'll calm down."

"She's flakier than usual," I said.

"Yeah, well, maybe it's PMS."

"Your wife know you talk about women this way?"

"Where do you think I get it from? Hey, thanks Meg. Keep me posted. You found out what happened yet?"

I hesitated. "Not quite yet."

"Deliberately wiped?"

"I think so."

He blew out a stream of air. "Inside or ... outside?"

I bit my lip. "I'm not sure yet."

"Inside's trouble."

I nodded, thinking of Danny Chen, not ready to broach the subject until I knew more. "I'm not ready to make any statements about it yet, sorry."

Henry ran a hand through his short-cropped hair, looking worried. "Let me know when you do, okay?"

"Sure."

He climbed into his p.o.s. Dodge and I climbed into my flashy red Hummer, dropped the transmission into drive and headed in the general direction of Ann Arbor. I needed to see Glen Blalock. It had been a long time—probably not long enough—but Glen could help me out.

By the standards of civilized society Glen was certifiably insane; by the standards of the computer industry, he was about average. When he worked for me at CyberConduits we got along fine as long as what he wanted to do happened to converge with what I wanted him to do. Otherwise he did what he wanted and no manner of coercion—sweet-talk, threats, bribery—could convince him otherwise.

Now he lived and worked out of a red-brick warehouse in the older part of Ann Arbor, running his own business, Blalockubus, Inc., consulting to digital imaging companies worldwide, and irritating students and faculty at the University of Michigan every time he opened his mouth.

Late afternoon was not a good time to be crossing from Troy, above the city, past the airport to Ann Arbor. About six million commuters were on the move. I listened to "Fresh Air" on National Public Radio and tried to ignore the fact that I was alternating between five miles per hour and seventy-five miles per hour in seemingly random spurts and stops. Finally I made my way to the creepy section of town where Blalockubus, Inc. was situated, a dingy, dirty, industrial section of town, warehouses whose birth dates ranged all over the last century, many abandoned, a few converted to lofts and businesses, some still warehouses. Truck traffic was heavy, but civilians like myself seemed in short supply.

I parked out front of a stately red-brick industrial warehouse, two stories tall, all the windows on the top floor, which was where Glen's loft was. The front door looked like a slightly shiny black steel door, but when I approached, the surface of the door crystallized into a full-sized image of Mel Gibson. Mel said, "M&M? That you?"

I stopped, impressed. It looked like Mel Gibson but sounded like Glen Blalock. I said, "Can you superimpose Mel's voice?"

"Of course. How you doin'?" Mel Gibson said, flashing me a supernova smile that made my toes curl.

"Who else?" I asked.

Mel Gibson disappeared and Sylvester Stallone materialized dressed as Rambo, complete with submachine gun. "Yo, Megan. Wha's up?"

"Nice. How about ... Hmmm ..."

William Hurt flashed on the screen. "Okay," I said. "Woody Allen."

Woody Allen took William Hurt's place and stuttered, "What are you waiting for? Come on in, for Pete's sake!"

I shook my head. "Nope. I want to see Glen Blalock, please."

A dumpy toad of a human being with a wispy ginger beard and shoulder-length hair appeared. He was enthroned in a complicated black leather chair with keyboards all around him, a headset perched on his ears.

"No," I said. "I wanted to see Glen, not Mel Gibson."

Glen grinned. "I love you, darlin'. Come on in."

As I reached for the doorknob the image shifted so I was grabbing Glen's crotch. Ugh. I suppressed my revulsion and entered. In the entry was another screen. This time Pee-Wee Herman was pointing to his left. He smirked and gave his patented giggle. Twenty feet down a brightly lit cement corridor was yet another screen. Kathleen Turner pointed me through a door— "Sexy ol' Glen's that way." —sounding breathy and sexually charged. I pushed through another door to find Glen grinning happily at me from his command module.

"I got your e-mail," he said. "You're back in business, huh? What was that, about a year? All that money and you still couldn't stop workin'?"

"It's a long story, Glen. How've you been?"

"Hey, great! I'm just about to have dinner. You want a Dove Bar?"

"Hell yes! Is that your dinner?"

"Sure. I lost about twenty-five pounds on one of those high-protein, low-carbohydrate diets, but I was depressed the whole time. Now I'm trying a high-fat and sugar diet, see if I'm any happier."

Prozac and other mood stabilizers, I thought. Give it a shot, Glen. Knock yourself out.

He climbed out of the chair and crossed to a chest freezer and tossed me a Dove Bar. Weaving his way through piles of electronic equipment, Glen settled back into his chair. About five-eight, he probably weighed two hundred and seventy pounds. He wore a sweat-stained T-shirt featuring a Star Trek Borg—Seven of Nine—and baggy jeans.

"You like my door?"

"Impressive. Who did it?"

"Toshiba. I helped with the programming. Still trying to debug it, too. That flat screen might be your new computer monitor. Pricey, but you could have a whole wall made of the stuff and you'd never suffer eyestrain." He peeled the cover off his Dove Bar. "What can I do for you?"

I pulled the videotape from my backpack and held it up. "This is totally confidential. We clear?"

Glen crossed his heart with his Dove Bar. One thing about Glen, he kept his mouth shut. In his business you had to or nobody would let you test prototypes. "You know me," he said, mouth full.

I handed it to him. He glanced at it. "$8.99 at Walmart. What else you want to know?"

I peeled the wrapper off the Dove Bar and cocked my eyebrows at him. Sometimes silence was the best response to Glen's humor. I took a bite of the ice cream and almost swooned. It had been a long time.

"Okay, okay," Glen said. "I'm gonna burn it on a disk, okay?"

"Sure, as long as I take it with me."

"Yeah, yeah, yeah. What you got, government stuff here? Top secret shit? What's the big deal?"

He moved to an imposing tower of high-end electronica, popped the tape into a player, clicked on a digital monitor, tapped at a keyboard, popped a disk into a burner, brought his computer into line and started the tape.

I nibbled at the Dove Bar, watching the rape video for the second time. It seemed even weirder now. Something was definitely strange about it, but I couldn't quite figure what that might be. When it came to the end, Glen said, "What, no cum-shot?"

"No—what?"

He fast-forwarded through the tape to make sure there was nothing else on it, then handed it back to me. "No cum-shot," he said. "What's a porn tape with no shot of the guy, uh, ejaculating? Usually in the chick's face, though I've never really figured the appeal."

"Yuck. Me neither."

"Yeah, well, you never know what some guys'll go for, I guess. Must be that degradation thing you feminists are always complaining about. So ..." He finished off his Dove Bar, tossing the stick across the room into a large waste basket. "Two points," he said, arms raised in mock-cheer. "You in the porn biz now? That part of troubleshooting?"

"No. Why do you think it's a porn, uh, movie?"

"It's not?"

I shrugged. "I thought it was a tape of a rape."

Strapping on his headset, Glen turned his big chair toward the monitor, gesturing for me to have a seat in a chair nearby. Into the headset mike he said, "*Glen command one. Drive E play.*"

The drive light clicked on and Barbara Walker once again appeared on the screen. To me, Glen said, "Camera angle one, your establishing shot. From the foot of the bed, elevated. Not quite looking straight down, like they're shooting from a ladder."

I stared, seeing it now. Glen continued. "Angle two. There was a cut. Hold it. *Glen command pause.*" He tapped a key, then switched controls over to a trackball mounted on one armrest. The video image moved in reverse. "There," Glen said. "A cut to the second camera angle. See it?"

"Yes," I said. And I did.

Now the camera angle was on the doorway, a wide view, Barbara Walker still visible tied to the bed, but off to one side. The rapist flung the door open and entered, the door swinging shut behind him with a bang. The camera moved in closer on the rapist, filling the screen.

"Angle three," Glen said, and this time I saw the next cut. Suddenly we were back on the ladder, not as high, looking down over the rapist's shoulder. He was holding a knife on Barbara. She said, "No! No! Don't hurt me!"

"Back it up," I said.

Glen did, working the trackball. I watched Barbara closely this time, concentrating on her face and her eyes, looking to see if she was really afraid. No, I thought. She was acting. *Wasn't she?*

Another cut and a close-up of Barbara, filling the screen, the rapist's hand holding the knife, running it slowly up her leg.

Barbara sobbed. Or was she holding back giggles? "No!" she said. "Don't hurt me! I'll do anything! Anything you want!"

"Yes," the man said. "You will."

Another cut, an extreme close-up. The knife slid under her black panties and sliced them off her body, leaving her bare and exposed. The gloved hand tore away the nylon.

Another angle, backing off. Barbara screamed.

Another angle, wide. The man tossed the knife away, dropped his jeans and mounted her. The angle shifted again—we don't actually see penetration. Barbara struggled and tried to get away from him. The images ended as abruptly as they began.

I got up and tossed the remains of the Dove Bar into the wastebasket. "You're sure it's a porn movie?"

Glen shrugged. "Hey, do you think I'm an expert?"

I tilted my head and gave him my best skeptical look.

"Okay, okay. Yeah, I'm pretty sure. It's better than amateur stuff, very smooth, and it's been edited. Most amateur stuff will be a fixed camera or a moving camera with a little stutter to it, you know? Bunch of tracking shots, but the camera's not steady. This was spliced together—all the camera angles—but the quality's not a hundred percent, though shit, M, semi-pro's the name of the game these days what with the Internet being the number one market for it."

"You think this is an Internet porn movie?"

Glen shrugged. "Mighta been made for video."

"What else can you tell me—any details you could zoom in on?"

Glen tickled one of his keyboards and a grid superimposed itself on the monitor, then he started the rape scene again. Only he trackballed through it, the equivalent of a frame at a time. He froze it on Barbara lying spread-eagled on the bed. "Anything stand out to you?"

"No," I said. "You?"

"Want to check out the ropes on her wrists," he said, and lit up the part of the grid around her arms, then used the computer to isolate and enlarge. The resolution skittered away, leaving the image fuzzy. He fussed for half a minute and enhanced the image. Finally I saw a close-up of Barbara's left wrist, the rope biting into the skin. No, I corrected. Not really biting into her skin.

"Fairly loose," Glen said. "From the looks of it. Like maybe she's not really tied too tight."

"Yeah."

He went back to the original image and we saw the door quickly open and the rapist enter. Glen locked in on what was behind the door, froze it, enlarged it, and worked on enhancing it. It was still a muddy mess. He shook his head and continued, freezing the picture of the rapist.

"Anything?" he asked.

"Jeans, plain white T-shirt, ski mask," I said. "Shoes?"

"Nike. See the swoosh? I could probably work out his shoe size if you really want it."

"No, not now. What else?" I asked.

"Not sure." He continued. Bit by bit we inched our way through the tape sequence. When the rapist dropped his jeans and tore off his shirt I said, "What's that?" Pointing.

"That there is a circumcised dick, Megan. Haven't you seen one before?"

"If you drop your pants to show me one now you're a dead man," I said. "No. On the, let me see, left bicep."

Glen moved in, enhanced. On the left bicep there was a tattoo.

"Can you enhance?" I asked.

He shrugged and started to manipulate the image. It improved somewhat, but was still indistinct. Glen said, "If you leave the disk with me I might be able to get something. I can work on it tonight, get back with you in twenty-four hours or so."

I frowned, wondering what the Reverend would want me to do. Slowly, I nodded. "Go ahead. Keep it. But it's confidential. This is P.I. work."

"Yeah, that's what I thought. How old's the girl?"

"Eighteen."

"Very well-developed eighteen."

I nodded. Very well-developed, very sexual. We tracked our way through the rest of the movie but didn't see anything else of particular interest. Glen said, "I'll enhance the background through the door, too. Might find something interesting back there, but I'll have to work on it."

"Thanks Glen. Send me a bill."

He waved a hand. "For the thrill? Hey, it's good t'see you again. I checked and CyberConduit's stock's up five points."

"Uh-huh," I said.

"You ever sorry you sold her?"

I sighed and changed the subject. "You think this thing might be on the Net somewhere?"

"I could look."

I gave him my skeptical look again. It was an expression I found myself using entirely too much with Glen, but he brought it out in me. "Glen, about a third of the Web is porn sites. How the hell're you going to track down a five minute video loop?"

Glen rubbed at his wispy beard, a thoughtful expression on his face. "Well, I'm working on a project with a private company out east that'll hunt for digital images on the Web. Scan in a photograph or a chunk of video, then it'll search the entire Web for a match or similarity. I might be able to find something that way. It's up and running, but it needs a lot of tweaking. It's got problems."

The complexity of what he described was staggering. It was taking a search engine like Yahoo! or Excite! to the nth degree and maybe more. "Who's the company, Glen?" I said.

He hesitated and something flickered in his eyes. He waved his hand dismissively. "Oh, just a little private company."

Oh ... Uh-huh. "This company happen to be in Maryland?" I asked.

Glen's face grew blank. "You want me to give it a shot, or what?"

"Sure, Glen. And thanks."

I put away the videotape and wondered about a little company "out east" that would want video-search capabilities on the Web. The National Security Agency, perhaps? A little company in Fort Meade, Maryland? The government agency in charge of tracking all codes, satellite, telephone, cable and digital communications? A government agency that made the C.I.A. look like Girl Scouts?

"Let me know what you find," I said, and handed him one of my business cards.

"I will, M&M. I will. Nice to see you."

I was almost out the door when he called out, "Hey, Meg?"

I turned. "What?"

"You never answered me. You ever sorry you sold CyberConduits?"

I nodded. "Just about every day," I said. "I ask myself that just about every day."

4

I stood outside Glen's warehouse feeling as if I'd just skinny-dipped in a waste treatment plant. It didn't help that I knew I was still being observed from a number of digital video cameras mounted around the building entrance. Glen had a dirty mind—a brilliant mind, but dirty. A hopeless adolescent, and when he'd left CyberConduits to pursue his own interests on his own time, ultimately I had been glad to be rid of him.

I revved up the Hummer with the remote, still thinking about the videotape. I turned and faced the door. "Glen!"

No response. I said, "I don't want you making any personal copies of that disk, you understand?"

Still no response. I climbed into the Hummer and found my way back into rush hour traffic—Ann Arbor rush hour to Detroit rush hour to northern suburb rush hour. I listened to "All Things Considered" on National Public Radio, just part of my daily info-fix, news junkie that I am. One of the top stories was about Solar Microsystems, the company that bought CyberConduits. My stomach clenched so tight I thought I was going to upchuck all over the dashboard. I sucked in deep breaths, willing myself to relax. Only when the news finally switched over to a bloody coup in Africa did my muscles return to normal. *Shit Malloy!—you need therapy*.

I finally made it to Rochester Hills and parked in the large, mostly empty parking lot of the Missionary Church of Jesus Christ Evangelical where Reverend Walker had told me he could be found.

The entire grounds had been made into elaborate botanical gardens with winding pathways through ornamental trees and flowers. The church itself was large, an appealing combination of traditional and modern, the traditional supplied by granite block, the modern by slanting sheets of mirrored glass. From where I stood the scarlet rays of the setting sun lit up the glass in a million shards, as if someone had frozen a rainbow and shattered it with a sledge hammer. For a moment my breath caught in my chest, at one with the architect's grand plan. Then I said, "Holy shit! That's gorgeous!"

Ah well. So much for reverence.

Steeling myself, I walked past the handful of cars parked near the entrance and went in through the main doors.

The first thing I heard was the Reverend's mellifluous voice, seeping into the foyer, which was carpeted in a muted burgundy. There were places to hang coats off to the right, and off to the left was the Serenity Chapel and a hallway leading to a meeting hall, rest rooms, offices and Sunday school rooms. Forward, though, was the main sanctuary behind a wall of glass.

" ... and God instructed Jesus to prepare himself by retreating to the desert. He took nothing. For forty days and forty nights the Son of God fasted and prayed and prepared for his greatest sacrifice. And it was here, in the blinding heat of the desert, that Satan appeared before Jesus."

I crept into the sanctuary and took it all in. Reverend Walker stood behind the elevated oak pulpit in front of an amazing triptych of stained glass. The image on the left was of Jesus performing a miracle, raising Lazarus, I thought. The central image was of Christ on the cross. The image on the right was of Jesus appearing before his disciples, floating above them, awash in a blaze of heavenly light. Beneath it all were the pipes of an organ and the pews for the choir.

" ... tested ... tempted," Reverend Walker said. "Satan offered Jesus everything a man could want. That's important. A *man*. He offered first that Jesus eat, that he drink, that he be comforted. He offered him power, a kingdom. 'All this can be yours, Son of God,' Satan said. And what did Our Lord Jesus Christ say to Satan? What did the Prince of Light say to the Prince of Darkness?

"Get thee away from me, Satan! Away!"

From off to the right a man said, "Jim, maybe you need to gesture there."

Reverend Walker looked over. "You think so?"

"It's pretty dramatic. Might need to emphasize the point."

Reverend Walker paused for a moment, then said, "And what did Our Lord Jesus Christ say to Satan? What did the Prince of Light say to the Prince of Darkness?"

He pounded the pulpit with his fist, the sound echoing to the soaring beams of the ceiling. *"Get thee away, Satan! Away!"*

The director, a tall, thin, bald man in jeans and a white shirt open at the collar said, "Get thee away from me, or get thee away?"

"What'd I say?"

"First time you said 'Get thee away from me.'"

"What do you think, Ms. Malloy?"

Startled, I said, "'Get thee away' probably works better, but is the 'thee' necessary?"

"It's the style the parish expects," Reverend Walker said mildly, rich voice booming from the speaker system. "'Get the hell out of my face,' may have been what Jesus said in actuality, but my viewers aren't going to go for it."

I laughed. "I suppose you're right."

"Can you wait a while, Ms. Malloy? Is this ... urgent? I'll be done with the actual rehearsal in a half hour, then I'll have time to talk to you before Larry and I go over the lighting and other technical issues. Would that be all right?"

"No problem. Mind if I watch?"

"Not at all."

Might even be good for me, I thought, and sat down in the last row, sinking onto the soft cushions of the pews. Not too soft, though; not so soft that anyone would fall asleep on a TV program syndicated to ninety-nine stations nationwide. From the shadows a lean man in gray Dockers and a white dress shirt and dark tie approached me. His features were thin, his brown hair cut short in a conservative style. I pegged him for a youthful forty. Light reflected off his wire-rimmed glasses so I couldn't see his eyes. There was something peculiar about his body language, a vague combination of confidence and discomfort.

In a voice as smooth as vanilla yogurt, he said, "May I join you?"

Shrugging, I gestured for him to sit. He said, "I'm Matthew DuPuis, the assistant pastor. You're Ms. Malloy?"

I held out my hand. "Megan Malloy. Should I call you Reverend?"

He took my hand and I noticed the solid gold wedding band on his other hand. "If it makes you feel more comfortable," he said.

"I actually find it a little confusing."

He flashed a boyish grin. "Me, too. You can call me Matt, or Brother Matt, or Brother Matthew, if you like. Most people do."

Reverend Walker was building up momentum, hinting at hell and damnation while talking about resisting temptation, just as Jesus had. Every now and then he was interrupted by the director, who made suggestions or called out a time.

"I'll stick with Matt," I said. "You can call me Meg. This is quite a production."

"This rehearsal? No, not really. You should see the dress rehearsal with the choir and organist. Takes a couple of hours to get the timing right, especially with the lighting. During some of the music they roll tape of scenes corresponding to the emotional ambiance of the hymn. Sometimes it's from the grounds; other times it's farms or waterfalls ... whatever."

There was a mild hint of rebuke to his words, as if he were apologizing. Not strong enough to be sarcasm, but enough so you knew he wasn't buying a hundred percent of the image his own church was selling.

Reverend Walker said, "Forgive yourself? In this modern new age, that seems entirely too easy. First we have to forgive ourselves, we say, and everything else will come. But I say NO!"

"Jim—"

Reverend Walker ignored his director and charged on. "Everything else will *not* come so easily. I think in these perilous times we've given ourselves entirely too much freedom to forgive ourselves; ask for forgiveness and all will be forgiven. God, we say, will forgive us in the end. But what about guilt?"

"He's on a roll," I said.

Matt shook his head. "No, not really. Something's bothering him. His timing's off. He acts distracted." He looked shrewdly at me, and now I could see the glittering gold-brown of his eyes. "He's thinking about something else. Something to do with you?"

I shrugged. "I'm helping him out on something."

"What is it you do, Meg? Meg or Megan?"

"Whichever suits." I fished in my backpack for a business card and handed it to him.

He read it. "Troubleshooter. You solve problems, that it? Get rid of trouble?"

"Yes, I suppose so. Short-term problems, with any luck. I don't know about trouble."

"You're working on our website crash?"

I nodded, throwing in a shrug for good measure.

Matthew turned his attention momentarily toward the pulpit, listening to Reverend Walker discuss the easy way modern society asked for forgiveness and returned to the same old bad behavior. "'No prob,'" Reverend Walker jived, getting into it. "'Father, forgive me for beating my wife. And if I do it again, I'll just ask to be forgiven again. No prob, right?'"

Brother Matthew winced slightly.

"He's got a point," I said.

"Life is a merry-go-round," Brother Matthew said, smiling.

"I hope not. There are stops on this trip I'd just as soon not revisit."

His eyes focused on me again, as if looking into my mind, my soul. "I suppose you're right. What's the nature of Reverend Walker's problem?"

"I don't think it's something I should talk about."

He nodded, squelching his obvious curiosity. He didn't think I was here just for the computer problem. He was right and I wondered why he thought so.

Before he could make another probe for information, I said, "This is quite a place. And you support how many missions around the world?"

"Twelve." Brother Matthew leaned back and seemed to take in the church as if for the first time. Columns of granite, polished oak beams, stained glass, modern glass that angled and diffused the late-fall light in glowing shafts of azure and gold and rose.

"You know the funny thing?" he said. "Reverend Walker'd give all of it up to have his wife back."

"She's dead?"

He nodded. "She was a missionary doctor. He was the missionary minister, running the mission. They were in Zaire, what's now Congo. They met there. She was the new person on staff. Very young and beautiful—I've seen pictures. This was maybe twenty years ago. They fell in love, had Barbara. Then Katharine—that was his wife—got one of the illnesses she was treating people for. Some intestinal parasite. She never recovered. I don't think Jim ... Reverend Walker's ever really recovered, either."

"And he's raised Barbara by himself," I said.

He nodded. "Have you met her?"

I shook my head. "No, not yet. What's she like?"

Brother Matthew cocked an eyebrow. "Oh," he said casually, too casually, "Just your typical P.K., I think."

"P.K.?"

"Preacher's kid." He grinned. "I've got three myself. Four, six and seven. Little hellions."

"Is Barbara a hellion?"

Brother Matthew sobered. "Do you think it would be easy to have a father adored by a million TV viewers who think his words come directly from God? Or that another million people who don't like television ministries think your father is some sort of con man wrapped in the Bible, bilking simple-minded people out of their hard-earned money?" His words were bitter, barely covering a very deep anger.

"No," I said. "I suppose not. What else can you tell me about Barbara?"

Brother Matthew focused on me again. "Is this about Barbara?"

I shrugged. "Is she involved with the church?"

Matthew hesitated. "She grew up in this church. Sang in the children's choir, grew into the adult choir, acts in the Christmas pageant. Over the years I doubt if there's any area of this entire ... operation that she hasn't been involved in. She even worked the phone lines when she was old enough." He smiled. "Those are in an office building in Southfield, actually. During and after the televised services are when the phone lines light up, and I thought maybe she volunteered to work there just to get out of services. She's not very involved now—some resistance there, apparently—but Ji ... Reverend Walker can still get her to read from the Bible for services or sing with the choir. Sometimes, anyway. Teenage angst, I suppose. Stretching her wings ready to fly from the nest." He didn't sound convinced.

"How long have you known them?"

"Them?" he said.

"Reverend Walker and Barbara."

"Oh. I worked in one of the missions—in Cuba, actually—for a few years after I graduated from seminary, before Reverend Walker asked me into the church." He looked bemused, a smile playing at his lips. "Although Reverend Walker gives the sermons and directs the entire enterprise, my job is to attend to the day-to-day spiritual needs of this particular parish."

"Are there ... others?"

He nodded. "Brother Lucas, Brother Steven and Sister Nancy. And about fifty full-time staff here, part-time staff in Southfield, and a couple of hundred around the world at the missions." He cleared his throat and gave a soft chuckle that sounded vaguely like the purr of a contented cat. "Brother Lucas is basically our financial ..." He trailed off and looked sharply at me. "Perhaps this isn't what you need to know?"

"*Need* to know?" I asked.

Now Brother Matthew looked very embarrassed. He glanced at the pulpit. Reverend Walker was saying, "What is the price of forgiveness? What was the price for Jesus? He took on the mantle, the cloak ... our sins were like a great weight he wore ..." He muttered, "Damn," and shook his head, losing the thread of his sermon for a moment.

Larry, the director, said, "Try that again."

Reverend Walker said, "What is the price of forgiveness? What was the price for Jesus? He took on the heavy weight of our sins and died, taking them to hell and leaving them with Satan, returning to Earth to reassure us, to provide proof—*proof!*—to his disciples that he was indeed the Son of God! What was the price for Jesus? To die as a *man*! To suffer terrible anguish and pain on the cross, that barbaric symbol of cruelty and torture the Romans used on common criminals! To descend into the depths of burning hell with our sins and leave those sins at the cloven hooves of Satan, to momentarily abandon everything that he was—the Son of God, a child of earth—and experience the pain and torment that those sinners would have experienced were it not for him."

Brother Matthew said, "Jim told me you were helping him with a problem and I was to provide any information you needed."

"I see. Did he tell you the nature of the problem?"

He shook his head, obviously bothered by this. It was apparent that Brother Matthew was the church's number two guy, but in this case Reverend Walker hadn't trusted him one hundred percent. I decided to follow the Reverend's lead.

"Well," I said. "Why don't you tell me about Brother Lucas, Steven and, uh, Sister Nancy."

Brother Matthew stared at me, brown eyes large behind the lenses of his glasses. After an awkward moment he said, "Brother Lucas Balkovic isn't actually a minister, so much as the chief financial officer of what in a normal business environment would be a corporation. We're rather complex, in terms of that, and Lucas has an MBA from the University of Michigan. He not only sees that we're all paid and that all the bills get paid, but he doles out finances to the twelve missions we support worldwide."

"Why the title of Brother?"

Brother Matthew shrugged. "Reverend Walker's the head guy. It's much less complicated for the parishioners—especially those on TV all over the country—to view us as a largely spiritual hierarchy. I'm not entirely sure I agree on this point ..." He paused. "I'm being very candid with you, Ms. Malloy. Can I trust you?"

"Yes."

His gaze was penetrating and skeptical. He lingered a moment more on my answer, then nodded. "I'm not entirely sure I agree that we need these titles. In my case I suppose it makes sense, since I'm actually a minister and I take over sermons when Jim is sick or traveling, and the parishioners are actually more likely to deal with me rather than Jim. I'm the one who visits them at the hospital or counsels them prior to marriage and very often performs the ceremonies for weddings or funerals. Lucas, on the other hand, is a businessman who runs our finance affairs."

"And Brother Steven?"

"Steven Major. Another MBA, from Harvard. He does the actual running of the organization. To keep the corporate metaphor, he would be the Chief Operating Officer. He built this building, essentially. Found the property, got the permits and permissions in place, zoning, everything. And he's the one who keeps it running, as well as all the missions and the actual dealings with the various governments and everything else."

"Impressive."

He shrugged.

"And Sister Nancy ... ?"

"Nancy Phillips. Head of Education and Missions. She travels almost as much as Steven. She's in Sri Lanka now. She tries to visit each mission at least once a year."

"She's on the road a lot then, I guess."

He nodded. "It's exhausting, but satisfying."

"She tell you that?"

Brother Matthew faltered momentarily. Voice suddenly cold, he said, "Is there something else I can do for you, Ms. Malloy?"

"How many parishioners in this actual church?"

"Around a thousand. Two services, the second one televised."

"How well do you know Barbara?"

He looked out at the triptych of stained glass, his face a study in conflicting emotions. Reverend Walker and the director were in close discussion near the altar. I had missed the grand finale of his sermon, concentrating on Brother Matthew. Finally Brother Matthew said, "This is about her, isn't it? You're not really a computer troubleshooter, are you?"

"Yes, actually. I am. Just like the card says."

He shook his head. "You're more than that, right?"

"I hope we're all more than what's printed on our business cards."

"This is about Barbara."

I shrugged. "I'm not at liberty to say. But anything you can tell me about her would be helpful."

Reverend Walker was wrapping things up with the director. Suddenly Brother Matthew nodded his head as if to himself and said, "Meet me tonight at Barnes & Noble on Rochester Road at ten o'clock. Would that be possible?"

I nodded. "Why?"

Reverend Walker was heading down the aisle toward us. "I'll see you there," he said, stood up and walked away.

I saw that the calm, serene and spiritually confident facade Reverend Walker wore on the pulpit was gone. Now he looked like a stricken parent listening to the names of the deceased after a plane crash. He stopped next to me. "Matt helping you out?"

"Yeah," I said, wondering. "Giving me some general info. Thanks."

"I didn't expect you tonight," Walker said.

I stood up and slung my backpack over my shoulder. "I've found out a few things I think you need to know. In your office?"

Reverend Walker met my gaze. "I —"

"In your office," I said again, using a little more force.

His eyes widened suddenly, his face showing fear and curiosity, not unlike a deer facing an oncoming International Harvester. He found his voice, though. "Of course. Come this way."

Of course, I thought. Let's go talk about your daughter, the porn star.

5

My first impression of Reverend Walker's office was its neatness, as if presentation was everything. And maybe it was, because everything from the large, simple desk made of blond wood to the meticulous gray furniture grouping seemed designed to look comfortable and neat, but not pricy. I wondered for a moment about the Reverend's attention to image, how far it extended.

My second impression was the wall of glass looking out on the gardens. The sun was still in its slow autumn process of sinking into the horizon, but right outside the windows was a large planting of well-cared-for rose bushes, gorgeous and brilliant in the fading light.

"Beautiful roses," I said.

Reverend Walker's face lit up for a moment, turning to look out the window at them. "Do you like them?"

I nodded. "I really like roses."

"Me, too," he said, standing to gaze out upon them, the expression on his face bemused, oddly self-aware. "Do you garden?"

I laughed. "Me? No. I hate weeding. Seems too much like work. But I like flowers."

He nodded, wistful. "My wife loved gardening. Even when we were in Zaire she kept a flower garden." He sat behind his desk and craned his neck as if to stretch out a kink. "Back then I felt pretty much like you do. I liked them, but I didn't like to garden." He turned in his gray leather chair to look out at the roses again. "But when Katharine died ..." He spun toward me and shrugged. "I missed her. So I started gardening. Especially the roses. Those are mine out there. No one works on the roses but me." His voice was soft. "I feel close to Katharine when I'm gardening."

"Well ... they're beautiful."

"Thank you." He steepled his hands and rested his strong chin on the tips of his index fingers. "I didn't expect you tonight. You've found something out?"

I nodded and gestured toward the grouping of sofa and armchairs. "Do you have a TV and VCR?"

"Of course. In the cabinet there. I use it to go over my services, to see how to improve the show."

Show, I thought. Such a practical side to their approach, all of them. I was under the impression TV ministers never thought about their televised services as being part evangelism, part entertainment. They all seemed to take themselves so seriously; but here, face to face, it seemed different. Watered-down show biz with a spiritual beat. Theater of the soul.

I crossed to the cabinet, popped in the tape and gave the Reverend a hard, searching look. "I'm going to have to ask you to watch this tape one more time, all right? I know it won't be easy, but I have to point out a few problems. It puts a very different spin on things."

He splayed his strong hands. "I ... this is important, right?"

I nodded.

He tipped his head slightly in reluctant agreement. I jabbed the PLAY button, snagged the remote and sat down in one of the gray upholstered arm-chairs. Scene by scene I explained what we were seeing, the changes in the camera angles, the shifting point of view.

Halfway through, the door burst open and the director, Larry, thrust himself into the room. "Jim, I've been going over the—"

He froze, taking in the images on the TV. I quickly hit the STOP button and the screen flashed blue.

"Hey," Larry said, face flushing red, his expression a mix of recognition and embarrassment. "Sorry. I should've knocked. I wasn't ..."

Reverend Walker said, "Ms. Malloy is helping me with a personal matter, Larry. I'll be with you in twenty minutes or so."

"Uh ... yeah. Hey, sorry. I didn't ..."

Closing his eyes in dismay, Larry left Reverend Walker's office just as abruptly as he had entered, the door slamming behind him. Reverend Walker gazed at me. "I wonder what he thinks."

"If you're lucky he thinks you brought me in here to watch dirty movies together."

Walker closed his eyes and snorted softly, almost a laugh. "I'll think of something to tell him. ... I don't think I need to see the rest. What's your conclusion?"

"My conclusion is your daughter wasn't raped. She took part in a porn movie of some sort. And for some reason somebody—possibly your daughter—delivered a loop of it to you."

Reverend Walker nodded, got to his feet and walked away from me. He silently stepped through a doorway and closed the door after himself. I heard water running and assumed it was a private bathroom. I rewound the videotape, slipped it back into its sleeve and left it on the coffee table in front of me. With nothing better to do I examined the photographs on the wall.

Reverend Walker with various people I didn't know except for Barbara and Brother Matthew. It didn't seem to be a memento wall, the Rev with famous people, the movers and shakers of the community, but family and friends. After a couple minutes Reverend Walker returned. He shook his head. "You wouldn't believe the headache I'm getting."

I wanted to laugh, but I didn't think he intended it to be funny. "I imagine," I said. "I'm sorry, sort of; I mean, I'm glad it's not a rape, but no father wants to find out his daughter's working in porn movies."

He sat back down, frowning. "Any idea when this film was made?"

I shook my head. "No. You mentioned her birthday was last month. If it was after that, it's even legal."

He closed his eyes again, thinking, maybe praying. He nodded his head as if liking what the voices in his skull were saying. "Can you find her?"

"Find her?"

He nodded. "She's missing, after all. And involved in ..." He gestured wearily at the tape. " ... in that filth. Can you find her?"

"How long's she been missing?"

"Since Sunday," he said.

Sunday, I thought. Well, that's interesting. "After the services?"

He nodded. "She was supposed to meet me at home for dinner, but she never showed up." Now he looked embarrassed, not meeting my gaze. "I made excuses to the family we were hosting, but frankly, Ms. Malloy, Barbara's been doing this a lot recently."

"Doing ... what?"

"Being unreliable. Coming and going as she pleases, staying out late, disappearing for days on end."

I took that all in. "Except for the disappearing for days on end it all pretty much sounds like typical teen rebellion. How often has she disappeared like this?"

He shrugged. "Few times a year."

"Is there any pattern to it?"

He looked puzzled, and ran an elegant, long-fingered hand through his thick white hair. "Pattern?"

"Did she leave after a fight? Was it over a weekend or weekdays? How many days does she disappear? What's she like when she returns? Does she tell you where she went or what she did or who she went with?"

His embarrassment seemed to intensify, as if he were a reluctant witness under the close scrutiny of a prosecuting attorney. "No, I can't say there was any pattern to it."

Now I felt my concentration intensify and I zeroed in on him. "There wasn't a pattern or you didn't notice it?"

"Really, Ms. Malloy!"

"If you want my help, you've got to answer hard questions. Here's a couple more. How old was Barbara when she got her first period?"

"*What? I—*"

"How old was she when she got her first bra?"

"That one I know. Eleven. Sister Nancy mentioned it to me, as a matter of fact, because ..." He trailed off.

"Because she was so developed that it was becoming an issue," I said.

He nodded and frowned at his hands. "Really, Ms. Malloy—"

"Meg."

"—I'm not as distant a father as this makes me seem."

Uh-huh. Maybe; maybe not. "Does she own a car?"

"Yes." He seemed suddenly reluctant to answer my questions. Get out the can opener, I thought, time to pry him open.

"What type?"

"Mazda Miata."

"Red?"

"Yes, how did you know?"

I shrugged. "License number?"

"I agreed to a vanity plate for her seventeenth birthday. THESPIAN."

"She wanted to be an actress?"

Mr. Mongoose, meet Mr. Cobra. Reverend Walker froze, ready to be dinner. "Y-yes."

We contemplated each other for a long moment. "I guess she is, isn't she?" I said, and instantly regretted it. "I can probably find her," I said, "if that's something you really want me to do. But it's possible she'll come back on her own. And ... she's a legal adult, so bringing her back is somebody else's job. I'll need her social security number, driver's license number if you've got it, any credit cards she might have. I'll also need the names and locations of any of her friends I can talk to."

"Her best friend is Lisa Dunn. She's a freshman at Oakland this year, living in the dorm. I don't have her number, but—"

"I can find it, no problem. Any boyfriends?"

"No! I discouraged her from dating. I mean ... there wasn't anybody regular."

Uh-huh. "Names?"

He looked cornered again. "I ... I guess I don't really know. I guess Joe Mason was a friend of hers, a ... boy ... friend." He buried his face in his hands, vaguely theatrical. "What kind of father does that make me? Oh God!"

I was the wrong person to hire if what he wanted was sympathy. I cut through the crap. "Look—Reverend? I'll find her. I can do that. But I've got a couple things I need to know, just sort of random thoughts, things that seem kind of coincidental that I need to consider. Okay?"

He nodded, staring me down, blue eyes rimmed scarlet. "Okay." He sniffled, retrieving a handkerchief from his pocket.

"What does your daughter know about computers?"

He shrugged. "Quite a bit. Don't most kids these days?"

"She have a PC at home?"

"Yes. In her bedroom."

"Access to the Internet?"

"Yes."

"I might want to check that, but we'll talk about it tomorrow. She ever show any interest in WebSpinners and the church's website?"

"What are you getting at?" There was a spark of anger in his eyes and I was glad to see it. I was much happier with people mad at me than begging for comfort and sympathy. Good old-fashioned rage I could deal with.

"It's an interesting coincidence that Chavez Tech's server crashed and burned right around the same time Barbara did her disappearing act."

"What are you saying?" He was on his feet now.

"I'm not saying anything," I said. "Just that it's interesting."

"Barbara wouldn't do anything to harm this church!"

Whatever. I wasn't going to argue the point. I said, "Your director, uh, Larry—"

"Larry Clinton."

"He work for the church, or is he some sort of subcontractor?"

"Larry? He's a member of the parish, and his company, LTC Video Production handles the broadcast of our services. Usually we have the same cameraman ..." He faded out, looking troubled.

"I may have to talk to him," I said. "I may have to ask him some pointed questions about the type of videos he and his crew do."

"No. I don't believe Larry would—"

I pulled the PDA from my backpack. "We'll talk about it later," I said. "Now, if you have the information I need ..."

6

I climbed into the Hummer, wondering if I actually knew what I was doing. It felt like I was being scattershot about this whole thing—no written contract, no money down, no coherent plan of attack. Shouldn't I have insisted on seeing her bedroom and her computer? For all I knew Barbara had left a note on her desk:

> *Dear Dad:*
> *I ran off with Joey. We're getting mar-*
> *ried in Vegas. Elvis is officiating. Frank*
> *Sinatra's going to be the best man. Love ya and*
> *see you after the honeymoon.*
> *Your loving daughter,*
> *Barb.*

With a sigh I dug out my phone and dialed Oakland University's information number from memory. Both my parents had been faculty there. I asked for Lisa Dunn's number, got it and punched it in. The woman who answered had to shout over Sheryl Crowe blasting in the background.

"Hello!"

"Can I speak to Lisa Dunn?" I said.

"*What?* Can you talk louder? I can't hear you!"

"CAN I SPEAK TO LISA DUNN?" I said louder.

"WHO?"

"CAN YOU TURN THE SOUND DOWN?" I shouted.

"WHAT?"

"LISA! IS LISA THERE?"

"LISA'S NOT HERE!"

"WHERE IS SHE?"

"AT *WORK*!"

"WHERE DOES SHE WORK?" I bellowed.

"MR. B'S!"

"THANK YOU!" I screamed and clicked off. Christ! The future of America in action. But I was in luck. Or so I hoped. Mr. B's was a restaurant and bar in downtown Rochester.

Well ... and in Troy and Royal Oak and probably a couple other places, too. But Rochester was closest and I was hungry.

I found a spot in the municipal lot on the west side of Mr. B's and entered through the back door, remembering walking by the place with my dad when I was a little kid and seeing a line of motorcycles parked all in a row. Harleys. In the 70s Rochester had a tough reputation, and Mr. B's had been something of a biker bar, back before bikers were mostly lawyers and accountants with too much discretionary income. It was hard to believe now, with Rochester being an upper-middle-class suburb with chi-chi shops and strip malls as far as the credit card could see.

I waded into the sea of dim light and clamorous noise. The crowd on a Wednesday night was mostly college students—the kind with a fair amount of discretionary income—and straggling families and couples who wanted pizza or miscellaneous deep-fried whatevers before the weekend crowds choked the place to a standstill. I tagged a waiter, a gangly redhead who stood about six-six, and said, "Lisa Dunn work here?"

"Over there," he said, pointing to a woman whose back was to me. "Thanks," I said, and waited to be seated, telling the hostess I wanted to be in Lisa's area.

She scanned the restaurant—hard-wood floors, wobbly tables, TVs pinned to the walls, a bar in one room, pool tables in another, the overly loud rasp of rock music, brewery and local memorabilia on the walls. "C'mon," she said, and I followed her to a small table for two. "Lisa'll be with you in a min."

It was longer than a "min," but not too long. It gave me ample time to watch Lisa in action. She was about five-five, sturdy in tight jeans and a green Mr. B's T-shirt. She was probably twenty-five pounds too heavy, but she wore at least ten pounds of it in her breasts, the rest on her hips. It worked well for her, anyway, and I noticed men watching her. She was a natural flirt; probably made great tips. She wore her hair in a layered style past her shoulders, a golden-brown mane that probably took three hours to wash, dry and curl in the morning. Her makeup was expertly applied, something I had neither inclination nor patience for. Dangling earrings—rhinestones, I thought—finished the pic; those and the long, blood red fingernails.

"You know what you want to order?" she said. "Or do you want to look at the menu for a while?"

"Slop burger and seasoned fries," I said. "Grilled, not fried. No tomatoes, hold the chili. Otherwise ... everything. Wait. Hold the onions, too."

"What'll you have to drink?"

"Corona, *por favor*."

"Ha! *Si, senorita!* Coming right up."

She trotted off with my order and I settled in to await my cholesterol bomb with a side of deep fat. In my endless search for the perfect hamburger, Mr. B's slop burger came very, very close to culinary nirvana. On top of a Dove Bar, well, I'd have to work a little harder at the gym and tack on an extra mile or so to my daily run, but considering my client, perhaps this is what God wanted. I could only hope.

When Lisa returned with my beer, I said, "You're Lisa Dunn?"

She stopped, hand on hip. "Yeah. I know you?"

"No, I don't think so. My name's Meg Malloy. I'm looking for Barbara Walker. I understand you're a friend of hers."

Lisa's expression grew wary. "Yeah, so?"

"Well, she took off a couple days ago. Her father wants to see her."

"You a friend of her father's?"

"No, not really. More like an employee. Why?"

"I don't like the Reverend. And neither does Barbara."

"Yeah, well, that's not really any of my business—"

"Sounds like you're making it your business."

Whoa! Hostility alert!

I took a deep breath and a sip of my beer, trying to figure how to approach this. "Look, something's come up. Re—Mister Walker's concerned that Barbara might be in trouble."

"Yeah, right. Try again. What's your name? Meg Malloy? What kind of a name is that?"

"Uh ... Scots-Irish?"

"Sure. Look, tell *The Rev* Barbara doesn't wanna talk to him, 'kay?"

"Then why'd she send him a videotape?"

Something changed in her blue eyes. Surprise, I thought, but she hid it well. She seemed caught off guard, momentarily speechless. "Hey, that's none of my business. And none of yours, either." She turned and took off, disappearing into the kitchen.

Five minutes passed. Then ten. I watched a baseball game on ESPN on one of the TVs—Atlanta and the Mets. I didn't have much interest in the National League, especially Atlanta. Fifteen minutes slipped by. I wondered if she'd bring my slop burger. I wondered if this investigation was worth annoying the person who was supposed to bring me my slop burger. Some things in life are more important than truth and justice, and my slop burger was one of them.

The red-headed kid came out with a plastic basket holding my slop burger and a mound of pepper-buttered seasoned french fries, death in a basket. "Thanks," I said. "Where's Lisa?"

"Dunno. She asked me to bring this to you."

"Thanks."

He left me to my carnivore special and I dug in, hoping she hadn't spit in the food. Gustatory celebration! I could almost feel my arteries harden as I ate. I gave myself over to the pleasure of the food, blocking out all notions of private investigation and computer troubleshooting. "Be the food," I muttered. *Be the burger. Become one with the cholesterol. Zen and the art of the heart attack.* Lisa came and went, dealing with other tables, not looking my way. Finally, when I was finished and staring at her, she sauntered back over to my table.

"That be all?"

"Uh-huh."

She slapped the check down on my table, shaking it. "Wait," I said, before she could steam away.

I whacked both my hands down on the table. Beneath my left hand was a ten dollar bill. Beneath my right were five twenties. I said, "If I leave without talking to you, what's under my left hand pays the bill and the tip. If you talk to me, what's under the left hand pays the bill and what's under the right hand is the tip." I shot her a look right between the eyes. "Am I speaking your language yet?"

Her gaze flickered. She reached for the money under my right hand. "Uh-uh," I said, holding out the ten. "I'll meet you out in the parking lot. I've got a red Hummer. You know what that is?"

"No." She was glaring at me, sullen, but most fish look that way when their lower lip's caught on a hook.

"Big, square, boxy thing, looks like a Jeep with a thyroid problem. Can't miss it."

"Okay."

"Me and your tip'll be waiting."

"I can't spend too long or the boss'll get after me."

"Talk fast, then," I said, and shot to my feet, leaving the ten on the table.

After ten minutes I figured she stood me up. I was sitting on the hood of the Hummer, taking in the evening. Fall was being kind this year and the temperature hadn't dipped below 65 degrees yet. There was a cool westerly breeze and the air felt thick and sensual. I could smell the fry grease from Mr. B's, something fishy from Kruse & Muir's, and something spicy from who knows where. One thing about Rochester, there was no shortage of decent restaurants. My kind of town.

The west municipal lot was surrounded by mature oak, maple and willow trees, swaying in the light wind. I closed my eyes and pretended I was in Maui. Nope. No ocean, different smells. Even the air felt different, not so seductive. Guess I was home after all. Above me the stars were coming out. I looked for my favorite constellation, Orion, and found it, counting the stars in the hunter's belt. Watch out for that bear, buddy!

"Where's the money?"

I turned to Lisa, who stood six feet away, hands cocked on cantilevered hips, giving me attitude.

"I've got it," I said. "We'll do this on the payment plan. Where's Barbara?"

"How ya think I know?"

I held up one of the twenties. "I'm guessing you do know."

"Well ... I don't."

She was lying. I tucked the twenty back in the pocket of my jeans and shrugged. "Let's try an easy one, okay? Who's Joe Mason?"

"Joey? He's a friend a Barb's. Why?"

"How do I get in touch with him?"

"He lives in town. Goes to O.U., but he lives in a house downtown. Over on Terry Street, you know, where the Spartan Motel is?"

"He and Barb date?"

She shrugged. "Maybe used to. Don't know. I kind of doubt it. Joey's not her type."

"Why's that?"

She shrugged again. "I don't know. He's a nice guy. Kinda ... young."

"She likes older men?"

"I don't know. He's ... he's a kid, you know? I mean, we're the same age, but Joey's a kid." She shrugged.

I handed her the first of the twenties. I said, "What do you know about the videotape?"

"Nothin'."

"Why don't you tell me what you were thinking when I mentioned Barb sent her father a videotape."

Lisa shifted her weight from one foot to the other. "Look, hey, I been on my feet all day. You mind if I sit down for a sec?"

I gestured for her to join me on the hood of the Hummer. She scooched up next to me with a sigh of relief. "You ever waitress?" she asked.

"Nope."

"Lucky. You some sort of P.I.? You act kinda like that."

"Some sort, I guess. Mostly I'm a computer troubleshooter."

"Oh. I don't know much about computers. Barb does, though."

"What's your major?" When I was in college that was a pickup line. I wondered if it still was.

"Interior design."

"Uh-huh," I said. "And Barb wants to be an actress."

"She can make it. She's got the talent and the looks."

"Why'd she decide not to go to school? Her father said he wanted her to go to Harvard."

"Ha! That's what *Daddy* wanted, no doubt. What she really wanted to do was go out to UCLA and go to film school and take acting classes, try to break in that way. They had a big fight about it. Taking a year off was, like, a compromise."

"When they had a big fight, is that when she took off for a few days?"

Lisa shrugged. I held up a twenty. She snatched for it, but I shifted it just out of reach. Lisa sighed. "Yeah. They fought, Barb took off."

"Where?"

"Usually she stayed with me."

"Usually?"

"Far as I know."

I gave her the second twenty. "What about Joey?"

"His mom wouldn't let her stay. Joey's mom's a very straight-laced Catholic. She makes *The Rev* seem like a party animal."

"Know any other boyfriends of Barb's?"

"No."

I wasn't sure if she was telling me the truth or not on that score. I said, "So what was Barb going to do with herself this year?"

"Well ..." She paused, rummaging in a purse for something. She pulled out a pack of cigarettes and a Bic lighter. Tamping one out, she lit up. "She decided as long as she was stuck in town, she'd try to get something going with one of the video production companies, see if maybe she could get some work as a model or actress in commercials or something."

"LTC Video?"

"That the one does her dad's church services?"

"Uh-huh," I said.

"Yeah, that one. She figured at least she could learn a lot about the business, the practical stuff. What scripts are like, camera angles, even all the, whatayacallem, digital stuff."

"She was into computers?"

"Kinda. I guess she went off to a church computer camp when she was about eight, got hooked. Not enough to, like, work in computers. She said that was for geeks." She eyed me. "I'm due another twenty."

Ignoring that, I said, "Any other video companies? Did she get any work as an actress?"

"Maybe. She mentioned something about doing some acting."

I leaned back and stared up at the stars, tilting my head to see Orion above the tree line. "Don't bullshit me, Lisa. What kind of acting?"

Deep sigh. "Maybe some ... adult films."

"Porn?"

"I guess. Just acting, isn't it?"

"Mmm." I handed her the twenty. "You know who with?"

"Nope."

Liar, liar, pants on fire. The little bitch was lying.

"I think you do," I said.

"Nope," she said, and slid off the hood. "Gotta get back to work or I'll get my ass fired." She looked me over. "You don't look like a computer geek."

"I am," I said, fishing out a business card and handing it to her. "I still owe you forty bucks."

"So give it to me. You make a lot of money at computers?"

"About twelve million."

Her mouth opened in shock. "*What!?*"

Was she the only person on the planet not to have heard of Bill Gates? I shrugged. It was my turn to shrug. I was due. "I dropped out of college to open a computer company with my boyfriend. I sold it about a year and a half ago for about twenty million. I split eight with my ex-husband and the rest of the employees."

"Holy shit! I didn't know there was that much money in computers. Maybe that's what Barb meant."

That was like tossing a live toaster in my Jacuzzi tub. I held out the last two twenties and said, "What'd she say?"

Lisa eyed the forty greedily. "She said she knew a way to use computers to make a fortune. And she was gonna do it, too."

"She say how?"

"Nuh-uh. Maybe she was going to open a company."

Somehow I didn't think so.

7

I made a quick call to information, then drove over to the Masons'. Terry Street was quiet and tree-lined, running east off Rochester Road. The houses were uniform and well kept, more rational in their size than the overgrown monstrosities developers were currently building. The Mason house was a tidy brick ranch with white shutters, an oak tree in the front yard and neatly edged sidewalks and shrubbery. The two-car garage was detached, the back and side yards surrounded by chest-high chain-link fence. I parked in the driveway and knocked on the door, which was answered by a worn-looking woman in her forties or fifties. Maybe even older. It was hard to tell.

"Yes?" she asked through the screen door.

"Is Joe Mason here?"

The woman wore her curly hair short, but didn't touch it up, revealing a lot of gray, which made her look older than she probably was. I adjusted her age downward. Dramatically. At one time she may have been pretty, but now she looked old for her years, and tired. She was probably only five or six years older than me, but she looked old enough to be my mother.

"Yes, Joey lives here," she said. "Who are you?"

A kid appeared in the background. "Who is it?" he asked.

"Don't know, Joey. Someone for you."

Joe Mason approached the front door. He was about five-nine, and stocky, carrying a lot of extra weight. He had curly dark hair that surrounded his moon face like a lion's mane. So far I had to agree with Lisa Dunn. Joe Mason seemed like a kid.

"Joe, my name's Meg Malloy." I held up one of my business cards, wondering if either of them was going to open the door. "Could I talk to you for a couple minutes?"

"What about?" Mrs. Mason asked, her voice carrying an undertone of tension. She ran her hands over her polyester-covered hips, her fingers twitching like baby bird wings.

"Mrs. Mason, I just need to talk to your son for a few minutes. It's—"

"I won't let you talk to him unless you tell me what this is about."

I intuitively understood that if I told her it was about Barbara Walker the inner door would be slammed in my face. I took a deep breath. "As my business card says, I'm a computer troubleshooter. Your name was recommended to me by a friend at the university. I can use some part-time help."

Mrs. Mason's frown diminished slightly, but Joey's expression grew confused.

"Really," I said. "Just odds and ends."

"Who told you—"

Joey pushed past his mother and stepped outside.

"Joey—"

It's okay, Ma. We'll just go for a walk and I'll be right back."

"You don't even know this woman. I don't like her story. What kind of employer drops in at nine o'clock at night without calling first? I don't—"

"Bye, Ma! Back in a few." And Joey Mason was off, hot-footing it down to the sidewalk. I hurried after him, acorns crunching underfoot.

We walked half a block in silence. Joe finally said, "I'm assuming that was a line of bullshit."

I laughed at his tone of voice. Suddenly he didn't seem like quite the kid he had before. "Well, you can maybe help me out. You want to go somewhere for coffee or—"

"Let's just walk. What's the name again?"

I handed him the business card. He stopped and angled it at the moon to read it. "Computer troubleshooter," he said. "That for real?"

"Yes," I said. "That's for real."

"Okay. I know a little bit about computers—"

"You know Barbara Walker?"

Joey's shoulders slumped and he sighed. "This doesn't have to do with my father? This has to do with Barbara? Shit. She run away again?"

"Uh-huh."

"Are you really a computer troubleshooter?"

"Yeah. But ... look, I'm working for Reverend Walker in a different capacity. Basically I'm looking for Barbara. You know where she is?"

"Nope," he said, voice flat.

I thought the simple declarative 'Nope' was a lie.

"And look," he went on. "If she wants to get away from her old man, more power to her. I'd give a million bucks to get away from Mom."

"Overprotective?"

"Shit, lady! Where were you five minutes ago? I'm eighteen, and she treats me like I'm in kindergarten. It's just her and me, but She-it! My stepdad died a couple years ago and didn't leave any insurance and Mom's an LPN at Crittenton, so I'm going to O.U. instead of somewhere else so I can get away from her. Money. You offering me a job or not?"

"Not really, no. Sorry."

"Figures. This is all about Barbara, then?"

"Afraid so."

"Well, fuck Barbara, okay? We went to school together and we were friends, but Barb and I are on different trails these days. She's got her head up her ass and I don't want to have anything to do with her."

"Hey, take it easy. Sorry. So no idea, huh?"

"None." There it was again. *None. Nope.* Something in the back of my mind distrusted his one-word answers.

"Let's head back before Ma calls the cops," he said.

We drifted toward the house. "Know anything about Barb doing some work in films?"

"My ass," he said. "I don't know what she thinks she's gonna do. You know how tough it is to make it in Hollywood? Better off playing the Lotto."

"Lisa Dunn says she was going to stick around here and get work with one of the local video production companies, learn the business, get some experience."

He snorted at mention of Lisa Dunn. "Sure. Old reliable Lisa. You have to beat it out of her?"

"Bribed her, actually."

"Yeah, how much?"

I didn't say anything. Joey shrugged. He apparently had no deep-seated drive to hit me up for money. "None of my business. Chances are Lisa knows where she is, anyway."

I stopped, forcing him to halt and face me. I said, "Joe, someone sent Reverend Walker a videotape that had Barbara in it. It was a very disturbing tape. Any idea why someone sent it to him?"

"What's so disturbing about it?"

I studied him, half-lit by the moon, most of his face in shadow. Brighter than he was given credit for. "It's confidential," I said.

"I don't know shit about it," he said. "I don't know why, but if it was something sexual, then probably Barbara sent it to her *Daddy* just to get in his face. She and her *Daddy* had *issues.*"

"Anything in particular?"

He plucked at his oversized white T-shirt. "Hey, I'm the Prince of Parental Issues, right? And my old lady isn't a sex symbol for the forty-five and up born-agains. Lucky me, I never had to pretend to be the perfect daughter in ninety-nine cities every Sunday morning. Who needs that kind of pressure?"

"Anything more specific?"

"Like, was *Daddy* screwing his little girl in the choir loft? I doubt it, but who really knows what goes on behind closed doors, right?"

"This all goes back to sex? You think Barbara has a thing—"

"I'm eighteen, okay? Not eighty. I know a little bit about sex—I surf the Net every night. Barbara's a cock tease. Any guy with one nut and half a brain can figure out what she's selling." He paused to look up at the sky. "False advertisement, you know? She doesn't follow through." His voice took on a silky falsetto. "'*Oh, Joey, let's just be friends.*'"

"She lead you on?" I asked.

He shrugged. He'd apparently already said more than he expected to.

"You said you and she were on different paths. What'd you mean?"

He shrugged again. "Like, she thinks she's going to go off and be rich and famous, livin' large. It's a fantasy. Not me. I got my feet on the ground." He laughed, harsh and self-deprecating. "Head up my ass, but feet on the ground."

"Pretty jaded for only eighteen," I said.

"Hey, my father dumped my mother when I was two. When I was nine she married my step-dad, who wasn't such a bad guy, but he didn't really like kids. He died a few years ago. Every now and then my father, the biological one, decides maybe he wants custody, probably for tax purposes. Ignore me most of my life and decide suddenly when I'm eighteen maybe you'd like to talk. Bullshit. He's an asshole. You see life like I've seen life, you get a sense of reality."

"Still," I said. "You don't have any dreams? Something wild and crazy you'd like to achieve?"

He laughed the wild, angry laugh again. "Yeah, well, maybe I'll be a rock star and get married to a super model. How's that? Fucked by a beautiful woman. Wild and crazy enough for you?"

I flinched at the self-loathing. "Stranger things have happened."

"Maybe to other people," he muttered. "We done here?"

"What are you majoring in?"

"Me? Engineering."

"How are you at computers?"

"Not bad, why? Gonna offer me a job now?"

"Sorry. Just asking."

"Yeah, well, shit. That's how it goes, huh? Tell the Reverend that Barb'll come home when she's done doing whatever shit she's doing. She's eighteen. An adult. Leave her alone and she'll come home ... wagging her little *tail* behind her."

I looked up and down the street, thinking over our conversation. "You know anything about porn movies?"

Cautiously he said, "Porn?"

"That's right."

He teetered from foot to foot, uneasy. "Nope."

Lie number three, I thought. "You sure?"

"Sure," he said. "I don't know a damn thing about porn movies." He turned and rushed up the driveway and into his house.

8

My conversation with Joe Mason left me feeling uneasy, not only because of the unexpected degree of self-directed loathing, but because I was sure he knew more than he was telling. So far, everyone seemed to know more than they were telling, leaving me clueless and confused.

If I was going to continue poking into other people's business, I was going to have to get used to being clueless and confused. Toss in annoyed and aggravated, and I was pretty sure I was well on my way to being a private investigator, at least emotionally.

I headed south on Rochester Road, through downtown with its shops and restaurants, over Paint Creek and up the hill to Avon Road, the Leader Dogs For the Blind training facility, past Winchester Mall, several upscale subdivisions, more strip malls, and finally into Rochester Hills and the Barnes and Noble where I was to meet Brother Matthew DuPuis.

I was early, but scoped out the Starbucks to see if Matthew DuPuis was there. He wasn't. I hit the periodicals section and snagged a *New York Times* and the latest *Wired*, then shifted into the mystery section to see if any of my favorites—Janet Evanovich, Sue Grafton or Aileen Schumacher—had put out a new book. They hadn't, but I found one by Dick Francis I hadn't read yet, and a new Harlan Coben. Then I drifted back to the computer section. I didn't find anything new I didn't already own, so I paid for my purchases and returned to the coffee shop, bought a double mug of the house java, no steamed milk, no "gourmet" flavoring, no Madagascar cinnamon, and settled down with all the news that was fit to print.

I didn't have long to wait. Brother Matthew appeared in front of me accompanied by a tall, thin man in a dark undertaker's suit. He reminded me of one of those Wegman photographs of Weimaraners all dressed up in people clothes.

"Ms. Malloy? This is Lucas Balkovic," he said, jumping right in with the introductions. "The financial officer of the church."

I took Brother Lucas's bony hand, flinching at the undisguised hostility in his blue eyes and on his horsey face. Without asking the two men sat across from me.

I said, "You guys want some coffee? Maybe some carrot cake or a brownie? I'll buy."

"Who are you?" Balkovic demanded, ignoring my offer, voice rough.

"Excuse me?"

"Show me ID," he said.

I glanced at Brother Matthew. His face was carefully expressionless.

"You sure you don't want some cake or something?" Coffee seemed unnecessary; the guy was hyped enough.

"ID," he said, voice cold.

"Sure," I said, puzzled, and supplied my driver's license.

Balkovic looked it over as if I'd handed him a Kleenex filled with snot. He held out his other hand, snapping his fingers. "You know what I mean. Your ID." He tossed my driver's license back across the table at me.

"Maybe you could—"

"Who are you?" he snapped. "Who are you with? Specifically. Stop playing games and—"

I handed him my business card.

"Not this! This is ... this is bull ... bull crap! Why can't you people just come out and deal honestly with us? I assure you I'll cooperate completely—fully—if you'll only come out of this ... this subterfuge! We're a ... a church! We're not trying to hide anything." Sweat beaded up on his high, bare forehead, his voice tight and reedy from tension.

I took a deep breath. "Mr. Balkovic ... I really don't know what you're talking about. My name is Megan Malloy and I'm—"

Brother Balkovic lurched to his feet, jostling the table, causing my coffee to slop everywhere.

"Enough! Tell your people I wanted to cooperate, but you insisted on continuing your evasions! Typical! Call me when you want to get down to the truth."

He flung a business card onto the table. It landed face down in the spilled coffee. Without another word he stalked away.

I tried to make eye contact with Brother Matthew, but his gaze was inward, thoughtful. He would not meet my eyes.

Voice low, he said, "I hope you're who you say you are," and stood up to leave.

I watched him disappear, then tweezed Balkovic's business card out of the puddle with two fingers and patted it dry. I entered the data into my PDA and discarded my coffee, soggy napkins and the card.

Well, it's official, I thought. *I have reached my aggravation quota for the day*. Time to go home.

9

I parked the Hummer in the gravel pull-off next to my dock. My house stands on the land side of Heights Road, which runs along the south shore of Lake Orion. On the water side—mostly—is sparse parking and private docks. I stood at the end of the rickety, splintery gray wood dock for a minute, listening to the soft lap of the waves, smelling seaweed and lake water. Lake Orion is large and amoeba-shaped, with several small islands dotting its surface. My house, a three-story cottage, overlooks two of the tiny islands, each seven-hundred-square-foot floor providing a wall of glass for the view. The back of the house faces a steep bluff, so steep it only supports shrubs, weeds and miniature mudslides.

Taking a final deep breath of the lake air, I crossed Heights, slipped in and punched off the alarm system. The entry level was the original summer cottage, which had been vertically renovated year after year until I bought and gutted it. It now consisted of two rooms: a small living room with thick gray carpet, a sectional sofa and a Steinway baby grand piano, and a laundry room that doubled as a spare bathroom. My renovations had cost more than the house had, but it was worth it. No garage, but no yard to maintain either.

Up a spiral staircase on the second level was a kitchen/dining room and another living area, this time furnished with a sofa and loveseat, stereo system and big-screen TV. I stopped there long enough to retrieve a pitcher of frozen strawberry margaritas from the freezer, a bag of tortilla chips from the pantry, and a jar of salsa from the refrigerator.

The third level was two rooms and a full bath with Jacuzzi. One room was my bedroom, the second my office. I changed into sweats and checked my answering machine. One message.

"Oh ... hi honey, it's Mom. Why aren't you ever in? Anyway, your dad and I are in Amsterdam now. You remember Kerrie Livernois? She plays viola with the Concertgebow? Well, we're going to stay with them for a few days. Kerrie wants to fit in an informal recital for the two of us if we can squeeze it in, but we'll see. Your dad and I have scheduled a Rhone tour in a week or so. We're having such a good time ... Oh, here's Kerrie's number in case you ..."

I dutifully jotted it down, smiling. After selling the company I had presented my parents with a handful of credit cards and explicit instructions to go travel like they had talked about all these years. Once their initial doubt and guilt disappeared they hopped the first plane out of Michigan. They return every couple months for a week or so, then go back storming other borders. I'm always receiving calls at odd hours from various time zones. Denmark and South Africa, Saudi Arabia and Russia. I received a very peculiar video-tape of them cavorting with penguins in Antarctica, a day trip they just couldn't resist. I had a sneaking suspicion they wanted to make love on every continent (or every country), but I didn't dwell on it—they were my parents, after all. I was glad they were enjoying themselves.

I took my PDA out of my backpack, and my snacks over to my office, which was crammed with the best computer equipment money could buy ... and buy and buy and buy. Sometimes it was irritating to be in a line of business that had built-in obsolescence requiring a change of equipment every three to six months. My computers were always on, linked to Chavez Tech via cable, various screen savers lighting up the monitors. I dropped the PDA into its cradle and instructed the two computers to talk to each other, then down-loaded my e-mail. One message on my answering machine, one hundred twenty-two on my e-mail. Yup. I was a cyber babe.

I shoved open the windows and gazed out at the water, as black and velvety as a dreamless sleep, marred only by the occasional home light. I didn't want to read the e-mail. I didn't want to check the computer system for intruders. I didn't want to get to work autopsying the Missionary Church of Jesus Christ Evangelical's database. I wanted Maui.

Or more correctly, I wanted the dream of Maui, the beautiful flower of Maui, not the bugs that went with it.

As I'd told Lisa Dunn, I had started a computer company with my boyfriend. On the surface that was a true enough statement. Mitch Freeman and I had been in love and together we had dropped out of college and formed a company called CyberConduits. Mitch and I were both computer majors at Michigan State University, and the whole thing had been sparked by a visit to my parents' house.

My father, at that time, was a professor of computer science at Oakland University, and the conversation at the dinner table had drifted into what Dad thought might be *The Next Big Thing*. In retrospect, I realize *The Next Big Thing* was always a preoccupation of Mitch's. Mitch wasn't happy to catch the big wave at the crest and ride it to shore; he had to jump off and look for an even bigger one.

At that dinner conversation over pot roast and redskin potatoes, Dad had talked about the Internet, which had been in existence since 1969, but was largely the slow-moving toy of academics and computer nerds. But he mentioned that, in his opinion, modem and processor speeds were finally getting to the point where the general computer-using public might be interested. But, he had added, the actual server computers that acted as conduits for digital data transfer needed to expand, too.

I remember Dad peering expectantly over his reading glasses at Mitch, waiting. Mitch immediately started brainstorming about a company name and what it would do, all ready with a marketing plan and nothing to market. Dad looked up at Mom, who was gazing at me, a thoughtful expression on her face. I caught the exchange—it has now crystallized in my memory. They both seemed to be waiting.

I said, "Is this locked into academia and government, or is there a niche for start-ups?"

Dad smiled, a gold star for the prize pupil. "There's a need for start-ups. I have all the contacts."

Mitch bubbled, "Then that's all we'd need," and continued blue-skying his business plan.

The subject changed to something else, probably an upcoming recital my mother was giving. She was a professor of music at O.U., a gifted violinist, first chair with the Rochester Symphony, third chair with the Detroit Symphony. I remember that Mitch kept bringing the subject back to the Internet. Dad listened and nodded, but didn't feed the frenzy. It was only later, when Mitch drove off to visit with some friends for a while that I asked Dad if he had any books. The smile he flashed me was what daughters live for. He handed me six books on Java, html and other languages relevant to conduit systems. Then he handed me a copy of an article he had recently submitted to a technical journal. It was on programming for server computers and hadn't been accepted yet.

I stared at the article for a moment, shocked. "If it's such a great idea, why aren't you doing it?"

"Just because it's a great idea doesn't mean it'll succeed," he said. "Just because it's a great idea doesn't mean the time is right." He shrugged. "And I'm old enough to know what I like to do, and running a business isn't it. It's not my bag."

I went back to school and pored over Dad's paper and the textbooks. Mitch saw what I was doing—my interest fed his enthusiasm. Using what I learned, I wrote a program for server computers linking the Internet, let Mitch package it pretty, and showed it to Dad. He took it to one of his contacts, who bought the program for ten thousand dollars and a job offer. We took the money, but not the job.

CyberConduits was born.

Mitch and I dropped out of school to run the company and got married six months later. The company grew, slowly but steadily, moving out of the second bedroom of our apartment into an office building in Novi. After our initial success, Mitch lost interest. Mitch liked ideas, not work, and once a company is formed, the only thing really left is the work. He had no interest in making a strong foundation and building on it. He wanted to chase fads and strike it rich. Unfortunately, that philosophy also extended to our marriage.

I worked seventy and eighty-hour weeks making the company go. When the World Wide Web was invented in '91, business boomed. The Web was built on the foundation CyberConduits helped create. By 2001 Mitch and I were divorced. I bought his half of the company for a quarter million cash and a percentage of any sale or stock options.

By the late 90s I had eighteen employees, a plush office and no life. I spent all my time at the company, had no husband, no kids, no friends. Just employees and money I did nothing with. We were not MicroSoft or IBM or Yahoo! We were a small company in a small niche of the booming Internet economy, providing non-glamorous software for server computers. Many of the big companies that understood what we did began to hint at possible buyouts or mergers. I listened, but didn't bite.

Somewhere in there, probably around the time my parents retired, I began to think a lot about what my father had said about not wanting to run a business. I liked technical challenges. I liked programming. I liked playing with computer equipment and solving complicated problems. I hated budgets and business competition and hiring and firing employees. I particularly hated being buttered up and stabbed in the back, often simultaneously. It had been two years since I programmed a line of code. Three years since I'd solved a technical problem, and four years since anyone asked me to or thought I could. I was the boss, and I didn't much like it.

Maybe it had to do with Dad's heart attack. It was a small one, but it scared me. I took two weeks off from the company to help Mom. In a lightning bolt of discovery that St. Paul would have appreciated, I realized how close my parents were; realized how distant their life of academic pursuits, family and quiet affection was from my own. Dad recovered, but I didn't.

Not long after, I received a call from Lyle Worthington of Solar Microsystems, coming right out about a possible buyout. I told him I'd think about it, and did. CyberConduits was in the process of redecorating. One day after Lyle's call I sat in a meeting with my managers, supposedly working on the directions we thought we should take the company. Instead it turned into a full-blown argument about what color the walls should be and interior decorating.

Halfway through a pitched battle over window blinds I stood up and walked out. I called Lyle and said, "Let's talk."

Six months later I packed all my belongings into storage, bought a string bikini—having neither the body nor the boldness for a thong—and moved to Maui. A month later I was the proud owner of an enormously overpriced beach house. I never missed a sunset.

For a year I pursued the life of the rich beach girl. I snorkled, learned to scuba dive, rode bikes down volcanoes, played beach volleyball, and chased and was chased by a string of sun-bronzed boy-men with flashing smiles and empty eyes.

Twice I flew to Seattle to consult with Solar Microsystems. I grew bored, not necessarily a bad thing at that time of my life. I rediscovered the joy of reading for pleasure, watching movies, playing the piano and a regular exercise routine, swimming and running and working out at the gym.

His name was Craig. No last name. I met him at a beach party over roast pork and mai-tais and took him home with me to my beach house with the sunset views. We rolled around in bed for a while and I fell asleep in his arms. In the middle of the night I woke up to find him going through my purse.

"What're you doing?" I asked, flicking on the bedside lamp.

Craig was typical—curly blond hair, chiseled features, deep tan, well-developed muscles, perfect teeth and eyes like chunks of glittering blue glacier ice. He took all the bills out of my wallet. "You think I do this for free?" he said.

"You're—"

"There's only two hundred here. You got more?"

I stared at him as if I'd invited an alien into my house. Into my bed.

He began to rifle through my drawers. I sat in stunned silence, sheet wrapped around me, Maui's warm breezes drifting through the open windows. Finally he found the little metal box that held my backup cash. He emptied it.

"See ya, babe," he said, and left a card on my dresser. Just Craig, it said, with a phone number.

I stayed up the rest of the night, restless, prowling the house, listening to the waves, thinking deep and bitter thoughts. The last year seemed like a waste. Maui spoiled, paradise lost. What I had become? A rich, idle woman with no purpose who paid for sex?

In the morning I packed up the beach house, contacted a company to maintain it and caught the first flight to Detroit.

To home.

It was too late to do anything about CyberConduits. And I didn't want to start another company. But I did want to work. Something where I could do short-term projects, solve problems, but not a nine-to-five job that tied me to a clock. I became a computer troubleshooter.

One of my computers beeped, jerking me from my memories. On the screen a window opened up.

BLACK GUARD ALERT

Beneath that, it said:

YOUR SYSTEM HAS BEEN APPROACHED BY A TROJAN HORSE

I tapped a key to inquire. A Trojan Horse is a hacker technique. Hackers program their computers to randomly dial numbers in hopes of hitting an open computer system. They knock on the door and try to park a Trojan Horse in the barn, a program that allows them to come back and explore the computer system or let them use the system as a false front for hacker activity.

Someone was trying to break into my system.

I waited. **Black Guard Alert** is a commercial program to warn and protect from attempts to hack into personal computer systems. It works fine against run-of-the-mill hackers. The screen flashed:

TROJAN HORSE HAS BEEN REPELLED.

I kept watching.

A new window opened on the screen.

This was a program I devised myself. Just in case a hacker got past **Black Guard. Trojan Horse Has Entered The Water Pit** was followed by a readout of the Trojan Horse's specifications. I read through it quickly, nodding.

I typed in:

<track>

The computer began to backtrack the Trojan Horse, to identify the location of the hacker. Suddenly the screen went dark and Water Pit came back on.

TROJAN HORSE HAS ESCAPED!

I stared at the green letters for a moment. Because I have a fast hookup and because I'm fairly well known within computer circles, hacker attacks, many coincidental, a few intentional, are not unknown. Only a few make it to the Water Pit. Nobody—as far as I knew—had made it past the Water Pit. It had successfully kept my hacker from entering the system, but it had not trapped the hacker, as designed. Nobody had escaped from it before.

Until now.

This wasn't just a randomly programmed attempt. It was deliberate. And whoever was trying to break into my system—specifically *my* system—had been skilled enough to escape my trap. Very skilled.

What the hell was going on?

10

I sat down to deal with my e-mail, beginning with a delete-frenzy of the spam that slipped through my filter. If I could write an effective program to kill spam I could build a bridge to Maui. Finally, down to mail I wanted, I took a sip of margarita and skimmed headers, to get to the important ones first, "Fwds" last.

To: Ms. Megan Malloy
From: Lyle Worthington, CEO, Solar Microsystems, Inc.

Hello Meg:
Hope everything is going well with you. Per our discussion of the 18th, the board has agreed that your input regarding new server applications would be more than welcome. Please let me know if you're still interested and if so, we'll discuss your fee. The meeting will be in Seattle on October 12th. Your presence would be greatly appreciated.
Sincerely,
Lyle

I replied *Yes* and asked for more details. The next was from my Dad.

To: Meg Malloy
From: Dad

Hi, sweetheart. Mom said you weren't home, so I thought I'd drop you a quick note. We're having a ball—thanks so much (again). Mom tells everyone we meet about how you're giving us a free lift around the world—they're as green as new peas, everyone. Kerrie Livernois wants your mother to do a joint recital—you know Mom, all resistance : "I can't, really, I haven't practiced in months (a lie), I don't know the pieces (a whopper), I don't have my violin with me." Well, Kerrie has a friend who's offered to loan

Mom her Stradivarius, so ... the recital's next Thursday. They're
practicing like crazy. Jek Livernois's taking me on a tour. Joke:
Amsterdam is very tolerant of homosexuality ... that's why there's
so many dikes! :)
Well, gotta go.
Love,
Dad

I replied at length, telling him about my current job as a P.I. He'd be pleased,
I thought. Both Mom and Dad had been understanding when I sold CyberConduits,
even supportive. But Dad had wanted to know what I planned to do. When I had
said I planned to do nothing, I was retired, he had shot me that frown parents learn
early. It suggested I didn't know what I was talking about. Mom told him to leave
me alone, that I'd figure it out soon enough. Both were right. I did figure it out
soon enough, and I wanted to work and stay busy. Maui was great, but it was
too far from Mom and Dad. Lake Orion felt like home.

There were undoubtedly people who didn't understand that, but they
probably wondered why Bill Gates keeps working even though he could retire a
million times over, why Stephen King still writes novels and screenplays though
he could afford to throw his word processing program away, why Sean Connery
keeps acting when he doesn't need to. The answer is simple: they like to work.

There were nine e-mails from friends around the world which were
low priority, most containing jokes I may or may not send on. There werefifty
obvious spam trying to interest me in on-line gambling, Internet porn or computer
hardware, which I deleted. There were a few business-related messages, which
I read carefully and answered in detail. Then there was Glen's message.

> To: M&M
> From: Glen Blalock, Head Poobah
> Blalockubus, Inc.
>
> I attached the image of the enhanced tattoo. Came out good. The
> background through the door of the "porn palace" needs more work.
>
> Resolution is shit, but I might have a few tricks up my sleeve. Am
> running SpiderLegs to see if I can get a hit on any images from
> the video. It'll take time. Great to see you.
> Don't be a stranger.
> Glen

I clicked the attachment and watched the image unfurl. A grainy "enhanced"
image of the tattoo appeared on the screen. A black cat.

I printed and saved it to a disk, unsure if it would help. Then I picked my way through my friends' messages, reading the short jokes, deleting the long ones. The last one I checked was a "Fwd: Fwd" from TFerguson@Juno.com and its topic read: DID YOU HEAR THE ONE ABOUT ...

To: Megan Malloy
From: Tferguson

Malloy,
If you're serious about poking into this, cover your ass. You are in deep, deep shit. No joke. The danger is very real.
A Friend

Oh great, I thought. What is this? I checked TFerguson's point of origin, quickly realizing its tracks had been covered. TFerguson was either a completely bogus alias, or someone else's name used without permission.

I saved it all for later consideration. I wanted to go hunting to see if I could track down my "friend," but I had promised Steph I'd finish the salvage work on the church's database. It was time to earn my keep.

I dropped CDs into the player starting with Brahms' Second Piano Concerto, and got ready to work. Closing in on midnight, I logged on to Chavez Tech, typed passwords, and went to work restoring Missionary Church's database of charitable contributions. Brahms turned over to Glenn Gould's version of Bach's "English Suites," which gave way to Mozart's Piano Concerto in D Minor. Daytime might be for classic rock and news, but midnight work demanded classical. My musical taste spun with the spheres.

It took me a while longer than I had hoped, but by three in the morning I was done. I saved all the changes and e-mailed Stephanie a bill.

Three in the morning was typically my bedtime. I'm a night owl, but I come by it naturally. When I was maybe five or six years old, I remember being awakened in the middle of the night by the sound of my mother practicing her violin. When I went to find out what she was doing, my father intercepted me, saying, "It's three o'clock, honey. What are you doing up?"

"Why's Mommy playing?"

"She has a big audition coming up."

I didn't understand that then, but Dad slipped me back into bed and together we listened to the gorgeous music resonating throughout the house until I fell asleep. Years later I woke up in the middle of the night to find my dad hunched over a computer screen. I was not a morning person, but at least I had the excuse that it was genetic.

Before I went to bed I considered Barbara Walker's disappearance. There were dozens of databases out there I could check her driver's license and credit cards on, but I had a short cut. There is no such thing as privacy, and the Internet makes it even worse. One of my contacts, a Ken Brynmore, interned at CyberConduits, but went on to be a programmer with NCIC, the National Crime Information Center. He had been a major source for Mitch in the brief time Mitch worked as a P.I. Hopefully, Mitch hadn't worn out his welcome. I e-mailed Ken with what I wanted, then dutifully checked the databases, too. By morning I hoped for results from all of them. I was too tired to go hacker hunting. I shut the system down, cleaned my dishes, brushed my teeth, set the alarm and went to bed. I'd be up at the crack of ten.

When the alarm went off I crawled out of bed, peed, hauled on a pair of running shorts, a baggy T-shirt and my Nikes. Stretching first (I'm too old not to), I ran, slowly, enjoying the warm fall day with just a hint of chill to come. I jogged up Heights to Shady Oaks, curving around the lake onto Dollar Bay Drive, cutting down Pine Tree to the canal, cutting through Marina Pointe Estates to Joslyn, past the library to Clarkston, finally wending my way back home. A UPS truck was just arriving. He handed me a box containing a large glass jar of M&Ms.
The note said:

> Good to see you again.
> A pleasure to work with you, as always.
> Take care
> Glen.

"Thank you, Glen," I said, "but, no, you'll still never sleep with me." So young and so cynical.

I took a fast shower, spread cream cheese on a bagel, poured O.J. and high-octane java and took to my computer. E-mail first.

To: Megan Malloy
 From: Stephanie Jones, President
 WebSpinners, Inc.

Hi Meg:
Went over your work this morning. Terrific job, as usual.
Thanks for bailing me out. The check, as they say, is in the mail. Henry and I want you to see if you can figure out what happened. If it goes past twenty hours, call me and we'll decide whether it's worth the effort.
Take care,
Steph

I e-mailed her that I would work on it soon, but was tied up for a day or two.
Then I checked the rest of my mail.

To: Megan Malloy
From: Kenneth Brynmore,
National Crime Information Center

Megan! How cool to hear from you. Taking over where Mitch
left off, huh? Good for you. I heard you sold CyberConduits—
couldn't believe it! Anyway, here's the stuff I found on your
M.P.—nada. No record, no credit card activity, nothing on
her car. Sorry. She's either dead or staying with someone
who's footing the bill. Good luck and stay in touch.
Ken
p.s. I'll help you when I can, but please be choosy about
what you ask. There are limits.

Ken's a good guy. Married with three kids, as of the last Christmas
card from him.
I mulled over what my next course of action should be and decided to
look into my hacker, TFerguson@Juno.com, *aka* A Friend. It didn't take long.
Whoever my "friend" was, he covered his tracks. The last address was
SmithJ189@aol.com, which was probably bogus as well. It wasn't a total bust,
but going any further would use more time than I currently wanted to give. I had
better go visit Reverend Walker and look over Barbara's bedroom. I made sure
my laptop, PDA, phone and wallet were in my backpack and headed out to the
Hummer, grabbing the M&Ms in case my blood sugar dropped. I walked across
Heights Road and punched the button on my remote to start up the Hummer.
With a deafening roar and a flash of fire, the Hummer exploded. I
was knocked on my ass, the glass jar of M&Ms shattering, scattering multi-
colored candy everywhere. Bits of glass and metal and plastic rained down
around me, drowning out my screams. I felt a wave of heat, a concussion like
a giant hand slamming against me, and something else. Wet.
Blood.
I tried to struggle out of the road, to run back to the house. When I
rolled over to my knees I was looking down at the blankly staring face of
Barbara Walker.
Just the head of Barbara Walker.
The body seemed to be spread in charred pieces all over the road.
This time I don't think anything could have drowned out my screams.

11

I scrambled backwards crabwise, trying to keep my distance from the rain of gore. My heart was triphammering in my chest, blood roaring in my ears, air burning in my lungs. Everything seemed to move in slo-mo, like struggling through Jell-O. A couple cars stopped. A kid jumped out of an old Honda Civic, shouting, "Are you okay?"

Yeah, sure, I thought, my skin pulled tight against my face, acid bursting up into my throat. Just peachy. I bit it back, along with my screams. The kid was coming closer, edging around the debris. Half a dozen paces away, he repeated, "Are you okay?"

I held up a shaking hand for him to stop. "Uh ... call 911," I said. "There's a dead ... a dead person all over the road."

He nodded, pulled a phone out of a pocket and punched in three digits, walking away, giving me space, but keeping an eye on me. A small part of my mind marveled at how calm he seemed. Must be youth. I sat by the side of the road, debating whether to put my head between my knees. Too proud? The Hummer was flaming up, the smell of burning gasoline, plastic, metal and body parts assaulting my nose. I leaned forward, thought I might throw up, or pass out. Sucked in air. Didn't pass out or puke. One good thing to happen to you so far today, Malloy.

If your back is ever against the wall. I mean, really against the wall ... your life's in danger ... My cousin Matalyn Malloy, an investigative reporter; bar chatter, talking about a friend of hers.

I snagged my backpack, dragging out my own cell phone and my PDA. The number was in the PDA, I was sure of it. My fingers were clumsy handling the stylus, but eventually I got my address book up on the tiny screen. I punched the number into the cell phone.

The kid from the Civic approached me again cautiously. "The Sheriff's coming. Your car explode?"

I nodded.

"I'll direct traffic, okay?"

He was probably eighteen with hair shaved up the sides and long on top, dyed fire-engine red. I gave him a relieved wave and he went off to move his car to block traffic in one direction. I didn't know who he was, but he was helpful. Thank God.

"Bear here," a voice said in my ear.

"Is this Jack Bear?"

"Yeah."

"This is Megan Malloy, Matalyn's cousin."

"The computer expert. Thanks for the work you did for me."

We'd never spoken personally, just by e-mail. I'd provided security protocols and encryption for his website as a favor to Matalyn. "Um ... Mattie told me if I was ever in trouble—*real* trouble—to call you."

"Tell me," he said.

I did, as succinctly as my nerves would allow. His questions were to the point.

"Are you in immediate danger?"

"I don't think so."

"The cops there yet?"

"No, but they'll be here soon."

"I can get there in an hour and a half if I fly in, but I won't have a car. You have an extra car?"

"No. Wouldn't you have to come to the airport?"

"I was thinking a seaplane into the lake you live on."

Damn. This guy doesn't fool around.

"I bet the cops'll have a lot of questions," I said.

"Yeah. Keep you pretty busy. I can be there in two and a half, maybe three hours if I drive. That way we can be mobile. You be okay that long?"

"I think so."

"Yes or no?"

I took a deep breath. "Yes. I'll be okay with the cops here. Aren't you in Traverse City, though? That's a four-hour drive."

"Three hours at the latest. Wait for me, though, okay?"

"How will I know it's you?"

"Black Corvette, license plate, U-R-S-I-N-E."

"Ursine?"

"Yeah. Anything else?"

"No."

"Sit tight. I'll be there soon."

The first Oakland County Sheriff's patrol car arrived only a minute later, two uniformed deputies taking it all in, hands resting on their gun butts, speaking with the kid in the Civic. He looked pretty confident despite the long baggy jeans and extra-long black Lords of Acid t-shirt he wore. My hero. He and the cops talked, they wrote something in their notebooks and the kid took off. I never got his name. In short order fire-fighting teams and another patrol car arrived, followed by a Chevrolet Caprice.

An older man, balding, with a parrot's beak for a nose, wearing khakis and a red golf shirt, climbed out of the Caprice. He stopped and stared at me for a moment before moving my way.

"That's a mess, for sure, eh?" he said to me. "You okay?"

"I'm not sure. Physically I think I'm okay."

"Sure, sure," he said. I estimated him to be in his fifties, his eyes brown and soft, his face a roadmap of wrinkles and creases. Long, narrow face, twinkling eyes, everyone's favorite uncle. He held out a badge, talking nonstop, giving me time. "Lieutenant Eli Rosenbaum, Oakland County Sheriff's Department, Major Cases ... naw, well, acting commander, Lake Orion substation. I'll be done with this tomorrow. They thought maybe they should promote me, make me a bureaucrat. I didn't want it, myself, but it's hard to ignore the money. I think I've proved I can't manage a budget, let alone people, so I'm back to the Detectives Bureau. I'd rather work Major Cases, anyway. How about you?"

"Huh?"

"What's your name, Miss?"

"Oh. Megan Malloy."

Lieutenant Rosenbaum held out a hand to me and helped me to my feet. "You see all this, Ms. Malloy?"

"Yeah. It's my car."

"Huh. What was that, a Hummer?"

"Yeah."

"No kidding," he said. He reached into his pants pocket and retrieved a notebook and pen and a cigar, which he stuck unlit in his mouth. "How'd it ride?"

"Ride?"

"Yeah. How's a Hummer ride? Mushy, like that Caprice? I hate that thing. It's got a Corvette engine in it in case I'm supposed to chase down speeders or something, but the suspension's got so much float to it I might as well be driving a pontoon boat. Steers like a bumper car. How'd your Hummer handle?"

"Like a tank," I said, put off-guard by the man's gentle babbling.

"Yeah? Blew up okay, though, didn't it? Who's this, uh ... this a woman?"

"I'm pretty sure, yeah."

Rosenbaum rocked back on his heels and stared again. The deputies were closing down the road, directing traffic and cordoning off the area. "You know her?"

"I think her name's Barbara Walker."

He scribbled in his notebook. "Why you think so?" he asked.

"I recognized her face."

He turned and shot me a quizzical look. "Face?"

I pointed to where the head lay. "I fell right about there. When I rolled over ..."

He tiptoed over to the head, careful where he put his feet. He hunkered down, gazing intently at Barbara's features. He nodded and tap-danced his way back to me.

"Hell of a shock," he said.

"It was."

"For her, too, I bet. Okay, Ms. Malloy ... so tell me, why would this Barbara Walker want to blow up your ride?"

"I ... I'm not sure."

"But you know her, right?"

"Well, not exactly."

He shifted the cigar from one side of his mouth to the other and wrinkled his nose like a rabbit. Rocking back on his heels again, he stared up at the sky for a moment, then back to me. "Let's pretend for a moment that you and I speak the same language, okay? You speak English like you learned from your mommy and daddy, and I speak English like I learned from my momma and poppa when they weren't speaking Yiddish to each other. Okay? Let's try this, maybe we can make sense of things. No, better yet, so *I* can make sense of things. Understand?"

"Go ahead, Lieutenant."

"How do you know Barbara Walker?"

"I don't. I'm looking for her."

"Well, hell, Ms. Malloy. I guess you found her. Or pieces of her."

"Lieutenant!"

He waved a calming hand. "Why were you looking for her?"

"Her father asked me to."

"Her father ... ?"

"The Reverend James Walker."

"Should I know who that is, because you say his name like I should know who he is."

"He's a TV evangelist."

"I'm Jewish. I never watched a TV evangelist in my life. I like to sleep late on Sundays, maybe watch *CBS Morning News*, though I liked Charles Kuralt a lot better than Charles Osgood. Maybe later, after breakfast, I'll watch George Stepha-what's-his-name, but I thought Cokie Roberts was a lot cuter. So, okay, Barbara Walker's father's a TV star of sorts. What do you do for a living?"

"I'm a computer troubleshooter."

Rosenbaum scratched his head and looked out at the lake. A seagull flew by overhead and his eyes followed it. "One of these houses yours, by any chance?"

I pointed.

"Good. Hang on." He walked over to one of the deputies, spoke to him for a moment, then returned to me. "Okay, Ms. Malloy. Let's go inside, get comfortable. Seems like you've got a story to tell me, and I like to get comfy, maybe have a cup of coffee if you've got some, while people tell me stories. People love to tell me stories. Over and over again. And I like to ask lots of questions. You like to answer questions, Ms. Malloy?"

"Not really."

"Well," he said, smiling. "You're just having one pisser of a day, aren't you?"

"Yes," I said, leading him to my house. "As a matter of fact, I am."

I started to make coffee in the kitchen when I realized there was ... stuff ... on my hands. Soot. Blood. Other stuff my brain did not want to cope with. I ran a hand through my hair and it came away with ... Spots did the hula before my eyes and I vomited into the sink, gripping the stainless steel as the world tilted and I threatened to fall off.

Rosenbaum patted my shoulder and in a soft voice said, "It's okay. It'll be okay. Come on. This way," and he led me to my bedroom and into the bathroom and in a matter-of-fact voice suggested I take a very hot shower. I did. I scrubbed my hair and my skin until the hot water ran out and my stomach calmed down. When I returned to the kitchen the coffee was made and Rosenbaum was sitting at my kitchen table drinking from a mug.

"Feel a little better?"

I nodded and poured myself a cup, debated adding a healthy dollop of whiskey and decided against it. For now. Jamieson's might very well be on the agenda later in the day.

"If you can figure out where it is," Rosenbaum said. "Maybe you should start at the beginning."

While I had been showering I had been debating how much to tell the Lieutenant. I decided: everything.

"To start at the beginning we need to go up to my office."

"Then maybe you can sorta give me a prologue to the beginning, you know, introduce it. Think of it as a trailer for a movie."

I eyed him. *What a nut.* "You mean, like, female computer trouble-shooter gets offer to hunt for client's missing daughter, but daughter tries to kill female troubleshooter but ends up killing herself instead?"

He sucked on the still unlit cigar. If he tried to light it in my house I would kill him. "I don't think Hollywood'll go for it, but you've got to admit, it's kinda catchy."

"Catchy," I said. "Anyway, here's my card." I handed him one of my business cards and explained why and what Stephanie and Henry had hired me to do for Chavez Technologies and the Missionary Church of Jesus Christ

Evangelical. He took careful notes without once interrupting. I was impressed.

I pointed to the stairs to my office. "Then the Reverend came into WebSpinner's offices wanting to talk to me," I said.

"When was this?" It was the Lieutenant's first interruption since I'd started the spiel.

"Yesterday. Tuesday."

"You make enemies fast, Ms. Malloy. Okay, no more questions. You go on and talk."

"Let's go to my office. I'll show you."

He followed me upstairs and I explained what the Reverend had wanted and popped in my copy of the disk and played the rape scene. Lieutenant Rosenbaum leaned forward in his chair, eyebrows raised. When it was done, he said, "*Oy vey!* The father shook up?"

"What do you think?"

"I'd be murderous ... and embarrassed."

"Bingo," I said. "I took the tape to a friend—he's the guy who converted it to disk—and we analyzed it. We don't think it's a rape. We think it's a loop of a porn film." I slipped a blank disk into my drive and made a new copy while I played it again for the Lieutenant, describing the cuts as I went along.

"My, my, my, my, my," he said. "So then what?" He held up his hand. "Hold it, just a second." He walked over to my windows and looked down. Fire-fighters were still spraying foam on my Hummer. A van and couple official cars were parked clear of the scene but close by. "That's the M.E.'s guys and the crime scene techs and couple more detectives. Gotta go talk to them. Be right back."

I nodded. When he was gone I labeled the new disk and stored it away, and printed up all my notes on the case so far, who I had talked to and what they had said. Full cooperation. About five minutes later I heard footsteps below me, and Lieutenant Rosenbaum returned.

"Okay," he said. "Let's continue. So what'd you do after you determined it was a porn loop?"

I described my investigation, and handed over my notes, as well as a printout of the enhanced cat tattoo.

"Whew-boy," he said, looking at it all. "You're organized."

I shrugged.

"Uh-huh, uh-huh," he said. "So you get home, play with your computers, find out what? Zip, zero, nada, and this morning someone tries to blow you up. Makes me wonder a couple of things."

"Me, too."

"One, you used that remote thingy to start your car. I'm guessing this bomb was attached to the ignition. I want to know, did this mad bomber— Barbara Walker, I guess—plan for you to be in the car when it blew up, kill you, or just to scare you? 'Cause I'm guessing if they were smart enough to hook up your car to explode, they woulda seen the remote gizmo attached to your ignition."

My estimation of Lieutenant Rosenbaum went up a few notches. "I don't know," I said, stomach clenching.

"Second thing ..." A heavy-set man with black curly hair appeared in the doorway. Rosenbaum grinned. "Leon, how ya doin'?"

"Interesting day so far. You got a second?"

"Sure. You want to talk to Ms. Malloy?"

"Eventually."

"Excuse me," Rosenbaum said, and walked halfway down the stairs with the man named Leon. They talked for a moment, then Rosenbaum came back up and sat down next to me. He adjusted the crease in his pants, took the soggy cigar out of his mouth and examined it, then stuck it back in.

"Don't smoke any more, but I've got the oral thing going. Great prop, too. Gives my hands and my mouth something to do ... not that there's ever a shortage of things for my mouth to do. My wife says I've got a motor mouth. Probably the Captain may've said something about that somewhere along the twisty-turny path, too. But hey, some of us, we just can't think as well without putting it into words, you know what I mean?"

"Uh-huh," I said, heavy with skepticism. Rosenbaum stared at the computer screen in front of him, the screen saver displaying slowly rotating geometric figures.

The Lieutenant picked up his coffee mug and said, "I'm going to have to go back over your story a couple of times, and then Detectives O'Connell and Frisch are going to chat with you, and probably Leon. Leon, the guy you just saw, he's an investigator for the Medical Examiner's Office. And I wouldn't be surprised if Mike or Sue, the crime scene techs, they might want to talk to you, too. Lots of questions. Then we'll type them up and you'll sign it. That's how it goes, pretty much." He took a sip of the coffee and grimaced. "Cold. Want a warm-up? I'll trot downstairs and get it."

"Okay," I said, and handed him my half-full mug. He trotted downstairs returning a minute later.

"Okay, Ms. Malloy," he said. "Most investigators, they wouldn't tell you squat. That's the old school and it's a good one, and frankly, most of the time I agree. But you, I seen what you've done so far, and I see you're a couple of steps ahead of me, you've got your suspicions—"

"I have no idea why she'd try to kill me. Scare me, maybe, but—"

Rosenbaum held up his hand. "Leon, you remember him? The M.E.'s investigator? What he wanted to tell me? He found a major part of this woman's body, her corpse ... I guess you wanna call it torso, okay? And part of the man's job—gross-out time, Miss—is to get what they call a core temperature. Usually stick a thermometer into your liver, see what the temp is inside you. Anyway, Leon managed it with what he found, and what he wanted to tell me is the woman was cold. You get what I'm saying?"

"I'm not—"

"What I'm saying, Ms. Malloy, is Barbara Walker's been dead a while. Leon tells me she's been dead since between eleven and one last night. More'n twelve hours. That, Ms. Malloy, puts a different spin on things."

12

True to his word, it was an afternoon for questions. Lieutenant Rosenbaum ran me through the story three more times, stopping me often to expand or repeat something he wasn't clear on. During the final go-round an investigative team with the State Police Bomb Squad showed up and I went over it another half-dozen times with the head woman while her team transferred the charred hulk of the Hummer onto the back of a flatbed truck along with any non-body parts they could find.

Then it was the other two detectives' turns, Frisch and O'Connell. Frisch was tall and dark and handsome in a cookie-cutter sort of way, vaguely generic, and he asked all the routine questions. His partner, O'Connell, was a woman around my age, and she mostly listened. When she did ask questions, they were typically hard to answer because it was obvious she was looking for inconsistencies and psychological nuances. She was very intense and obviously the alpha dog of the duo. I wondered how she and the Lieutenant got along.

Finally ... finally, finally, finally, the questions came to an end. The crime scene techs and the Bomb Squad people were still at work, and it looked like uniformed cops were knocking on my neighbors' doors. My days as a corporate honcho reared their ugly head and I did a quick calculation of the cost of so much manpower. I shivered. There were a lot of levels to the cost of a murder, I thought. Philosophical *and* pragmatic.

My kitchen was a mess—I had opened up my fridge and pantry when it became obvious there was not going to be a quick end to this. I wasn't much of a cook, so the pickings were slim, but there were bagels and cream cheese, peanut butter and grape jelly, bread, grapes and chips, Coke and coffee. Lieutenant Rosenbaum, munching on a bagel, led me outside now.

"You've been very helpful, Ms. Malloy," he said. "Quite a story. Why you think she was in your car?"

I'd been asked this same question at least two dozen times by half a dozen people in a dozen different ways. It was a dirty dozen type of question, number one with a bullet, I guess, and I hadn't supplied a decent answer all day and didn't have one now. "I don't know," I said. "I wish I did."

"Me, too. Next, I gotta go inform the father. How you think he's gonna take it?"

"Poorly."

"Yeah. No surprise there. You think ... you think there was some hanky-panky goin' on, you know, between Daddy and daughter?"

"Hanky-panky, Lieutenant?"

"Yeah, hanky-panky. The low-down dirty boogie. The deed. The dirty deed. Sex."

"Dirty deeds done dirt cheap," I said. "Like the song."

Rosenbaum grimaced. "AC/DC. My oldest listened to them. I let him live though ... barely. Anyway ..."

"I don't know. Joe Mason hinted, but I sure don't know. The Reverend seems naive ... blissfully naive ... about his daughter."

"Maybe it's an act."

"Maybe. But what does it have to do with blowing up my car ... with her in it?"

Rosenbaum shrugged, popped the last bit of bagel in his mouth and brushed off his hands. He found another cigar and stuck it unlit into his mouth. Around it he said, "Sure made a statement. Dramatic."

"Yeah. I guess I must have been onto—"

A black Corvette sped around the curve, slowed, then pulled off the road behind the Lieutenant's Caprice. The door opened and a set of long legs slipped out, followed by the rest of the man. Must be Jack Bear, I thought. He looked around, seemed to take everything in, saw me and nodded slightly. I felt something inside me ... clench.

Jack Bear was about six feet tall with broad shoulders and a narrow waist. He wore white tennis shoes, tight jeans and a red sweatshirt with the sleeves cut off. Tall, dark and, oh boy! Long black hair, chiseled dark features, a strong jaw. My toes curled. Jack Bear was a man you noticed. At least if you were a woman. He crossed the road toward us as if he had all the time in the world, an easy panther's gait, athletic and effortless.

"Hi," he said.

"Jack," I said as if we were old friends. "This is Lieutenant Eli Rosenbaum with the Sheriff's Department."

Jack nodded, then said to me, "You all right?"

"Better now."

Rosenbaum chewed on his cigar. "This the friend you called?"

"Yes."

Rosenbaum nodded. "Nice t'meetcha, Jack. I didn't catch your last name."

"Bear," he said.

"Where you from, Mr. Bear?"

"Traverse City."

Rosenbaum shifted his gaze back to me. "What time you call him, Ms. Malloy?" Always cross-referencing; always a suspect.

"Right after my car blew up. Around twelve-thirty."

Rosenbaum took out the cigar and inspected it absently, as if it had presented him with a mild puzzle. "You got from Traverse City to Lake Orion in less than three hours?"

"I caught all the lights," Bear said.

Two hundred and forty-some miles of expressway, I thought. Uh-huh.

Rosenbaum tucked the cigar back in his mouth. "Well," he said. "Nice to meet you."

"Yeah. Same here."

Jack Bear looked at me. He jerked a thumb at the house. "Want to go in?" I nodded.

"Let me get my gear," he said, and loped across Heights to his Corvette and returned a moment later carrying a blue and white nylon gym bag.

"Need anything else, Lieutenant?" I asked.

He was watching the techs go over the scene. "No, Miss Malloy. I'll probably get back with you in a day or two."

I led Bear into the house. Once inside he looked around, taking in the view and the piano. "You play?" he said.

"Yes."

He nodded. "Let's take a look at the whole place, then talk. You okay? Cops treat you decent?"

"I cooperated."

"They tend to be relentless."

"They were."

We went through the entire house. Jack seemed concerned about all the glass, but didn't comment. From my office we stood at the windows and looked down on the scene below. Rosenbaum was conferring with the other two detectives, then headed for his car. "Okay," Jack said, a smile ghosting his face. "Third floor seems safe from snipers and fire bombers. At least while the cops are still here."

He turned and held out his hand. "Jack Bear."

"Meg Malloy," I said, taking his hand. "Thanks for coming."

"No problem. I know you've probably answered about a million questions already, but why don't you run it through for me."

We sat down and I reran it, including showing him the disk of the tape and the enhancement of the tattoo. Jack sat intently, leaning back in an office chair, head cocked, arms crossed. He let me tell the whole thing uninterrupted. Finally I said, "I think that's it."

He nodded. "Okay. What you need to do is decide ... what do you want to do?"

"Do?"

"Sure. Someone either tried to scare you off or tried to kill you. The cops are going to work to figure out who and why. You can turn it completely over to them and get on with your life, or you can try to figure out on your own what's going on. Either way I'll stay and watch your back and help out until you think you don't need me anymore."

I thought about it, about what he was saying. I said, "I told the cops everything. We'll be tripping over each other."

"Everything?"

"Well ... I think so. Everything relevant."

"Why did the server crash?"

Crash, I thought. Why was it wiped? "I'm not sure ..."

Jack cocked an eyebrow at me. "But you have some ideas?"

Slowly, I nodded.

"You tell the cops you think Barbara's murder has something to do with the server crashing?"

"Um ... not ... explicitly."

Jack smiled. I felt that clench again inside me, a sure sign the man was pinging my hormones. But he was my cousin's lover. I knew very little about him, and what I did know was a little ... disturbing.

Jack said, "Why not?"

"Look," I said, suddenly defensive. "I told the cops how I got involved and what I was doing when Reverend Walker hired me. I don't know if there's a real connection between the crash and Barbara's disappearance. Both the Reverend and Stephanie are ... touchy about P.R. where the website's concerned."

Jack was quiet a moment. "Why didn't Stephanie do it entirely inside WebSpinners then? I know you're good, but if she's that worried about image, why not keep it to herself?"

I explained about Danny Chen quitting ... or what had Stephanie said ... *Disappearing.* I thought she'd been exaggerating. Steph's so high-strung ...

Oh shit. I told Jack about Danny Chen.

"You tell the cops about that?"

"No." I shook my head. "No, I didn't."

Jack said nothing. Just looked at me, waiting.

Did I want to look into this? Did I want to keep being a P.I., amateur or not?

I thought of Barbara Walker's head rolling across the road, of my Hummer blowing up. I realized I no longer felt afraid ... well, not too much. What I felt mostly now was pissed off. Somebody had targeted me. *Me*, damnit!

I had run away once, selling CyberConduits and fleeing to Maui. I regretted that decision, probably always would. When I returned to the mainland, I'd vowed to never run away again.

"Let's find out what's going on," I said. "Let's do it."

"Good."

"I need to talk to Reverend Walker first."

"The cops'll be there for a while," he said.

"Right." I stood up, began to pace my office, scuffing my heels on the denim blue plush carpet. "We'll talk to Reverend Walker later. Let's go talk to Danny Chen."

"You know where he lives?"

I turned to my computer system. "I can find out."

"Sounds like a plan." Jack unzipped his gym bag and drew out two leather carry-alls.

"What're those?" I asked.

He held up the smallest leather case. "Lock picks."

I stared. "We're going to break in somewhere?"

He shrugged.

I let it go. "What's the other one?"

He unzipped it and withdrew a handgun. "Beretta 9mm. I've also got a sawed-off shotgun in the car."

"You're ... well armed."

He grinned again. "Didn't Mattie tell you? I'm a dangerous guy."

13

Danny's last known address was a house in Troy, only about two miles from the offices of WebSpinners, a two-story colonial in a middle-class subdivision of colonials, ranches and split-levels. It was going on five-thirty and people were coming home from work, collecting their kids from latchkey, deciding what to cook or order for dinner, contemplating the first martini, beer or glass of white wine, wondering what was on TV, hoping the kids didn't have much homework, deciding whether the lawn needed mowing. And Danny, single man, computer geek, former ... former? lover of Stephanie Jones, had lived in the midst of it all.

Jack slowly drove by Danny's house, then circled the block.

"Looking for something?" I said, conscious of his physicality, conscious of the sawed-off shotgun beneath his seat and the Beretta he had stowed in the glove box.

"It's a good idea to know what your escape routes are when you're going to break-and-enter."

"We're not going to break-and-enter, Jack," I said. "We're going to knock on the door—"

"Or ring the bell."

"—and Danny's going to answer and we'll go in and talk to him."

"Sure," Jack said.

"Nothing illegal," I said.

"Okay."

"Nothing, Jack."

"Got it."

I stared at him, able to look at his profile unblinkingly because he was driving. Not classically handsome, too ethnic to be a GQ model, but striking ... attractive.

"You're ... Native American?"

He grinned. "How'd you guess?"

I smiled back. "The name kind of gave it away."

"Chippewa," he said. "That's what we're called in Michigan. Algonquin, other places. I don't have much use for 'Native American.' I'm okay with 'Indian' though I'm glad Columbus wasn't trying to find Turkey."

"You live on the ..."

"Reservation? Up in Peshawbestown? No. I live on a boat at the Clinch Park Marina downtown Traverse City. The *Canowakeed*. That's the name of the boat. A forty-foot sloop."

"The *Canowakeed*?" We passed Danny Chen's house again. It looked deserted, a modest colonial with robin's-egg blue vinyl siding, black shingles and white trim. The garage door was closed and the driveway was empty.

"It's a Chippewa word," he said, and pulled the Corvette into the empty driveway.

"What's it mean?"

He retrieved the gun from the glove box and leaned forward to slip it into the small of his back underneath the sweatshirt. He angled his way out of the car without answering. I joined him, slinging my backpack over my shoulder.

"No breaking-and-entering," I said as we walked to the front porch.

Jack gestured to the door. "Knock or ring the bell?"

I punched the doorbell. From inside we could hear the chimes. We waited. Nothing. Birds sang from a sycamore tree in the front yard. Half a block down kids yelled at each other, high-pitched but indistinct. Sounds of suburbia.

I rang the door bell again. Again, nothing.

Two more times.

"He's not here," I said.

Jack leaned forward, cupped his hands around his eyes and peered inside the house. He straightened up and swung open the screen door and turned the inner door's knob. It was locked. Jack slipped the leather pouch containing the lock picks from a pocket.

"Your call," he said.

I cupped my hands around my eyes and peeped through the window. I winced at what I saw, my stomach dropping. Closing my eyes for a moment, I sighed. "Go ahead," I said.

"Talk to me like we're supposed to be here, okay? This takes a few minutes."

Jack began manipulating the picks. I began to chatter. "I haven't talked to Mattie in a while. How's she doing?"

Jack, without taking his concentration off the lock, said, "Talk about something else."

"You don't want to talk about Mattie?"

"Talk about Maui," he said.

"No."

"Okay," Jack said. "Don't talk about Maui. Talk about ... read any good books lately?"

"*Charlie's Bones* by L.L. Thrasher."

"What's it about?"

"Well, this woman is having a pool put in, and they dig up some bones—"

"Charlie's?"

"Uh-huh. And the ghost of the guy whose bones they belong to suddenly shows up, saying, 'I was an undercover cop who got shot in the back of the head. You have to help me find out who did it.'"

Jack turned the knob and the door swung open. "Sounds like a good book ... for a ghost story. You believe in ghosts?"

"No. You?"

"Yes," he said flatly. "Let's go." He led the way in, stopping to polish the doorknob with the edge of his sweatshirt pulled over his hand, then closed the door after us. He wiped the inner doorknob then leaned down to upright a lamp that had been knocked over, his shirt still over his hand.

I couldn't help but notice two things. One, Jack had six-pack abs, and two, he had a vicious scar that ran horizontally across his stomach.

"Let's see if they broke the bulb."

"They?"

He didn't answer, just clicked the switch with his elbow. The living room was suddenly bathed in light.

"Shit, Jack! Someone'll know we broke in here."

"A car in the driveway of a dark house doesn't tell you that, too?"

I stepped over and pulled the drapes shut. Then we took the time to look around at the mess we had seen through the windows. Every lamp had been knocked to the floor, every end table tipped over, every cushion yanked off and cut to ribbons, stuffing spewing onto the carpeting. A dozen framed photographs had been smashed to bits and lay in tattered ruins on the floor in glittering piles of glass, wood and shredded paper.

Jack had the gun in his hand now. "Stay behind me."

Instinctively I lowered my voice to a whisper. "You think someone's here?"

"Shh."

We crept from the living room into the kitchen and dining room. The refrigerator hung open like a broken jaw, empty. I looked around, puzzled. There was no food spoiling in the open, no rotting trash at all. In fact, despite the overall destruction of glass and tableware, there were signs that the contents of the refrigerator had been cleaned up. Weird. Food-obsessed burglars?

"Try not to touch anything," Jack said.

"Why?"

"Fingerprints. Don't want to leave any."

"Good God! You don't think—"

"Shh."

The possibility we might find Danny Chen dead somewhere in the house had not occurred to me until that very moment. Oh sweet Jesus, I thought. Oh God no! My skin suddenly felt very far away from me, my nerves stretched, sending out signals so weak and faraway they could have been transmitted from Pluto.

Jack turned abruptly and caught my wrist. "Keep it together," he said, voice gentle and even. "Now's not the time."

I felt like a collapsing star. Instantaneously back in my skin, back in Danny's house, back in the real world, back in the moment. Jack wasn't panicking. Why was I?

I breathed in a deep lungful of air and felt my heart slow. I nodded. "Okay."

From the kitchen we climbed the stairs to the second floor; three bedrooms and a bathroom. The destruction was the same, as if a hurricane had torn through, systematically wrecking everything.

"Malicious," Jack murmured.

I nodded. It looked like whoever had been here had been searching for something, but the level of violence was way beyond what a thorough, orderly search would have required. It was as if the searchers had vented an uncontrollable rage on the house's contents.

Had they also vented it on the house's owner? We saw no blood.

One of the bedrooms had been Danny's home office. The computer had been smashed to pieces, glass and plastic and circuits, broken keyboard keys, an alphabet soup of plastic lettering, scattered everywhere.

Jack was still relaxed in a taut, vigilant sort of way. Aware, but not expectant. The gun was still in his hand, but down by his side. He no longer prowled, but still seemed in a state of heightened awareness.

We went through the rest of the house, including the basement and the garage. Jack even peeked into the attic. It was the same, a depressing display of secondary violence—we saw only the aftermath, but that was enough.

Finally we were done, or at least we'd seen all we cared to see. We stepped out onto the porch, waving goodbye in a crass attempt at subterfuge if some observant neighbor saw us leave. Back in Jack's car we pulled out of the driveway and headed out of the subdivision.

Casually, Jack said, "You can freak out now."

I smiled and shook my head, thinking back to that moment in the kitchen, my supernova interval. "I don't think I need to now."

"Good. Where to?"

"Might be a good idea to go talk to Steph before we do anything else."

"I need ..." Jack fell silent.

"Cut north on the next road, take a left so we can get over to Long Lake Road."

Instead of following my directions Jack headed out toward Big Beaver Road. "Where are you going?"

He shook his head and pulled onto Big Beaver, smoothly merging into rush hour traffic.

"Jack?"

"Shh."

"You've got to stop shushing me. I won't—"

"Shut up then," he said. "You like that better?" He pulled onto the ramp to southbound I-75 and brought the Corvette up to eighty miles per hour.

"What the hell are you doing?"

"We're being followed."

"What!?"

"Middle lane, about two hundred yards back. The black Taurus. Two guys."

I peeked back, saw it and turned to stare at Jack. "Are you sure?"

"That's what I'm trying to find out." He pulled over to the right and got onto the entrance ramp for westbound I-696.

"Where are we going?"

"You tell me," he said. "You want to lose 'em or ID 'em?"

I hesitated, thinking of the destruction of Danny's house and the explosion of my Hummer, Barbara Walker inside.

"Can we do both?"

Jack shrugged.

"Let's try then," I said.

"Okay," Jack said, suddenly pulling onto the shoulder of 696 and slowing to a halt. "It's your party."

14

Jack flipped on the emergency flashers. The black Taurus sped by.

"Got the plate number?" Jack asked.

"Yeah. That was kind of anti-climactic."

"Good." Jack clicked off the flashers, shifted into first and accelerated into the right lane, taking the first available exit, which was Ten Mile Road. "Having them pull up behind us and jump out with machine guns would be more than I care to deal with today."

"Has that ever happened to you?"

"Hmm," he said. "Not recently." He glanced up. "Are we in Detroit?"

I followed his gaze. The water tower of the Detroit Zoo, festooned with painted animals, loomed above us. "Royal Oak," I said.

"The Detroit Zoo is in Royal Oak?"

"Uh-huh. Ever been there?"

"The Zoo?"

"Yeah."

"No. I've been to the Clinch Park Zoo in Traverse City."

"Isn't that a kiddie zoo?"

"I suppose. But I live right behind it, so I see some of the animals every day." He paused. "Why is the Detroit Zoo in Royal Oak? Is the Royal Oak Zoo in Detroit?"

"I don't know. Odd, isn't it? Isn't the Chicago Zoo in Lincoln Park?"

"Is it?"

"I'm not sure. I think so."

"Huh. Why don't I drive around for a while, make sure we've lost them, make sure there isn't another car."

"Sure. I'll trace the plate number." I rummaged in my backpack and withdrew my PDA and a small collapsible keyboard that I mounted it on. I turned it on and flipped up the antenna on the PDA.

"You're using that thing like a laptop?"

"Sort of. It's limited, but I've got e-mail and Web access on it. The mini-keyboard helps."

We were driving through a middle-class subdivision, dramatically different from the one Danny Chen lived in. It was much older, with much smaller houses. I would be willing to bet the median income was different, too. Almost every house was a ranch, often white or red brick, with a dense growth of trees and shrubs. It was probably built in the forties and fifties when this was what middle-class Americans aspired to.

"I can't hack with it," I continued. "But ..."

Jack looked amused. "You kind of light up when you go digital."

"I'm not 'going digital'."

Jack checked the rearview mirror. "Going, going, gone."

"What are you trying to say?"

He made a dismissive gesture with his right hand.

"No," I said. "Tell me."

He shook his head. "You ever go a day without logging online? Ever *not* turn on your computer? Check your e-mail?"

"You have a website!"

He shook his head. "Not any more."

I opened my mouth to snap back at him, but he'd caught me by surprise. "You don't?"

"No."

"Why not?"

He shook his head and gestured at the PDA. "Now's not really the best time for this, you know? It'd be nice to know who was following us. Do your thing."

"Mattie said you used a laptop—"

"Just—do—your—thing. Okay?"

Irritated, I logged onto the PDA's Web server and started to surf. The tiny screen was impossible to work with, but I lost myself in it anyway. The Web is the universe, a huge city with all sorts of interesting and beautiful structures, parks, theaters and museums. Also, like a city, it has many scary, ugly things. It also doesn't have a road map, or even very good Yellow Pages.

I started by looking for databases for license plates. If I was working from my computer system I might try to hack into the DMV, but it would be too much hassle with this thing. There were a number of relatively legal sites that collected information about license plate numbers, though most seemed to be for collectors. None of them could ID the plate on the black Ford Taurus.

"How's it going?" Jack said a little while later.

"Slow."

"I'm surprised."

"By what?" I couldn't keep the crankiness from my voice. I was bouncing off the mild skepticism and sarcasm in Jack's tone, but figured I was entitled. I'd had a bad day.

Jack grinned and said, "Mind if I try?"

"Just drive."

He leaned forward and snapped on the power button of a phone mounted under the radio. He tapped two keys and a number flashed across the little screen. After a moment a deep male voice spoke from the stereo speaker system. "Hello?"

"Roger, Jack here."

"Hey Jack. What do you want?"

"*Hi Jack! Nice to hear from you. How's it going? How's life treating you?*" Jack said.

"Hi Jack. Nice to hear from you. How's it going? How's life treating you? *What do you want?*"

"Nice to talk to you, too. Going okay. I'm fine. I need a trace on a license plate number."

"Where are you?"

"Royal Oak. Roger, you know the Detroit Zoo is in Royal Oak?"

"Do you know the Detroit Pistons are in Auburn Hills?"

"As a matter of fact, I do."

"You would. Of course, the Detroit Lions used to be in Pontiac, but they moved back to the city."

"Change is good," Jack said.

"Bullshit," Roger said over the phone. "Bullshit change is good, and coming from you I don't believe it. What the hell are you doing in Royal Oak?"

"Helping out someone."

The silence was long and drawn out and I thought Jack showed very little irritation.

Roger's voice said, "Anyone I know?"

"Actually, her name is Megan Malloy."

"Any relation?"

"Cousin."

The silence was even longer and emptier this time, but finally Roger, whoever he was, said, "What's the plate number?"

I read it off to him. Roger read it back to me. "That it?"

"Yeah," Jack said.

"I'll call you back in a half hour or so. Keep your phone on."

"Sure."

Jack pulled the Corvette out onto Woodward, what in the Detroit Metro area could reasonably be called Main Street, running from the Windsor Tunnel downtown all the way north to Pontiac and Bloomfield Hills. "I'm hungry. How about you? Know someplace decent around here?"

"How are you on Italian?"

"Love it," Jack said.

"We need to head south then," I said, "but it's on Woodward. Pasqualle's. Pretty decent Italian food."

As Jack changed our course, I said, "Who's Roger?"

"Roger Johnson, retired cop, Traverse City P.D. He was a captain, chief of detectives. Also a cherry farmer."

"And he'll have it traced for you?"

"For me, yeah," Jack said. "Sort of for me, I guess."

"You're friends?"

Jack slowed to a stop at a red light, frowning. "Friends," he said oddly. "I guess so, yeah. I guess we are."

Jack parked the Corvette around back of Pasqualle's, rear of the car against the wooden fence. Hide the license plate and all set for a quick get-away. We went in and were quickly seated. Jack made a fast scan of the menu, nodded and put it aside. He glanced around. We'd requested seating near a window close to the emergency exit. All Jack's idea. I couldn't decide if it was paranoia or healthy precaution. Then I thought of my Hummer exploding and Barbara Walker's head rolling toward me and voted for healthy precaution.

"You okay?" Jack asked.

I nodded, debating on whether I had any appetite or not. I decided I did, but not much of one. It had been a very strange, very surreal day. If Salvadore Dali were God, this was the sort of day he would have made. If the afternoon hadn't been so exhausting, answering a gazillion questions, the transition from being at home to searching Danny Chen's house would have been bizarrely abrupt. As it was, I had been glad to get away from the house, glad of any activity that took me away from the char-spot on Heights Road by Lake Orion.

"Jack," I said, looking him square in the eyes. He didn't flinch away. "Why'd you shut down the website?"

I wasn't sure he was going to answer. His expression didn't really change, although something in his eyes did. He seemed almost ...

I thought of him blithely saying "Yes," when I jokingly asked him if he believed in ghosts. The look in his eyes seemed almost ... *haunted*.

"I had a career change," he said.

The waitress arrived and Jack ordered chicken parmigiana with salad and breadsticks and a side of spaghetti. He also ordered a half-bottle of red wine, some sort of Burgundy I'd never heard of, but then again, what I knew about wine could be written on the cork ... or screwtop, as the case may be. I ordered cheese ravioli and said I'd try the wine, too. What the hell.

After she left I propped my chin on my hands, elbows on the table. "Career change?" I said.

One of Jack's eyebrows raised slightly, but he didn't say anything. Jack had been a bookie; the website had been his way, apparently, of staying out of the path of the cops and the Feds. His server was out of Las Vegas—my suggestion—and I had built in some very intense encryption security to fold the site if there was any indication of law enforcement trying to hack in. It had essentially been a message board, gamblers leaving their bets and using their credit cards.

"Career change," Jack said.

"Okay. So what do you do now?"

He smiled. "Help people like you."

"We haven't discussed your fee," I said.

He shook his head. "I'm doing this ..." He trailed off.

"You're doing this for Mattie," I completed.

Clearly uncomfortable, Jack shrugged. "I guess. At least partly. It's what I do, though. Help people."

"Like a P.I.?"

He looked troubled, glancing away, eyes scanning the parking lot for black Tauruses. He shook his head slightly. "Not really. I mean, yeah, someone comes to me and says their kid's gone missing, or whatever, I'll look for them. I guess that's what a P.I. does, but I'm not licensed, I don't have an office, I don't advertise."

"You charge for this?"

He nodded. "Sliding scale. If it's something of value they want found, I'll do it for a percentage."

"Found," I said.

He nodded. "Suppose somebody's boat gets stolen. Lot of that up in TC. If I can find it and return it, they'll pay me a percentage of the insurance money."

I thought about what he was saying. "You mean they don't tell the insurance company you found the boat?"

He shrugged. "That's between them and the insurance company."

"That's not ..."

"Right?"

"It's kind of ... dirty," I said. "You're sort of an accessory to insurance fraud."

"Except I don't know for a fact that's what's happening."

"But ..."

He held up his hand. "I've found missing kids, too. And you know, sometimes, maybe, they were better off not at home. If I can determine that, I try to help them out, find a reasonable alternative. So they don't have to resort to hooking out of the back seat of cars. You know what I mean? I work in the gray areas because that's most of what's out there. Dirty deeds, you know what I mean? But somebody has to do them."

"But you're not going to charge me?"

He smiled. "I work cheap."

Dirty Deeds (Done Dirt Cheap), I thought. Like the song. I opened my mouth, then shut it a moment. Swallowed. Then I took a deep breath. "There's something I need to ask you, and it's kind of important to me, but ..."

He raised the eyebrow again.

I plunged on. "Mattie said you were ... *connected*."

He made a head-dipping movement as if he were laughing to himself. "'Connected'? You mean mob-connected?"

"Mafia. Yeah. That's what she told me."

He laughed softly and took a sip of his ice water, eyes again scanning the parking lot. "Well, Mattie always had a sense of the dramatic. You know what the mafia is?"

"Organized crime," I said.

"It's not all that organized," Jack said. "Basically it's a bunch of guys, usually ethnically related. You know, the Italians are La Cosa Nostra and the Chinese got the Tongs and the blacks have their gangs and the Russians have whatever the Russians have. There's a kind of hierarchy, with bosses and lieutenants and as far as the Italians go, the Feds have pretty much picked them clean. That's what they say, anyway. I'm rather skeptical, but that's not really the issue, is it? Like here in Detroit, the FBI put almost all of them in prison just a couple of years ago. There's still some around, I hear, but ..." He shrugged.

"So ... you worked with them?"

He rubbed his jaw, thinking. The waitress brought the salads and bread sticks and I found myself in unexpected possession of an appetite. I began to eat my salad, but Jack ignored his.

"This is important to you?" he said.

It was; I wasn't sure why. I knew the low-level criminal and Mafia stuff had been part of Jack's appeal to Mattie, who had been an investigative reporter down in Tampa. About a year ago she accepted an assignment in London and left. I'd hardly heard from her since. Maybe Jack hadn't either.

"I think it is," I said. "I'm sorry, but ..."

He nodded. "No, it's all right. You see, my dad ran a sports book, too. Back when Traverse City was rural, real hicksville. Most towns have a guy that'll cover your bets. As TC grew, though, so did his business. Back in the early 70s the first casino opened on the reservation. That's when a couple of guys from St. Louis and Chicago appeared, opening up a vending company."

"Mafia," I said.

"Uh-huh. They wanted the res casino to rent slot machines from them. They also wanted a piece of whatever illegal was going on up there. A sort of northern Michigan branch office. They told my dad he had to have their permission to run his book up there and pay for the privilege." Jack went silent.

"And?"

"He said No, and he got beat up a couple of times. That's called racketeering, by the way, and it's part of the whole RICO statutes thing. Eventually my dad decided if he was going to stay in business—or stay alive—he was going to have to cooperate. And I sort of inherited the business from my dad. I did my thing—it's a misdemeanor, by the way—and I paid money to these St. Louis guys and they stayed off my back. That doesn't mean I was mobbed up or anything. It was just the way you do business." Jack started to eat.

"What did they think of you quitting?"

"Oh, I think they were glad I was gone. Not that it matters. Their influence up there was getting strong enough to interest the Feds. It was time for me to get out. Too much heat."

I doubted that. He didn't sound like that was what had happened, that the mob and the Feds turned up the heat and he got out of the kitchen. Something had ... happened. Something ... I knew there had been a big mess while Mattie was there, and that was how she met Jack, but I had been involved in the CyberConduits sale and not paid much attention. My own mid-life crisis. If it wasn't computer news, I hadn't been much interested in current events. That, like many other things, had changed.

I sensed Jack wasn't going to talk about it anymore, so I switched the subject. We chatted, or I did, about restaurants and sports and the weather. The cell phone rang.

Jack punched the talk button and said, "Bear here."

He listened for a moment, face expressionless. "How well?" He was silent as Roger talked into his ear. "No," Jack said. "I'm not sure. No, honest. Uh-uh. Not as far as I can tell, but I may be ... Yeah ... I appreciate the offer ... Thanks, Roger. I mean it. Thanks."

He clicked off the phone, holding it in his left hand and gazing out the windows again.

"Well?" I asked. "Did he trace the plate?"

"Uh-huh," Jack said. He put the phone away and looked down at his plate as if he couldn't remember having ordered the food.

"Who is it?"

Jack took a sip of wine, his expression thoughtful.

"Jack! Quit screwing around. Who is it?"

Slowly Jack said, "Car belongs to a guy by the name of Bradley S. Meyer. Roger, by strange coincidence, has met him."

"What?"

"Brad Meyer is an agent with the FBI field office in Detroit."

15

Jack reattached the cell phone to his belt. He contemplated his dinner for a moment in silence, then took a bite of his salad.

"FBI," I said, my appetite going, going, gone.

"Uh-huh."

"Following us."

"I was pretty sure of it."

"Did they pick us up at Danny's house?"

"Makes me wonder," he said. "I didn't notice anybody following us from your house, but it's possible. Especially if they're using a multi-car tail."

"Breaking and entering." I rubbed my forehead. "A couple Feds might have witnessed us breaking and entering?"

Jack nodded. "But they didn't stop us, or arrest us or anything."

"Small comfort."

The waitress brought our food. Jack sampled his chicken parmigiana and nodded. "Not bad."

I stared at my cheese ravioli. My stomach did a slow roll. I closed my eyes and shook my head. "Maybe this isn't such a good idea."

Jack didn't comment, kept eating. I opened my eyes and stared at him. "Maybe this isn't such a good idea," I repeated.

"Hmmm," Jack said. "Spaghetti's pretty good, too."

"What do you think?"

"I think the food here's pretty good."

"Damnit," I hissed. "I'm not talking about the damned food."

"I know you're not," he said. "But you want me to tell you what to do. I told you already. If you want to try to figure out what's going on, I'll help you and watch your back while you do. If you want to sit tight and let the cops do their job, I'll stay around and keep you safe."

"How long?"

"As long as it takes," he said.

"For Mattie," I said.

Jack shook his head. "For Mattie, yes, partly. But it's what I do."

"Sort of a private eye."

"Sort of, I guess. I'll help you. I'll cover your back. I'm good at it. I used to work with a P.I. off and on, Conrad Wilson, so I can help investigate, too. I have resources—"

"Like the retired cop."

"Yeah, like Roger."

I stared at him for a long time, attracted to him physically, but disturbed by him as well. Mattie had said I could trust him. But the FBI ...

"You're not concerned about the Feds in the Taurus?"

"Have you broken any Federal laws recently?"

I shook my head. "Not that I know of."

"Glad to hear it."

"How about you?"

"Broken any Federal laws? No, not recently."

Not recently. "Is it possible they're following you, not me?"

Jack smiled and wiped his mouth with the cloth napkin. "Anything's possible."

"Answer the question."

"I don't think so."

I sighed and nibbled at a ravioli. It was good, but getting colder every second. I took a bigger bite and felt my appetite return. A part of me wanted to find a motel room, post Jack at the door with his Beretta and his sawed-off shotgun and hide under the bed. Another part of me wanted to figure out what was going on.

We were at a crossroads, because it was up to me. I said, "If I threaten to quit every time things get weird or dangerous, what's the point?"

Jack didn't answer. He took a sip of wine.

"You're not very damned helpful," I said.

"I agree with you," he said. "Do you quit when things get tough?"

Loaded question and I wondered if he knew it. "Do you?"

"No."

"Me neither," I said. "Not any more, anyway. Let's not worry about the guys in the Taurus. Eventually the Feds'll come talk to us, right?"

"Very likely."

"Yeah, that's what I think, too," I ate another ravioli and thought a moment. "What do you think? Talk to Stephanie Jones or Reverend Walker?"

"Who's closer?"

"Steph."

"Steph it is, then."

Except when we got to the Troy office of WebSpinners, Inc., we couldn't talk to Stephanie. We couldn't even get near the building because it was surrounded by police cars and fire trucks. We parked three blocks away and walked, pushing our way through gawkers to get a closer look. I scanned the crowd, looking for Stephanie, or anybody from WebSpinners. It was 7 pm, but people at WebSpinners worked odd hours, coming and going as they pleased, often working from home, depending on what sites they were actually working on, depending on whether or not they had customers to deal with in person.

I finally recognized someone I knew, Dee Fontaigne. I nudged her and she spun, startled, green eyes wide. "Meg! Oh God! Meg. *What's going on?*"

Dee stood five feet tall, with curly reddish-brown hair. Chunky with an oval face and too much makeup, Dee was given to hysterics over very small matters, but her reaction seemed honest this time.

"That's what I wanted to ask you," I said.

Dee's eyes flickered to Jack. "He's with me," I said. "Jack, this is Dee Fontaigne, one of the programmers for WebSpinners." Jack nodded and she smiled at him, but her distress quickly reasserted itself.

"Oh, my God. Meg, WebSpinners caught on fire! And, and, ohhh, you heard about Stephanie, didn't you?"

I tensed and my hand shot out to grab Dee's elbow. "What's wrong with Stephanie?"

"You haven't heard? Oh my God! Meg, I can't believe nobody contacted you. Everything's going crazy, everybody's absolutely in shock, and now this, this—" She flailed wild arms toward the three-story building.

I shook her. "Tell me what happened to Stephanie."

"She was shot! Oh my God! She went out for a business lunch today and—"

"*Where is she?*"

"What? Beaumont, in ICU. She's—"

My heart was racing, my stomach in free fall. "Dee, calm down! Is she going to make it?"

"She's ..." Dee began to wail, tears coursing down her plump cheeks, smearing inky mascara across her face. "We don't know! I can't believe this is happening!"

Jack, voice quiet, said, "Were you in the building when the fire started?"

She stared at him. I was on the balls of my feet, ready to race for the Corvette, to get over to Beaumont Hospital as fast as we could go.

"Y-yes," she said. "There were three of us th-there."

"What happened?" Jack said. "Describe it."

"I-I don't know. I mean, there was a kind of ... whooshing noise—"

"Like an explosion?"

"Uh-huh. And—"

"In your offices?"

"Um ... outside, I think. Outside the front door."

I thought about WebSpinners' setup. They had half the second floor.

You either took a flight of stairs at either end or in the middle, or an elevator in the middle. The central stairs and elevator opened into an entryway and if you went right you hit the entrance to Webspinners, Inc., double glass doors engraved with the company and the spiderweb logo it was superimposed on. That opened into a reception area. Beyond the reception area were offices and cubicles.

"In the entryway?" I asked.

"Yes."

"What about Henry?"

Dee's eyebrows raised and she wiped her cheeks, smearing her face with black mascara. She looked like one of the firefighters. "I don't know," she said. "When we ran for the entrance we realized the whole entryway was in flames, so we went out the emergency exit. I've never been so scared in my life."

I was torn. Head for the hospital or look for Henry Chavez?

I bit my lip, looked at Jack, in a low voice said, "If they trashed the server and WebSpinners, they've managed to destroy almost any evidence of what was going on with the church's website and what caused the crash."

Jack, body coiled, was scanning the crowd. He said, "This isn't a safe place for you, you realize that."

"I do now."

"Let's get outa here, then." He turned to Dee. "We've got to get going. What can you tell me about what happened to Stephanie?"

Dee focused on Jack, her body language altering subtly. She canted her hips in her skintight black jeans, angling her orange silk blouse to stretch across her breasts. "Well, she had a meeting with a prospective client—"

"Who?"

Dee frowned. "I don't know. Somebody called this morning, said they wanted to put together a website for their corporation, something major, and could Stephanie meet them—"

"Them?"

Dee shrugged. "I don't know. Maybe just the head of the company."

"Go on," Jack said.

"She was meeting them—him—at Lelli's—"

"It's in Auburn Hills," I said. "By the Silverdome."

"And—and—" Dee sobbed into her hands, more dramatically this time, for Jack's benefit.

He touched her shoulder and she flung herself on him, bawling into his chest. Jack, expressionless, patted her back and muttered at the top of her head. I rolled my eyes and wondered why this annoyed me as much as it did.

"What else?" I said.

"Oh, my God! Meg—Somebody shot her right here in the parking lot." Dee snuffled. "She was lying on the ground—blood was everywhere."

16

As Jack drove west on Thirteen Mile Road toward Beaumont Hospital, the platinum sun still above the tree line, I jabbed buttons on my phone, trying to reach Henry Chavez. At his home number I heard his answering machine message, and I told him to call my cell number as soon as possible. I clicked off, frustrated. Jack was driving calmly, keeping an eye on the rearview mirror.

"Anybody back there?" I said.

"I don't think so."

Next I punched Henry's number at Chavez Tech. A recorded voice informed me that the number was "*temporarily out of service.*"

"Shit."

Cell phone in one hand and PDA in the other, I noticed Jack glance over at me and grin at my juggling act. "Wipe that smirk off your face," I said.

"So much more convenient than a little black book," he said.

"Shut up."

He smiled, but said no more. I finally found Henry's cell number in the PDA, punched it into my phone, and hit send. I was informed—yet again— that the number was "*temporarily out of service,*" but after the tone I could leave a message on Henry's voice-mail. I cursed again, told Henry to call me ASAP and left my number.

Hiding the PDA back in my backpack, I cradled the phone in my hand, power on, waiting—hoping—that Henry would call me soon. Within minutes we were back in Royal Oak, searching for a parking space at Beaumont Hospital.

The Intensive Care Unit was brightly lit, hushed, and smelled mildly of disinfectant. The nurse at the desk said Stephanie could have only one visitor at a time, and there was already someone in with her.

"Who?" I asked, knowing that Stephanie's parents were now retired and living in Texas, her brother on a military base in Saudi Arabia.

The nurse shrugged his shoulders and went back to updating the chart opened in front of him. Jack and I moved down the hallway to Stephanie's room, peering through the glass window to the unit within. "Uh-oh," I said.

Jack followed my gaze. Through the window we could see the curtained area where Stephanie presumably lay in the hospital bed. We couldn't see her. What we *could* see, though, was a man sitting at a chair next to the bed. He heard our voices, turned and immediately crossed the room and stepped out.

"Well, well, well," Lieutenant Eli Rosenbaum said. "If it isn't Little Miss Disaster. You think you could shed some light on why somebody tried to kill your friend and business partner this afternoon? On the same day somebody tried to blow you to pieces, not to mention Barbara Walker?"

I shook my head, feeling my jaw tense. Before I could say anything Rosenbaum plowed on. "I think I've seen that look before, Ms. Malloy. This one means you're going to contradict me, when you start grinding your teeth, kind of lower your head like you're gettin' ready to charge and headbutt me." He held a notebook in his left hand and a pen in his right that he now pointed at me, emphasizing his words.

"But I'm not in the mood," he said. "I heard about your friend in there completely by accident. After I left your place I swung by the D.B. at the Sheriff's—"

"D.B.?" Jack said.

"Detectives Bureau and don't interrupt, I'm on a roll here. I swung by the Bureau at the Sheriff's to coordinate with the Cap'n and one of the other detectives mentions that Troy has a murder attempt, looks almost professional, and lo and behold, the victim's name is Stephanie Jones, who just so happens to be in my notebook as somebody I need to talk to concerning a *freakin'* bombing in Lake Orion this morning. If this is a coincidence, Ms. Malloy, it's one hell of a coincidence. You got something else to tell me, like maybe what all is going on here? You want to maybe share with me why somebody's trying to assassinate all the people involved with The Missionary Church of Jesus Christ Evangelical? You think, just maybe, you could shed a little light on all this mess before somebody else gets killed?"

"Easy," Jack said.

Rosenbaum turned on him. "Bear, you keep out of my face, you got me? I checked you out and I'm not too wild about what I found. No arrests, but for some reason you seem to be linked to an awful lot of nasty business up north. You think, maybe, you'd like to talk to me about Joe Eaglefeather—"

"—no—"

"—or Conrad Wilson?"

"Uh-uh."

"How about Robert Cordella?"

Jack smiled. "Not much to say, I guess."

Rosenbaum tapped Jack on the chest with the pen. "How about Raphael Bear, smart guy. Want to talk about Raphael Bear?"

Jack wasn't smiling now, and it occurred to me that he hadn't been smiling when Rosenbaum mentioned Joe Eaglefeather and Conrad Wilson, either. He'd smiled when the detective mentioned Robert Cordella but his face had turned hard and stony at the name Raphael Bear.

"How's Stephanie?" I said.

Rosenbaum, an irritated expression crossing his face, turned to me. "She's sleeping now, but she'll live."

"Is there ... ?"

Rosenbaum softened momentarily. "Here's what we think happened. If you think something else, maybe you could share it with me. She took a call to meet somebody at Lelli's in Auburn Hills, on Opdyke Road. Nice Italian place, been there a couple of times myself. She leaves her office building there in Troy and somebody popped her from about eight feet away with a small caliber gun. .38, maybe even a .22, though if it's a .22 this guy's showboating. She's lucky. Bullet fractures her skull, ricochets away, doesn't penetrate. Must've hit her at an angle. No follow-up shot. Here's where we're guessing. This wasn't a really well-thought-out hit. Too busy, too exposed, wrong time of day. As far as we can tell, there was only the one shot. Ms. Jones probably saw it coming. She held her hands up in front of her and twisted away. The bullet clipped her left hand and glanced off her temple. A half inch the other direction and she'd be dead.

"Now," Rosenbaum said. "Either the shooter's stupid or he got spooked. I'm betting on a little of both. Instead of quickly popping another shot into her skull, he skips out."

"Any witnesses?" Jack asked.

Rosenbaum glared at him. "Did I ask you to speak?"

"Any witnesses?" I said.

Rosenbaum glared at me. "No. Now shut up and let me talk."

"Screw you," I said, and shoved past him and into Stephanie's room. Stephanie was sleeping, her head bandaged, her left hand wrapped in gauze like she was wearing an oven mitt. There was an I.V. into her other hand and I thought Rosenbaum had been downplaying the wound. From the hallway I heard Bear and Rosenbaum talking, a tense, wasp-like whine, but I tuned them out.

Time drifted. The I.C.U. was like its own little world, a high-tech bubble of isolation with its own sense of time and space. It reminded me of my father's heart attack and I felt my throat close, my chest burn. I shook my head and tried to calm down. I took a deep breath and listened. Nothing but the electronic hum of the monitors and the idle clinks and whirs of the machinery, the nearly inaudible drip-drip-drip of the I.V. solution. If this was as minor as Rosenbaum hinted, she wouldn't still be in I.C.U. A bullet wound to the head. It didn't penetrate. I wondered how much damage ...

A nurse slipped into the room and began to chart Stephanie's vital signs. She said, "Visiting hours are about up."

"How is she?"

"Lucky," the nurse said, brushing dark hair back off her forehead. "Fractured skull, severe concussion, some swelling of the brain, but nothing we can't manage."

"Will she ... will there be brain damage?"

"Are you a family member?"

"Friend."

She pressed her lips into a thin white line. "The neurologists don't think so, not long-term. Short-term, it's hard to say. She's not completely conscious. She keeps drifting in and out of a coma. The longer that happens, the more likelihood there is of damage."

I watched Stephanie while the nurse recorded all the information, then left, saying, "Five more minutes."

I had met Steph in college, a partner in my first computer lab, Introduction to FORTRAN. Both Steph and I had been weaned at computer keyboards, so most everything in the class was a boring rehash. The thing we agreed on most was that the Teaching Assistant, a Glen Blalock-type computer geek, needed to wash his hair and brush his teeth more often.

"He gives us tech nerds a bad name," she'd said.

"That's right," I said. "We're proof you can be a hot babe and have a brain, too."

The next lab session Stephanie had handed me a red T-shirt that had HOT BABE W/BRAINS stenciled across the chest. It was identical to the one she was wearing.

We'd been friends, though never roommates. I thought she was too emotional, too high-strung, too flighty and insecure to want to live with her. Stephanie, showing great insight, thought Mitch was an asshole and tended to fade whenever he was around me, which was most of the time. We'd stayed in touch over the years, first with irregular phone calls, later through regular e-mails.

"Ready?" Jack called to me.

I slid off the chair, touched Stephanie's hand and told her to get better, and joined the two men in the hallway.

Rosenbaum glared at me. "You going to tell me what's going on?"

"I don't know what's going on, but it might be a good idea to put a guard on Steph until it's over."

"Yeah? And you got Mr. Bear here to keep you safe, huh?"

"That's right, but you might talk to the Troy cops, see what they know about a fire bomb attempt on the building WebSpinners and Chavez Tech is in. You might see if you can find Henry Chavez. He runs Chavez Tech."

Rosenbaum wasn't taking notes. "You're holding out on me. You know something I don't."

"Hell, Lieutenant, you were doing all the talking. Maybe if you tried asking questions you'd get some answers."

Rosenbaum reddened, his long thin face twisting into a look of extreme displeasure. "I think maybe it would be worthwhile dragging you down to the D.B. and putting you under protective custody."

"I think it might be worthwhile if you spent more time trying to figure out who blew up my Hummer with Barbara Walker's corpse in it."

Jack cleared his throat. Rosenbaum and I wheeled and glared at him. Simultaneously we said, "*What?!*"

"Does it bother you, Lieutenant, that these two murder attempts have been unsuccessful?"

"No. I'm happy Ms. Malloy and Ms. Jones are still breathing. Why?"

"A bombing and a shooting?" Jack said.

"What you're trying to say," Rosenbaum said, "is that either the perps are total amateurs or they're just trying to scare these ladies."

"Or we're lucky," I said.

"You're both lucky," Jack said. "But this thing with Stephanie Jones doesn't ring like a professional hit."

"Yeah, Bear? You, with all your experience, how would you do it?"

Jack's gaze was as level and flat as a CD-ROM. "I wouldn't pick an office building parking lot at one in the afternoon, then panic if the shooting didn't go down the way I wanted it to. A second shot—bang! bang!—and she wouldn't be here, she'd be at the morgue. Whoever did this either hasn't done it much before or they don't really know what they're doing."

Rosenbaum glowered at Jack, yanked the cold, chewed-on cigar from a pocket and stuck it in his mouth. A nurse, walking by, said, "Sir, there's no smoking here."

"I look like I'm smoking, lady?"

"Please take it outside," she said, unyielding.

We began to walk down the corridor to the elevators.

"You got a point to this, Bear?" Rosenbaum said.

Jack nodded. "A car bomb and a fire bomb and an execution-style shooting have the hallmarks of a professional, maybe even mob work—"

"Something you'd be an authority on?"

Jack continued. "But if this had been real mob work, both Stephanie and Megan would be dead and WebSpinners would be ash instead of being scorched."

"This guy's 0 for 3, that what you're saying?"

Jack shook his head. "One in four," he said. "no matter how you look at it, Barbara Walker's dead. But how did she die? You said she was dead before the explosion."

Rosenbaum looked uncomfortable. "M.E. says there were petechiae on her eyes."

Jack met his gaze.

"What's that mean?" I demanded.

"Probable strangulation," Jack said. "The blood vessels in the eyeball hemorrhage."

"You know too much, Bear," Rosenbaum growled.

"I'm well-informed and not surprised. Strangulation isn't organized crime, is it? A strangulation is a crime of passion, rage, spur of the moment, usually. And you've got a videotape of someone in some sort of bondage porn film. You figure it out."

"So now you're a profiler, " Rosenbaum said, but he wasn't as irritable about it. He seemed to be thinking about what Jack said as we rode the elevator to the main floor.

"No," Jack said. "I'm no profiler, but I do have a question."

"Was Barbara raped?" I said.

"Yeah," Jack said. "That's the question."

Rosenbaum shook his head. "She had sex sometime before her death, but the M.E. doesn't think it was rape."

"So the real question," I said, "is who'd she have sex with?"

"Any ideas?" Rosenbaum said.

"No. You?"

"Nope. But I sure think that'd be a handy thing to know."

17

"Pull over," I said to Jack.

He shot me a questioning look, but I just gestured out the window. Jack obliged, sliding the Corvette onto the shoulder of Adams Road.

"What's—"

I put a finger to my lips and held up my hand in a 'be patient' gesture, then climbed out of the Corvette. This was probably one of the last undeveloped stretches of Adams Road, occasionally referred to as the Billion Dollar Mile. The houses being built along this road started at half a million. I walked away from the car and stood on the edge of a bare farmer's field strewn with disintegrating remnants of a corn crop.

"Your days are numbered," I said to the corn field. "Be prepared to become a subdivision. Resistance is futile."

In the west the sun was sinking behind the trees like a fiery-red coin dropping into an arcade slot. It set the sky on fire, flames of scarlet and pumpkin and plum scorching the horizon, turning it an indescribable cerulean around the edges of the burn.

I rubbed my face with my hands and thought about Barbara Walker, Stephanie Jones and Danny Chen. I wondered momentarily about Henry Chavez. And Jack Bear and those names: Joseph Eaglefeather, Conrad Wilson, Robert Cordella, Raphael Bear.

Was this what I wanted?

A few cars raced by on the road. The temperature was dropping with the sun, into the low sixties. A gentle wind from the southwest caressed my cheeks like a great aunt's kiss. Birds sang. A crow cawed from the field. Something—a mouse?—scuttled beneath the cornstalk debris.

As a corporate exec I had been used to making decisions. Then I had made a major life-changing decision and still couldn't decide if it had been a good one. Every decision had multiple consequences, I now knew, even minor ones causing a chain reaction that affected other people directly and indirectly.

I had a decision to make.

I watched the sun set. In Maui it had become a habit—settle on the beach, watch our nearest star sink into the ocean.

I missed Maui. The urge to flee back to Paradise was strong. Most people would say I was crazy. Here I was, involved in a multiple murder investigation, very much torn between the desire to complete my work, whatever it might be, and the desire to hop the first plane to Honolulu International.

Was there an in-between? Could you still work and take your retirement as you went? Could you stop and smell the turned earth as you went along? And watch sunsets?

I turned and saw that Jack was sitting on the hood of the Corvette, not looking at me, but watching the sky. I strode across the dirt clumps, stepping over corn stalks and climbed up next to him.

Jack didn't say anything, didn't look at me, his gaze fixed on the descending orb.

"What's *Canowakeed* mean?" I asked.

"'He Who Rides Before The Wind,'" he said, voice low.

The sun was starting to slip behind the distant trees. The breeze was picking up. "You like living on a boat?"

"Yes."

"Watch a lot of sunsets?"

"Yes."

"If I decided to quit and go to Maui, what would you think?"

After a moment he said, "That would be sensible."

"Do you think I should?"

He shrugged.

"I want your opinion. I *value* your opinion."

He shook his head. "I can't make that decision for you. Nobody can."

"I don't want you to make the decision for me. I want your opinion."

"What's Maui mean to you?" he said.

I turned away from the sunset to look at him. His profile was strong, handsome, undeniably Native American, chiseled from some dark stone or hard wood. "Paradise lost," I said.

"Maybe it was never found," he said.

"Maybe."

"According to Mattie you sold the company and moved to Maui. That's an American Dream if there ever was one. Worldwide dream, you'd think."

"Yes."

"It wasn't what you thought," Jack said.

"No. At first it was, but I guess I found the serpent in Paradise."

He nodded and the sun began to disappear in the coin slot, going, going ...

"What else?" Jack said.

"What else?"

"Sure. What else did you find in Paradise?"

I thought about that. The sun disappeared, the twilight enveloped us like a warm coat. "I'm not sure ..."

"Did you run away from ... here?"

I bristled, then stopped myself. "I suppose so. Yes."

"What else did you find in Maui?"

"Me, I guess."

"Like what you found?"

"Are you a shrink, Jack?"

"God forbid."

I took a ragged, shuddering breath. "I think I found the same person who left CyberConduits."

"Exactly the same?"

I shook my head. "No."

"Maybe that person wasn't all that happy in Paradise. Most people want, when you get down to it, to feel useful."

"Do you?"

"I try to be useful."

"Helping people?"

He shrugged, more felt than seen in the encroaching darkness.

"Do you believe in ghosts, Jack?" I asked.

"Back to that."

"Do you?"

"Sometimes."

"Who?"

He didn't answer.

"Joseph Eaglefeather," I said. "Conrad Wilson. Robert Cordella. Raphael Bear."

"Not all of them," he said.

"Who?"

He didn't answer. Cicadas began their melody.

"Raphael Bear," I said.

"My youngest brother."

"Is he ..."

"Dead? Yes. Murdered."

I caught my breath, not completely surprised, but caught off balance by actually hearing it.

"And—"

"I'm not talking about this any more tonight. Okay?"

I didn't know what to say. *Maybe that person wasn't all that happy in Paradise ...* Was I happy now? Contented, at least. Fully engaged, that was for sure.

I felt alive. I climbed off the hood of the Corvette. Jack cocked his head.

"Let's go visit Reverend Walker," I said.

18

The Reverend Walker lived in a chi-chi new neighborhood off Adams Road, where the houses started closer to a million bucks than half a million. His house was some sort of elaborate Tudor, probably somewhere in the range of five to six thousand square feet, and all I could think of was: Only two people live here?

When we rang the buzzer at the front door an attractive blonde woman in her forties answered. She had the kind of fresh-scrubbed neatness one sees in attractive blonde women in dish detergent commercials. I introduced myself and added that I was someone the Reverend would want to see.

"Oh yes," she said, letting us into the foyer. "Jim wondered what happened to you. This is so awful. He'll be so glad to know you're all right."

Jack and I stood quietly and waited on the oak floor beneath a crystal chandelier for this woman to move, to take us to the Reverend, to do ... something. Instead she stood silently in front of us for a long awkward moment as if uncertain of what to do. Like maybe she wanted to tell us to go away, but didn't think it would be polite. It was a very odd pause, then she said, "I'm Melinda DuPuis," and offered each of us her soft handshake.

"Brother Matthew's wife?" I asked.

"Yes, Matt's my husband. I really wish Matt was here to talk to you. I'm sure he'd have a lot of questions for you."

And I for him, I thought. "Well," I said. "Perhaps later. Where is he?"

"Matt?"

I looked into Melinda DuPuis's faded blue eyes and realized she was operating in a mild state of shock. Her even, unblemished skin seemed a little stretched and lines around the corners of her mouth were deeply etched from worry or stress. She wore sensible navy blue flats, gray slacks and a lightweight off-white sweater. But her reactions seemed screwed up, and she acted very much like she had something on her mind that she wanted to say.

"Yes, Matt," I said. "Where is he?"

"He's ... helping make arrangements for Nancy Phillips to come home for the funeral. She and Barb were close ... closer than most, I think."

"Sister Nancy Phillips?"

"Yes. Matt's been at the church since we found out, helping her with plane arrangements. Knowing her, she's halfway here by now. She's in Sri Lanka. She'll be devastated, of course. She practically raised Barbara."

"I see," I said.

We stood there awkwardly until Melinda said, "Well, I suppose you'd like to talk to Jim now."

"Yes," I said.

Melinda frowned, as if trying to remember something important. Slowly she said, "I know you've introduced yourselves ... but perhaps I could see some identification."

Jack and I exchanged a glance. I said, "Mrs. DuPuis, what's going on?"

"What do you mean, 'What's going on?'" she said, suddenly vivid and in-the-moment. "Isn't it enough that Barbara's been ... been murdered? And not only that, as if that isn't bad enough, her body was ... her body was *mutilated*. Do you know what this has done to Jim? Do you know what this could do to the *church*? The media have been calling all day long. I finally just put the answering machine on and let it listen to all those people. And frankly, Ms. Malloy, *if* that's who you really are—" Her gaze drilled into me like laser beams.

"If that's who really I am?"

"—we're not only unclear as to your involvement, we wonder if you aren't making matters worse."

"It was *my* Hummer that got blown to pieces," I snapped, feeling my lips peel back from my teeth in anger.

"Yes, but why?"

I was trying to appreciate this woman's point-of-view, but my temper was starting to buck against the gates like an unruly bull.

"Who do you *think* I am?" I asked.

Melinda DuPuis rolled her eyes and shrugged her shoulders as if she couldn't believe I was going to continue with this line of thought.

"Only you know what your agenda is, Ms. Malloy. But Jim seems to vouch for you, though it's not as if he's the best judge of people." She bit her lip, clearly having said something she hadn't meant to. "I think I'll let you talk to Jim now."

Jack shrugged when I shot him a questioning glance, then we hurried to follow her through the house. She led us through the formal living room, all blue plush carpeting and velvet furniture, a room that gave the impression it was never used. We cut through the large, shiny kitchen with its granite counter tops and shiny stainless appliances, past a formal dining room with a huge glass-topped table, and finally through the more casual family room with comfortable, plush sofas and chairs, a big-screen TV and built-in shelves filled with books. One bank of windows overlooked the backyard with its deck and privacy fence.

Melinda knocked on one of the doors. "Jim?" she said, then opened the door a crack and peered in. Her face tightened even more, the line of her posture becoming even more rigid, like a broom handle or ironing board had been shoved up her spine. "A Megan Malloy and Jack Bear are here to—"

Low, slow and slurred, Reverend Walker's deep voice said, "Yes, of course, Melinda. Send them right in. I want to talk to ..." Everything else was an indistinguishable mumble.

Directing a deadly disapproving look my way, Melinda said, "You can talk to him now."

"Thank you."

We stepped into Reverend Walker's home office. It was different than the office at the church, which had been partly for show. This was much smaller with two low windows overlooking yet another rose garden. An outside spotlight was aimed at the roses, which lit up in rainbow hues. I wondered what he was thinking now, the connection between his dead wife, the roses and his now-dead daughter. The maple desk was cluttered, the bookshelves overflowing with textbooks, Bibles and concordances. There were framed photographs on the wall of Barbara and the Reverend and of a woman I assumed to be his long-dead wife.

"Reverend—"

"I think calling me Jim might be appropriate now," he said. He sat behind his desk in a wrinkled white shirt, the sleeves rolled up over his elbows. "That detective, uh, Rosenbaum, indicated the explosion may have been meant for you."

His diction was a little sloppy, but his words and meaning were clear. His snowy white hair was disheveled, the lines in his handsome face much deeper than before. He had lost much of his healthy color, the skin of his jowls already seeming to have sagged. But it was his eyes, the blue eyes that had seemed so electric before, that had changed the most. Now they were dull and lifeless, tarnished blueberries.

"I may have gotten lucky," I said, taking a seat. As I did I noticed the tall glass of a dark liquid on a corner of the desk. My gaze darted around the office, finally settling on a bottle of Jim Beam on a lower book shelf within easy reach of where the Reverend was sitting. "How are you holding up?"

The Reverend reached out and fumbled at the glass, then raised it to his lips, knocking back about three ounces. If the man wasn't toasted now, he would be soon.

"Someone ... someone murdered my baby," he said, his tone as flat and lifeless as cardboard.

"I'm helping the police find out who did it," I said.

The Reverend drained the glass, carefully lifted the bottle off the shelf, even more carefully unscrewed the top, and with the deliberate caution of a full-out drunk, splashed the remnants of the bottle into the glass.

"Good, good," he said. He focused on Jack. "Who's your friend?"

I introduced him. Walker nodded, seeming to track what I was saying. "You have any children, Mr. Bear?"

"No."

"My daughter died, you know."

"Yes," Jack said. "I'm terribly sorry about your loss. However, would it be okay if Megan and I went through your house, especially Barbara's room?"

"Sure," Walker said with a flip of his hand. "Cops already did that." He rubbed his face with his left hand, then took another swallow of the Jim Beam. "They found some mari—mari ..." He contemplated his desktop for a moment. "They found some marijuana in one drawer and some pills. I ... I didn't know ... .They called the pills ecstasy. I don't even know what that's for. Do you? My baby was taking drugs and I never even knew. I wasn't much of a father, I guess. I thought God wanted me to run missions, to preach, to save souls. Now I wonder what I did wrong. I missed the soul right under my own roof. My very own daughter."

His expression was bleak and I thought he might cry, but he didn't, just rubbed at his eyes and took another drink of the Beam.

Jack said, "I think we ought to get you up to your bedroom, sir. I'll help you, if that's all right."

"I'm just fine right here," Walker said.

"I don't think so, sir," Jack said, and walked around the desk. He took the glass out of Reverend Walker's hand and helped him to his feet. Jack raised his eyebrows and looked at me. "Any questions while he can still answer them?"

I shook my head.

One arm under the Reverend's shoulders, Jack eased him around the desk and out of the office. Walker's head was starting to loll, his gait very unsteady. Jack supported most of his weight and led the way.

Melinda rushed to help us, saying, "He rarely drinks. You won't tell anybody?"

You people worry too much about appearances, I thought, but said, "No, of course not."

The master suite was on the main floor and Jack and Melinda managed to get Reverend Walker into it. Jack effortlessly lifted Walker onto the king-sized bed and undid his belt and took off his shoes. He pulled the blinds and ushered Melinda and me out, closing the door behind us.

"I'm so sorry," Melinda said. "He's usually so under control."

I tried not to roll my eyes. "He said we could go through the house, especially Barbara's room. I'd like to see her room now. Is it upstairs?"

"The police already did that."

"Yes, and they found drugs. I'm not looking for drugs. Where's her room?"

"Who are you?" Melinda asked.

I shoved my business card into her face. "That's who I am. If you think I'm someone different, I'd appreciate it if you told me who, because this is starting to really tick me off. What do you and Matt and Lucas Balkovic think I'm doing?"

She hid her hands behind her back and wouldn't meet my gaze. "That's really none of my business. You say you are who you are and I guess I'll just have to accept that."

"Look—"

Jack took me by the elbow and led me upstairs before I could finish. I hissed at him. "What are you doing?"

"She's not going to help you with this. Let her go. Come on. Are you looking for something specific in Barbara's room?"

"Her computer, hopefully."

It was a large bedroom with a queen-sized waterbed. The walls were painted a light blue, the bedspread a maroon comforter. There was the slight smell of incense, probably used to dilute the odor of pot. One window looked over the front yard. There was a dresser with a built-in mirror, makeup mirror, an overstuffed armchair and a computer desk with computer, printer and scanner. I gravitated toward the computer, but Jack started at the closet, opening the slatted bi-fold doors.

"Looking for anything in particular?" I asked.

"Trying to get a feel for her," he said. He glanced over his shoulder and said, "Maybe it's just me, but I have a gut feeling she's not completely a victim."

"I don't think so either."

"Something you're not telling me?" he said.

I shrugged. "No proof, just a thought. Ecstacy's the rave drug, right? Everyone's solution to Quaaludes?"

"Yup."

"Ever take them?"

He smiled. "Booze is my drug of choice, thanks." He took a shoe box off the top shelf and opened the lid. "Photographs," he said, and sat in the armchair and began to methodically sort through them. "Of course," he added, "I don't know what the hell I'm looking at. Maybe you should do this."

"I will, but go through them first." I gazed longingly at the computer, then began to go through her dresser drawers. A lot of t-shirts and jeans and lacy underwear. Thongs and string bikini panties, whisper-thin bras, a fairly impressive collection of Victoria's Secret lingerie. I had no idea if any was missing. Did she leave voluntarily, going off to a tryst? One she expected to return from? Or did she plan on starting anew? Of course, her car was gone. So was she.

I held up a black bustier and said to Jack, "She's eighteen and she's got one of these things. I've never even owned one."

"That doesn't surprise me," Jack said.

"Shut up."

He grinned. "I don't imagine her father knew what she owned. But I wonder who did the laundry?"

"I'm betting they hired somebody."

"Whoever they did probably knows quite a bit about what goes on in this household." Jack held up a 4X5 print and squinted at it before putting it on the bottom of the pile. "What's your take on Barbara and Daddy?"

"I don't know."

"You don't know or you don't want to think about it?"

"Yes."

"I'll be upfront about it then. Do you think there was something sexual between the Reverend and his daughter?"

"I don't know."

Jack pointed to the bustier. "Did you want one of those when you were eighteen?"

"I was then, and always have been, more into sleeping in a t-shirt and underwear. Bustiers and other lingerie aren't really about sleeping, though. They're about sex. It wouldn't totally surprise me if a lot of teenage girls were into lingerie like this, especially if they grow up in households where their parents don't really know what's going on in their lives. There's a fantasy element to lingerie. Of course, Joey Mason said she was a tease who liked older men."

"We should talk to him."

"One thing at a time."

I went completely through the dressers, but found them uninformative. To hell with it. I powered up the PC, double-clicked on the My Computer icon and began to scroll my way through Barbara's hard drive. Behind me Jack finished sorting through the photographs and returned to the closet. We worked in silence, broken once when Jack muttered, "She's got a lot of clothes."

"Actress wannabe," I said.

"Any luck?"

"Maybe."

In a flash he was behind me, one hand on my shoulder, leaning over to read the monitor. I liked his clean smell. Soap, a hint of masculine pheromones and something else indefinable. I was overly aware of his proximity.

"What is that?"

"She's got some hacker programs here," I said.

"Yeah?"

"Yeah."

"Like the one you said tried to break into your system?"

"She's got a Trojan Horse here, but it's different than that one. A lot simpler. She probably downloaded them from the Web."

"Anything else?"

I nodded and brought it up on screen. Jack frowned. "What is that?"

"It's a version of the database that I've spent the last couple days restoring."

"Part of the church's website."

"Right. Not something you see in the website, but it's there in the server. It shouldn't be here. And there are modifications here."

Jack made a face. "I'm not sure I understand."

I sighed. "Henry had everything burned onto backup disks. Once a day he backed up everything on the servers and kept them stored somewhere else. Maybe at his house, maybe in a safe deposit box somewhere. I don't know, and at the moment it doesn't matter. After the servers were wiped, Henry was more interested in getting Chavez Tech back up and running, so he loaded all the programs and data back on the servers Sunday afternoon and most of the night. But any data, like the church's Web donations Sunday, were gone for good. Except nothing's gone for good unless you incinerate the hard drives. That's where I came in, trying to restore the data."

"Interesting. So what's different?"

I turned to look at Jack. He was inches away, almost touching. With a faint smile on his face he edged away from me, giving me room.

"What's so different," I said, "is that there are changes here that neither WebSpinners nor I programmed in. I bet that when it came to data, Henry loaded the latest backups. But when it came to actual programs, like this database and encryption system, he may have loaded it from the originals. Anyway, there are differences from what I've been working on."

"Like?"

"Well, I mentioned I had my suspicions about the site and how the server was erased."

"I'm following you so far."

I nodded at the database I had found on her hard drive. "Remember what Danny Chen and Stephanie argued about?"

Jack raised his eyebrows. "I'm sort of lost."

I leaned my head back, stretching a kink out of my neck. "Danny said he wanted to audit all their commercial websites. Meaning, he was concerned there were irregularities in how the credit card information and financial data was being stored, encrypted and sent to the bank."

"Okay," Jack said, pointing to the screen. "So what are you seeing here?"

"What I wasn't sure about, but was suspicious about, had to do with the encryption and transfer programming. See, this is a fund-raising website. People can log on, put their credit card numbers in and make donations to the church. As you know from your own website, the card numbers get encrypted and sent to the church which then decodes it. Some businesses then process the

"When did she get home last night?" Jack asked. He'd taken over because the little bitch had begun to act as if I were invisible. I jammed my hands in my jeans pockets so they wouldn't reach out and slap her.

(*Chew, chew, chew*). "Dunno. I mean, she worked till closing, two o'clock, I was asleep by then. And I didn't see her this morning. Maybe she was out all night, or maybe she just got up early. I don't know."

"Is that unusual?" Jack said, arms crossed over his chest, standing a few feet away from her.

(*Chew, chew, chew*). "Well, maybe. I wasn't really paying attention, you know? But sometimes she stays out all night. Depends on who she's dating."

Jack took a step closer and rested his hand on her upper arm. His voice deepened. "Who's she dating?"

She looked up at him and for a moment I thought she was going to rip her clothes off. Instead she arched her back so her tits were aimed right at Jack. He didn't seem to notice, but I was sure he did. In fact, to his credit, he seemed to be using her attraction to his advantage.

"Well," she said. "Nobody, I don't think. Doesn't mean she didn't meet somebody and, you know, spend the night. Sometimes she does that. Not often, I mean, makes her sound like a slut, but ... hey, we've all had hot dates, right?"

"I'm sure we have," Jack said. "I bet you're a hot date."

Cindy giggled. "Yeah."

Oh cut it out, I thought.

"Does Lisa have a cell phone?" Jack asked.

"Sure."

"Do you know the number?"

"Uh-uh. Sorry, she never gave it to me."

Jack nodded his head toward Lisa's desk and the PC on top of it. "You mind if my friend and I kind of look around?"

"Well, I don't know ..."

Jack held up a hand, motioning her to silence. "My associate and I are working closely with the authorities. If we have to, we'll get a warrant, but we'd greatly appreciate it if you gave us permission to go through Lisa's things. We have reason to believe she's in serious danger."

Cindy's contact-lens-enhanced green eyes grew big. "Really?"

Gravely Jack nodded. "It's of the utmost importance that we find her."

"Oh. Well, sure. Go ahead."

Jack nodded to me and I hurried to the computer and began to rummage through Lisa's hard drive.

By 10:15 we were in front of Joey Mason's house on Terry Street just off downtown Rochester. Like the night before when I had visited Joey, the street was very dark, the trees mature, their leafy branches providing a protective canopy from moon and starlight, from the lamps on the far ends of the street. All up and down the street blue TV light could be seen between pulled curtains or through windows.

Except for the Mason's house, which was dark.

"Try again," Jack said. I did, punching in Lisa Dunn's number. In her desk we'd found the most recent cell phone bill, which conveniently had the phone's number on it. I had tried it as soon as we left her dorm, but the line had been busy. This was probably a good sign. Now I wanted to try it again, so I did.

"Hello?" I recognized Lisa's voice.

"Hello," I said. "Is this Lisa Dunn?"

"Yes, who is this?"

"Where are you, Lisa?"

All I could hear was her breathing. Finally she said, "Who is this?" a little more urgency in her voice.

"Lisa, don't hang up," I said. "It's Meg Malloy. I talked to you yesterday at Mr. B's? I was looking for Barbara—"

"I can't talk long, I'm in—" The line went dead. I promptly dialed again, but was given the message that the phone was either out of the service range or was turned off.

I looked at Jack in the darkness, could barely see his eyes. I said, "She's scared."

"I would be if I were her," Jack said.

"You think she knows who killed Barbara."

"Uh-huh."

"So I could turn her number over to the cops and they could try to track her down."

"Could. Can you?"

"No," I said. "I could probably figure out which cell she's in, but they're huge so that'll only narrow things down. To track a cell phone signal you need triangulation. It's supposedly possible by triangulating between cellular towers, but I don't know if it's real-time yet, and for me to do it would require I hack into the company's computers and co-opt their entire system, which I can't. The cops would do it if they had the motivation and the resources. With the Sheriff's I'm not even sure they have the resources. Probably the State Police. And they'd have to get her on the line and keep her there. At least, as far as I know. I don't know all that much about cell phone systems."

"Well, everything you've said so far is what I've heard, but you're right, technology keeps changing, so who knows. What do you want to do?"

Go home, crawl into bed and sleep for a week. Instead I said, "Let's see if the Masons are home."

We climbed out of the Corvette and walked up the leaf-littered walkway to the front door. I started by hitting the doorbell. We could hear the chimes inside, but nobody answered. I rang it a couple more times, then pounded on the door. Still no answer.

Jack said, "Want me to pick the lock?"

I rubbed my forehead, thinking. Finally, "Yes. Go ahead. You want me to talk so we look like we belong here?"

"Not this time. I want you to hold this so I can see." He handed me a penlight about the length of my index finger.

"You're prepared for everything."

"Not everything," he said. "They have a dog?"

"I don't know."

"Let's hope not," he said, and inserted his picks in the lock.

In five minutes we were inside. No dog. Jack flicked on a light. I said, "Won't somebody see it?"

He shrugged. "You want to stumble around in the dark?"

"Good point." I paused to take in my surroundings. Small and clean with comfortable furniture. Too much furniture. The living room had a couch, three big chairs, a coffee table and a TV set, but aside from that, nothing stood out. Cautiously Jack and I walked through the house. It felt empty. It felt ... abandoned. The refrigerator clicked and hummed and I jumped. My nerves were twitching, reminding me that this was breaking and entering, that I didn't belong here.

I stopped at the answering machine in the kitchen, took a second to figure it out, and replayed the last couple messages. Nothing that told us anything. Then I hit the redial button. After two rings a woman picked up and said, "Crittenton Peds."

Mrs. Mason was an LPN at Crittenton Hospital. I said, "Could I please speak to Mrs. Mason?"

"Linda Mason?"

"Yes," I said.

"Well, she doesn't usually work this shift. But, something ... wait, why did her name come up? In fact ... just a second." I was put on hold, listening to public service announcements for parenting workshops and breast feeding classes. After a moment the woman came back on and said, "Yeah, I thought her name came up. Linda called in, some sort of family emergency. She said she had to go out of town for a few days. We're not sure, but we think it was her aunt's funeral. It might have been one of her parents."

"Her aunt's," I lied. "That's what I was calling about. I guess Freddie already got hold of her, then. So sorry to bother you."

"Okay. Thank you." I hung up. Jack just shot me a questioning look. I told him.

"Lisa and Joey found out about Barbara and took off," he said. "They know what's going on."

I thought how that might have happened. After I left him the night before I imagine she jumped all over him wanting to know what I had talked to him about. Had he lied, told her it was about a job, like I originally had? Or had she gotten the truth out of him?

If they took off, if Joey knew something about Barbara, if, if, if ...

They were gone. Real family emergency? I doubted it. Too much of a coincidence.

"Joey got his mother to agree," I said. "So she must know something, too. This is scary shit, Jack." We headed for the front door. I couldn't wait to leave, to get out of this hollow-feeling place where I didn't belong.

"What do you want to do next?" Jack said.

"Go home."

Jack shook his head. "Bad idea. It's better to keep moving. Or find someplace to hole up. They—whoever the hell 'they' are—are going to know you're still alive."

"I need to get to my computer," I said. "I need—"

The front door burst open with a bang that shook the house and two men exploded into the living room, guns drawn.

20

When I was about six years old my parents took me to my Uncle Walter's house on Kearsley Lake to go ice skating. It must have been an extremely cold winter because the ice was very thick and people were driving their cars on the lake, revving the engines and braking into long skids.

At six I wasn't much of an ice skater. I'm still not. I kind of slithered and slid and fell and crawled around on the slick ice while my parents and relatives gracefully glided along.

I remember being bundled to within an inch of my life with snow pants, a coat, a scarf and a hat with my coat's hood pulled over that and tied so tight that only my face was exposed. I remember the sharp tingly sensation of the cold on my skin. I remember the helplessness of ice skating, of being unable to stand, unable to move where I wanted to move.

And I remember that one of the cars went into an uncontrolled slide toward where we were ice skating.

I remember my father coming out of nowhere and plucking me off the ice, tucking me under one arm and skating out of harm's way.

And what I remember most, second only to the undercurrent of fear and panic in my mother's voice, was the odd way everything slowed down. How my cousins seemed to move so deliberately, how the sound of my mother's soprano hung in the bitter winter air, how my father seemed unhurried, how the whirling car seemed to float toward us.

That's how it felt in the living room of the Mason's house when two men burst through the door.

With a sweep of his left arm Jack knocked me behind him, barking, "Run," as he did so. At the same time he lashed out with his right leg, exploding the lamp into a wall, slamming the room into darkness.

The first man through the door aimed a gun at Jack. In the dim light I saw movement, heard a grunt and a shout, then a clunk as a heavy object hit the carpeting.

I didn't run.

I threw myself toward the extinguished lamp on the floor, thudding and rolling on top of it. I snagged it and lurched to a crouch, spinning, trying to figure out what was going on in the darkness. I sensed three shapes struggling, grunting as blows were traded.

I swung the lamp like an unwieldy baseball bat. There was a crash and a vibration that ran all the way up the ceramic lamp to my arm, to my shoulders, to rattle my teeth. The man I hit groaned and slammed into the floor.

Someone uttered a low, guttural gargling sound, then the house shook as someone else collapsed to the floor.

"Jack?" I whispered.

Another light flicked on and I saw two men in dark suits on the Mason's living room carpeting. One, closest to me, was feebly struggling to get up amidst shards of off-white pottery. The other was motionless. Jack, his movements sure and unhesitating, pulled a knife from his pocket and flicked the blade out.

"*Jack?*" I said.

He didn't look at me, but quickly cut the cord from the lamp and bound, hands and feet, the man I had clobbered.

"Get outside," he said. "Now."

"Jack—"

"Hurry up."

He cut another cord from the room's third lamp and bound the second man, jamming his fingers against the man's neck. "Go," he said.

As if in a trance I picked my way around the men and out of the Mason's house. Turning as I stepped through the doorway, I watched Jack reach inside one of the men's jackets and pull out what looked like a slim leather wallet. He flipped it open and read it before tucking it back inside the coat. Something flitted across his dark features like bats across the night sky, then he pocketed their two guns and followed me out the door.

"You drive stick?" he said.

"Yes."

He handed me his keys. "Get the car going and get out of here. I'll meet you in the parking lot of the Spartan Motel. Don't park in the light. I'll be just a minute."

He melted into the darkness of Terry Street. Confused and shaken, it took me a moment to pull it together, then I slid behind the wheel of the Corvette, adjusted the seat, fired the engine to life and drove to the Spartan Motel. Five minutes later Jack knocked on the window and waved for me to move into the passenger seat. I did, scrambling over the gearshift, unnerved, unwilling to leave the relative safety of the car.

He said, "Okay?"

My hands were shaking and I felt like I might burst into tears at any moment, but aside from that I was completely uninjured. I nodded.

"Where to?" he said.

The only place I wanted to go was home and I said so. Jack, without commenting, pulled the Corvette out onto Rochester Road and headed south, which was not exactly the direction of Lake Orion. After a moment, when we had passed through downtown Rochester, I knew we definitely weren't heading for Lake Orion. "Where are we going?"

"I don't know," he said. "Your house isn't safe, though."

"I need my computers."

"You've got your laptop with you."

"Um ... yes. But ..."

"It's not safe to go to your house," he said. "I agree we could use a break, but we can't go to your house. Whoever tried to kill your friend Stephanie and whoever firebombed the offices knows where you live. Whoever it is might try at your house and it's not a very defensible position. Too much glass, really only one exit. Could be wired already, for all we know."

Could be wired already ... A bomb? Another bomb? My stomach cramped and for a moment spots tangoed before my eyes.

I leaned forward, head on my knees, sucking in deep breaths until my vision cleared. Sitting up, I stared out the window, wondering when my life took a left turn into the Twilight Zone. We continued south. Rochester Road was primarily stores—Borders Books and Old Navy and Target and Kmart and Barnes and Noble and strip mall after strip mall after strip mall interspersed with restaurants from McDonald's, Burger King and Wendy's to the middle-level chains like Red Lobster and Olive Garden. There are swankier restaurants like Kruse & Muir's and delis and small businesses, all lit up in a glare of fluorescence and neon.

"We could go to a motel," I said.

"We could," Jack said. "But we'd probably have to use a credit card and that might not be a great idea at the moment. Is there anyplace else? A friend who can keep their mouth shut, anybody like that?"

I nodded and Jack glanced at me. He reached out a hand to touch my leg. "Let's keep it together, okay? You were great in there. Really great."

"Who were they? Who were they, Jack?"

He patted my knee then retracted his hand to shift gears. He said, "Next time I tell you to run in a dangerous situation, though, I'd really appreciate it if you listened to me. It's hard to protect someone who doesn't do what you tell them to do. If I tell you to hit the dirt, hit the dirt, okay?"

"It worked out," I said.

Jack didn't comment.

After a moment Jack said, "I've got to make a call," and pulled into the parking lot of a darkened strip mall that boasted a bakery, a real estate office and a deli. There was a pay phone mounted against the white brick wall next to a bank of newspaper vending machines. "Stay here," he said. When he opened his door I involuntarily lurched forward, not wanting to be separated from him. He held up a hand. "I'll be right there," he said, pointing at the phone. "Quick call, okay?"

"Who are you calling?" I asked, not liking the tremor of fear that ran beneath the words.

"911. To tell the cops about those two guys back at the Mason's. Hang on."

He made it to the phone in five quick strides, leaving the engine running, the door to the car opened. I watched as he dropped in coins, punched the three buttons and spoke into the phone. Then he hung up and within seconds was back in the car and we were back on the road.

"Turn here," I said, gesturing to the next intersection, which was Auburn Road.

"You have a place for us to go?" he asked.

"Yes. For now, anyway. I need some time to think."

"Sure," he said, and followed my directions. After about ten minutes he said, "We're doubling back."

"More or less. Back to Rochester, anyway."

"Where are we going?"

I looked out the window at the lights of the streets. We were now back on Adams Road, heading north toward University. We passed the subdivision where Reverend Walker lived. I wondered how he was doing since we had left. If, hopefully, he was still asleep. The days ahead were going to be a living hell for him. He had lived through that before, no doubt, when his wife died. As a minister, even a TV minister, he must have overseen an uncountable number of funerals, stood by the bedside of the dying.

I doubted if he was prepared for it. I doubted if anyone was.

Finally I said, "To my parents' house. They're close to the University."

"They have a garage?"

"Yes," I said. "We can hide the Corvette inside. I have a key and I can use my Dad's computer system to look up some things."

"It'll work temporarily."

I watched Jack as he turned left onto University Drive. I said, "Jack, temporary's all we've got. We can't do this forever."

He nodded.

I gave him directions and eventually he pulled the Corvette into the blacktopped driveway of my parents' low-slung brick ranch, the front yard hidden by the shadows of my favorite weeping willow.

"Hang on," I said, and climbed out of the Corvette, let myself into the house through the front door, flicking on lights as I went. I plucked the keys to my mother's Buick off the key rack, set the garage door opener into motion and backed her car out of the garage. Jack slipped his car into the Buick's spot. I shut down the Buick and scuttled into the garage, ducking under the descending garage door.

From the trunk of his car Jack was retrieving the sawed-off shotgun and a duffel bag.

Once we were inside the house I stood in the kitchen, my back to the butcher-block counter top and said, "Who were the two men in the Mason's house? I need to know, Jack. I really need to know."

Jack's jaw clenched. He said, "His name is Michael X. Zilway."

"That's not what I mean."

"I know," Jack said.

"Who did I knock out with a lamp, Jack," I said. "How deep are we?"

"Deep," Jack said. "Very deep. We are in *way* too deep. And I don't really know how to get us out."

He gazed at me, his eyes dark, expression tense. He seemed, for a man who showed all signs of being totally unflappable, a little worried. He set the duffel bag on the vinyl-tiled floor and gently rested the sawed-off shotgun on the butcher block counter next to me. He sighed and seemed to visibly relax. "Michael X. Zilway," he said. "According to his ID, Zilway's an agent with the Secret Service. His partner, the guy you nailed with the lamp, is Bradley Meyer, the FBI agent with the black Ford Taurus. The two guys who've been following us."

The strength left my legs and I sank to the floor, resting my head on my arms. A low moan escaped my lips. "Oh Jack. What have we done?"

21

I sat there head on my hands, hands on my knees, adrift. I wasn't thinking analytically. I wasn't thinking about how I had assaulted an FBI agent. I wasn't even thinking about how someone may have tried to kill me this morning by blowing my Hummer to scrap. I wasn't even trying to figure out a way to extract myself from this mess.

I just let emotions wash over me like waves, pretending to be a piece of driftwood, inert and oblivious.

After what could have been five minutes or fifty, Jack nudged me. I opened my eyes and saw that he was offering me a shot glass filled with something dark. I took it from him and sipped it. And began to laugh.

It rolled out of me, inappropriate, slightly hysterical laughter. Jack leaned back against my parents' white side-by-side refrigerator and sipped his own shot of Dad's Jamieson's Irish Whiskey. Eventually, like a storm squall passing by, the laughter left me as well.

I said, "When I was twelve and Mattie was fourteen my parents went to a funeral with her parents for some relative of ours and they left us here. Mattie and I started talking about funerals and I asked her what they meant when they talked about an Irish wake. She said it means everybody drank a lot of Irish Whiskey and made toasts to the memory of the dead person."

Jack smiled and took another sip.

I continued. "So Mattie got out Dad's Jamieson's—" I held up the near-empty shot glass. "—which was almost full, and she and I took two shot glasses and started making toasts to all the dead people we could think of." I laughed some more and held up the shot glass to Jack. "One more, but only one, okay?"

He took it silently, disappeared for a moment, then reappeared with another shot for me. He didn't take one. I drank, remembering. Remembering in that visceral, total-body way you do when the memory is stimulated by a taste or an odor.

"We drank toasts to two or three people—relatives, I think—who had died. And we drank a toast to John Lennon and Martin Luther King and Elvis and John F. Kennedy, I remember that. And we started getting silly, drinking toasts to

Genghis Khan and George Washington and Abraham Lincoln and all the people who died on the Titanic and all the people who died in Vietnam and all the world wars ..." I giggled. "We were thorough, you have to give us credit for that. We were Irish through and through and we threw one hell of an Irish wake."

Suddenly Jack disappeared, reappearing with the bottle of Jamieson's and his empty shot glass, which he filled. Without a word—he hadn't said a word since I fell to the floor—he raised his shot glass in a toast, something indescribably sad crossing his face—and knocked back the whiskey. He screwed the bottle shut and put it aside.

"Who did you drink a toast to?" I didn't think he would answer my question. The sad look—sorrowful look—disappeared and he didn't say anything for the longest time. Then he said, "To dead friends and relatives." He sighed, thoughtful. "To lost loves, dead friends and relatives."

"Your ... brother?"

He shook his head. "I think we should probably get to work. Or, you should get to work if you think there's work to be done."

"Sure," I said, climbing to my feet. He reached out to help me and I clutched his hand, not surprised by his strength. I stood close to him, looking up at his features, the impenetrable depths of his dark eyes, the thousands of generations of Chippewa genes that had shaped his appearance. I said, "Did you see the picture in the living room of Mattie and me?"

He nodded. It was hard to miss. Dad kept it on the liquor cabinet, the only photograph he kept there. Mattie and me, twelve and fourteen, both of us with red hair and ponytails, arms around each other in cut-off jeans and tank tops. Cousins and best of friends. The picture had been taken the morning of our Irish wake. The morning *after* our Irish wake had been miserable and I think Dad wished he had a picture of us both barfing into the toilet as a reminder. We had finished off most of the bottle of Jamieson's—enough for a twelve-year-old and fourteen-year-old to experience the first and worst hangovers of our entire lives—and had been grounded from TV for a week by our respective parents. Mom had argued that we suffered enough, and Dad said he agreed, but it wouldn't hurt either one of us to go without TV for a week. Positive reinforcement, he said.

"What happened between the two of you?" I said to Jack.

Jack picked up the bottle of whiskey and walked into the living room to put it away in the liquor cabinet. "You considered what our options are?"

I sighed, wanting to throw something at him. "Why don't you talk about yourself?"

He glanced over his shoulder. "We're up to our eyebrows in shit and you want to talk about me. But the clock's ticking and it'll only be a matter of time—if those guys are looking for us—before they wonder about your parents. We have to consider our options and we have to consider them soon."

"Well," I said. "We could go to jail. That particular option has occurred to me. Are there others?"

"It might help with the Feds if we had something to bargain with when they finally catch up to us."

"And they will, won't they?"

He nodded. "Probably."

"We could call them up now and turn ourselves in, explain that we acted in self-defense, we didn't know who they were. That we knew someone was trying to kill me so we were justified in our actions."

Jack nodded. "Might work."

"But ..."

He sighed and sat down in my Dad's favorite armchair. "If it were just you, I'd say that was a pretty good idea. They could arrange for a safe house and you'd probably be just fine, hiding out until this whole thing goes away."

"But ... ?"

"But," he said slowly, "it wasn't just you. It was me, too. And I hate to tell you this, but law enforcement, local, State or Federal, isn't going to be likely to cut you any slack because of my involvement. Maybe especially Federal."

"Why?"

He frowned and sighed again. "They think I was responsible for the death of an FBI agent a couple of years ago."

I felt a tingle of electricity. "Were you?"

"Let's just say that on this particular issue the FBI is wrong."

"But you were associated with—"

"Organized crime?" Jack closed his eyes. "Yes. They know that, too. Another complication, to say the least. I may not have been the right one to call in this particular instance."

I sat down in my mother's rocking chair and regarded Jack Bear. I had known him a very short time, knew very little about him, but I liked him. Liked him a lot. Probably too much because for all I knew he and my favorite cousin still had a relationship. But Jack worried me, too, because he was something I didn't think I was prepared for. Jack was hot like flames, and like fire, you could be burned if you didn't know what you were dealing with.

And with Jack, I thought, you never really knew what you were dealing with.

If your back is ever against the wall. I mean, really against the wall ... if your life's ever in danger ...

I trusted Mattie, who had told me to trust Jack. And now Jack was worried because the two of us had gotten in over our heads. I climbed to my feet. Jack shot me a questioning look. "Come on. I'll show you Dad's office, but I've got some work to do."

"You want to solve this?"

"We *have* to solve this. By the way, what'd you do with their guns?"

"Put them in their car. I didn't want them shooting at the cops when they showed up. I thought about trashing their car, but I figured they were probably going to be pissed off enough."

"Good call."

Dad's office was in the basement, which had been finished off. He had paneled the walls in tongue-in-groove pine, applied a light stain and let it age. Occasionally it still smelled of evergreen forest. It was a windowless room with a built-in desk along two corners, each side ten feet long. The rest of the room was lined with bookcases crammed with textbooks. I powered up everything. On the computer screen—the *very large* computer screen—the system flashed through its startup ritual.

"He's a bigger computer geek than you," Jack said.

"Computer science professor at Oakland University," I said. "Retired, but still consulting. And yes, he probably is a bigger computer geek than me."

"Where are your parents, anyway?"

"Traveling. As far as I know, they're in Holland at the moment." I sat in Dad's black leather swivel and swivelled, lasering my gaze on Jack. "Okay, Jack. Tell me about the Secret Service. What do they do besides guard the President and despicable third and fourth-world dictators dropping by for a visit?"

"Investigate counterfeiting," he said.

"Right," I said. "They're Treasury Department, aren't they? Or are they part of the Department of Homeland Security now?"

"If they're part of Homeland, nobody knows what they do," Jack said. "Including the White House."

"Cynic," I said. "If they're Treasury ... I wonder why the Treasury Department is in charge of presidential security. Anyway, what else?"

He gestured at the computer. "You going to look?"

"I think I know already," I said. "They're big into computer crimes, which is where they overlap with the FBI. But they also investigate bank fraud and credit card fraud. Essentially they investigate crimes against any institution which is insured by the Federal government."

"Credit card fraud," Jack said. "Well shit."

"Exactly. Someone was siphoning money from the Missionary Church of Jesus Christ Evangelical's website, which was credit card donations. They also have a telephone answering board that takes donations over the phone— they're in Southfield—but their database is separate from the website. They share info—want to make sure all the money-paying parishioners are alerted to chances to donate—but they're essentially separate.

"Now," I said, my brain kicking into gear. "We know Barbara was behind this, though I don't think she was alone in it. I know money was siphoned and I know that on their biggest contribution day—Sunday, just a couple hours after the church service aired—all the money was shifted to a foreign bank account and then the website, the server and the database were trashed. Along, by the way, with the error and entry logs. But I think it was done by someone sneaking into the server and manually wiping the hard drives."

I thought some more, then snapped my fingers. "I didn't tell you about Balkovic, did I?"

Jack dropped down into an armchair where my mother sometimes curled up and read while Dad did his work on the computer systems. "No," he said.

"Brother Balkovic is the rough equivalent of the church's Chief Financial Officer. Last night, when I dropped in and talked to Reverend Walker at the church, Brother Matthew—he's the assistant pastor, remember?—asked me to meet him at Barnes and Noble on Rochester Road. When I met him, Balkovic was there, too. And he was acting paranoid and cryptic, demanding to know who I really was, wanting to know what I really wanted, wanting to know why we—"

"He said 'we'?"

"Well, 'you'. He wanted to know why 'we' wouldn't just come out in the open and ask them for what we wanted."

Jack clenched his teeth in a shark's grin, then relaxed. "You think Balkovic got wind the Secret Service was investigating the church because of credit card theft related to the church?"

"It makes sense," I said. "Let's say a couple hundred—maybe a couple thousand—people all over the country are having problems with someone using their credit card numbers illegally."

"Hell," Jack said. "There's a booming business in counterfeit credit cards. The guys—and sometimes they're Organized Crime, sometimes just guys who've figured out a way to turn a buck—get hold of people's real numbers, either by dumpster diving or by using them from legitimate business records—"

"Like the church's site!"

"Let's not call this church a legitimate business, okay? I know people who'd call organized religion just another form of organized crime." Jack grinned, a real grin this time. "Both want your money and both want you to behave in a certain way for fear of the afterlife. Anyway, they get hold of the card numbers and have new cards made to order with those numbers. Sell the cards for a price and the people who buy them have a card with a legitimate number, at least until they get flagged. And that can take quite a while sometimes."

"So the Secret Service investigates, and somewhere along the line they find that one thing all these people have in common is they donated to the Missionary Church of Jesus Christ Evangelical by way of the website. So they start poking around ..." I hesitated. "WebSpinners," I said. "Because WebSpinners and Chavez Tech are the actual source of the site and the computer programming, not the church."

"And Danny Chen wants your friend Stephanie to audit all the commercial accounts they have," Jack said.

"Then Danny knew!"

"Yeah. But who broke into his house?" Jack said.

"I don't know, but the Secret Service had it under surveillance afterward. *Afterward*, Jack."

"Did they have the Mason's house under surveillance?" he said. "How'd they know we were there? What, for God's sake, gave them probable cause to break in like that? If they were honest Feds, then did they think it was us or someone else?"

"Hell if I know. If we start keeping a list of questions we don't have answers to it'll take up all my hard drive space." I started rummaging through my backpack, yanking out my PDA, flicking it on and using the stylus to find the number I wanted.

"What's up?" Jack said.

I punched numbers into Dad's office phone. Waited for the phone to pick up. After two rings Glen Blalock picked up, saying, "Blalockubus, Inc. What do you want?"

"Glen, it's Megan. I need your help tracking down a remote user."

22

Dad's printer spewed out paper while I stared at the monitor and tried to think laterally. Tried to think around corners. It seemed clear we were dealing with some sort of scam—computer crime and credit card fraud—but who was behind it, and who had actually killed Barbara, remained a mystery.

Jack suggested it had all the hallmarks of organized crime. Or at least, he speculated, *some* of it did. The porn video and the credit card fraud, connected, seemed very mafia-like.

"Are the mafia still in Detroit?" I asked. "I thought the FBI really cleaned house a few years ago. Didn't you mention that?"

Jack shrugged. "So they say. That doesn't mean there aren't a few low-level guys trying to keep things afloat. Which makes sense, in a way. I mean, this thing hasn't been run very professionally. You're still alive, Stephanie's still alive ..."

And it seemed to me that Danny Chen, Lisa Dunn, and Joe and Linda Mason had a clearer idea of what was going on. But they had all disappeared.

Were they dead? Or hiding?

Now I was trying to find them, or at least, find clues to their whereabouts.

I had sicced Glen Blalock on the trail of my 'friend' who had left me a warning e-mail only yesterday, warning me that the case was very dangerous, to be careful. Just this morning—was that all it was?—I had attempted to track him or her down myself, only to get hung up in the America Online system.

When I had reached Glen on the phone he had said, "Their security's getting better."

"I didn't try that hard," I said, "because I didn't think it was all that important. I had a hacker, too, but I'm not sure they're the same. The hacker didn't actually get into my system—"

"Yeah, the Water Pit. I know. I got through, did you know that?"

I was flabbergasted. "Glen!"

"Hey, it wasn't easy. But ... M&M, this is *me* you're talking to."

I demanded he tell me what he did so I could make changes. Reluctantly he confessed and I was once again forced to admit that Glen—creep though he might be—was—a computer genius. A run-amuck computer genius with few or no scruples, but a genius nonetheless.

"Anyway," I said. "I've got other things to do—and besides, you can slip in and out unnoticed. As you've demonstrated. I might bring some unwanted attention my way."

"Yeah, you might. Hey, I've got the enhancements finished on the background of the video. Want it?"

"Is it any good?"

I could almost hear Glen shrug over the phone. "So-so. I'm not real pleased with it, but I've gone as far as I could. I'll e-mail you the enhancement."

I gave him my father's e-mail address then asked whether he'd had any luck tracking the porn loop. Uncomfortable silence. "Well, not in any practical way. My program narrowed it down to 3,472 different websites."

"That many?"

"You have any idea how many websites there are featuring video porn, and how much video porn is on each of them?"

"I actually don't want to think about it."

"Okay, Snow White. Basically my program located porn video segments featuring women spreadeagle on beds with a guy coming into the room, no pun intended."

"Three thousand four hundred and seventy two of them?"

"Well, I haven't looked at them, but that's how the program works, more or less."

"Let's call that a dead end."

"Yeah. Let me get on your *friend*."

And I was still waiting. But I had broken into the Oakland University computer system and rummaged around through the student records looking up Lisa Dunn and Joe Mason's vital data in hopes it might lead us to where they went. Ditto with Crittenton Hospital's personnel files. The patient records were more or less secure, but the personnel files were like an open door. And now I was printing out everything I could find on them.

In the meantime ...

I listened, staring at a photograph of my parents and myself taken on stage at Orchestra Hall in Detroit, after a concert where my mother was a soloist with the Detroit Symphony Orchestra. Good memories. Proud memories.

It was 2:35 in the morning and I could hear Jack moving around above me, a slow cycle from room to room followed by silence as he settled into the living room or the kitchen to sit and wait. Jack wasn't taking any chances. He thought our own personal Feds would be on to us eventually.

"And the bad guys?" I'd said. "Would they think of looking for us here?"

"Hard to figure these guys so far. If they think you're just hiding, they might leave it alone. Depends on their resources. But you can't plan for that. You have to plan for what they *might* do, not what you figure they *will* do. I'd like to get back on the road no later than four o'clock. We've got to find a place to hide out for the day, someplace we can hole up and get some sleep."

"Let me work on it, okay?"

"Fine, just don't work too long."

I listened for Jack upstairs, IDed his location as the kitchen, then typed "Joseph Eaglefeather" and "Traverse City" into the search engine. The headline from the Traverse City Record-Eagle screamed:

FBI AGENT KILLED IN CASINO BOMBING

Special Agent Joseph Eaglefeather, assigned to the Federal Bureau of Investigation's Northern Michigan Field Office, died in an explosion that ripped apart the New Peshawbestown Casino Saturday, July 10th. It is believed that Eaglefeather was attempting to defuse the bomb that destroyed ...

I skimmed the article about how a group of criminals attempted to knock off the Chippewa tribe's casino on opening day. It was the third incarnation of the the tribe's Traverse City casino and the gang's attempts had been semi-successful—three of the robbers had died in an explosion while attempting to flee from the casino's marina in a speedboat. Along with the boat had been approximately ten bags of coin and currency estimated at a value of $750,000. Very little of the money, which was either incinerated or ended up on the bottom of Suttons Bay, was ever retrieved. The dead were Robert Cordella, Fulton Smythe and Leonard Crane. Little was known about Smythe and Crane, but Robert Cordella was a local businessman with suspected ties to St. Louis organized crime. Held for questioning were local resident Jack Bear and Florida resident Matalyn Malloy.

Jesus. Mattie, you never told me.

I quickly typed in "Conrad Wilson" and "Traverse City" and was rewarded with a dozen articles about how Conrad Wilson, a local private investigator, had solved one case or another, often locating missing persons. But the one I was looking for—at least I thought—was how Conrad Wilson had been killed in a boating accident. A second article, something of an afterthought, made a connection between Wilson's boating accident and the casino bombing—the unidentified boat was similar to the boat owned by the now-deceased Robert Cordella.

I felt as if a cat with very sharp claws was climbing up my spine. Jack had told me that Conrad Wilson was a friend of his, that he had, in fact, worked with Wilson. According to the article Wilson had died while riding his Jet Ski on West Grand Traverse Bay, apparently run down by a "purple and red speedboat." A day later Robert "Bobbi" Cordella and two other men died in an explosion on Cordella's "purple and red cigarette boat."

"Mattie never told you?" Jack asked.

I jumped, a shriek leaving my mouth. Turning I said, "Yikes, Jack! Don't sneak up on me like that!"

He gestured to the computer screen. "I hope you got what you were looking for."

I glanced over my shoulder. "I'm not sure. Did you kill Robert—"

"Bobbi."

"Cut it out, Jack. Did you kill Bobbi Cordella?"

"Bobbi was a very bad guy," Jack said. "And getting worse every day."

"Just answer the question."

His dark gaze met mine. He said, "It's actually sort of a complicated question, but you're not looking for a complicated answer. So I'll give you the simple one. Yes, Meg. I killed Bobbi."

"You put the bomb on his boat."

He hesitated. "Why is this important to you?"

"What kind of man are you?" I said. I heard my voice tremble. "You killed three men! Three men! You put a bomb—"

Jack tensed. His expression shifted to a listening one, his attention focused upstairs and outside. Holding up a hand he headed upstairs.

Heart in my throat, emotionally conflicted, I checked the e-mail, downloaded the information Glen had found me, burned the image onto a disk and started to clean up my mess. Jack returned, said, "False alarm, but let's get out of here. You know where you want to go?"

I held up a sheaf of papers. "We're going to find who my 'friend' is."

In the rearview mirror of the Corvette I watched my parents' house—the covered front porch, the split rail fence, the weeping willow tree—shrink and vanish into the darkness. It was just after 4:00 in the morning and in this outer limit of exurbia some of the more diehard commuters were starting their day. Lone kitchen lights burned like beacons.

"Maybe we should just turn ourselves in," I said. The sheaf of printouts was now stuffed into my backpack—clues to ... where? What? More tragedy? Another narrowly avoided catastrophe?

"Okay," Jack said.

I slammed my palm down on the dashboard with a sharp whap! "Don't be so damned agreeable!"

"Sure," he said. His teeth gleamed from a reflection off the dashboard lights.

"I mean, what's the downside?"

"Now you sound like a corporate exec."

"Fuck you."

He chuckled softly, barely heard above the purr of the engine. I lapsed into silence. We took M-59 west, past the Pontiac Silverdome, arcing sinuously through downtown Pontiac. The buildings looked old. Red and brown brick boxes, depressing and industrial. But there were swarms of lights ablaze, and I knew that Pontiac's downtown appearance was a facade. Techies and the twenty-somethings had discovered Pontiac: cheap rents, high-tech infrastructure, decent night life and an emerging arts and music community. The school system and the government hadn't caught up, but downtown Pontiac—once a no-man's land—was cutting edge.

"The downside to turning ourselves in," Jack said, "is we assaulted two Federal agents while committing a felony—breaking and entering. They didn't announce themselves and they didn't appear to have a warrant, but they probably witnessed us go into the house and viewed it as a crime in progress—hence, probable cause."

"And they probably weren't too thrilled about us giving them the slip, so they were especially anxious to talk to us."

Jack hesitated, quiet as he threaded his way off M-59 onto Telegraph Road and headed north. "I wonder why they had Chen's house staked out."

"Me, too." We passed Summit Place Mall, then the county service center—the courthouse with 1200 emblazoned in huge numbers across the top of its high rise, the Department of Public Health, the morgue, the Sheriff's Department. "I wonder if Lieutenant Rosenbaum knows what's going on," I said.

"Mmm," Jack said.

"You don't think so?"

"No."

"Why?"

"Because *we* don't know what's going on, and we know more about it than he does."

"Good point."

At the corner of Telegraph Road and the Dixie Highway was a Trini & Carmen's Mexican Restaurant, a swap center with a huge mural painted on the side of whales and dolphins, and the Highland Motel complete with a billboard of a Scotsman in complete highland regalia—kilt and all. It was where Glen Blalock had tracked my 'friend.'

Jack idled the 'Vette and looked over at me. "Who do you think your *friend* is?"

"I hope it's Danny Chen."

Jack nodded. "But you're not sure."

"Nope."

"Did you ask Blalock to try to verify?"

"Um ... no."

Jack stared out the windshield toward the Highland's office. In the window was a neon red VACANCY sign. The Highland was L-shaped, one-story and uninviting. Its proximity to the jail made me wonder about its clientele. Its location on the corner of a commercial strip that boasted strip clubs, bars and other, even less-classy motels that offered hourly rates, did not bode well for its AAA rating.

"B&E hasn't worked too well for us today," he said. "Maybe we should try something with a little more finesse."

"Will it be legal?"

"Yes. Not, maybe, completely ethical, but it seems to me we're probably past that kind of hair-splitting."

"Way past," I said. "What's your plan?"

"Go in and ask," he said, shoving open his door.

As we walked across the parking lot, in and out of cones of illumination alive with fluttering moths and sluggish mosquitoes, Jack said, "Let me do the talking. Just play along."

My backpack slung over my shoulder, I just nodded. *What the hell, Jack. Give it your best shot.*

Jack pushed his way through the door, hand reaching for his wallet. The clerk behind the high, Formica-topped counter was alert, already aware of our presence. He'd probably been watching us since we pulled into the lot. I suppose a certain amount of paranoia went along with the graveyard shift at a motel.

"Good morning," he said. "Can I help you?"

He looked to be about twenty years old. Either Indian or Pakistani, with close-cropped black hair, dark inquisitive eyes and narrow features. I pegged him for a college student with a third-shift job that allowed plenty of time for study. A laptop was open on the desk in front of him.

Jack flipped his wallet toward the kid. "I'm Conrad Wilson, a private investigator. This is my associate, Lauren Singer. We're trying to track a missing person name of Daniel Chen. We have reason to believe he's staying here."

The kid shook his head. "Nah. He checked out early yesterday morning. I was still working. He left around seven o'clock. We talked about computers. He knows a lot."

"You're sure it was Daniel Chen?" Jack said.

The clerk nodded, reached down and came up with a registry. "See for yourself. We do it both manual and computerized. The boss doesn't completely trust computers. Go ahead, look."

Jack and I scanned the book and saw that he spoke the truth. Danny had signed in—and out—with his own name.

"Missing person, huh? Who hired you?"

"His wife," Jack said.

"Yeah? She know he's gay?"

Jack and I pinned him with our stares.

"I mean, hey, it's none of my business. You see a lot of things in a place like this, and this guy seemed okay to me. But he had a male visitor late the other night."

"A man," Jack said.

"That's the point I'm making. Yeah. Tall guy, older. Came in close to midnight. I had just come on duty, came in a little early. Midnight to eight, that's my shift. Then I usually go to school and sleep in the afternoon."

"How old was this guy?" Jack said. "Can you describe him?"

"How old? Don't know. Looked about sixty, but coulda been younger because he moved like he was, you know, in good shape. He had white hair."

I slung my backpack on the counter, hauled out my laptop and fired it up. I inserted a disk I'd burned from Steph's system and brought up a version of the Missionary Church of Jesus Christ Evangelical's website. There was a page devoted to all the "officers" of the church. Brother Matthew. Brother Lucas. Brother Steven. Sister Nancy.

I pointed. "Him?"

The kid studied the image of Reverend James Walker. "Yeah," he said. "That's him. Definitely."

23

It was after six o'clock and the burnt-ivory of pre-dawn had given way to the blue-gray light of a cloudy, overcast morning. Jack and I pulled up in front of the Reverend's house and stalked to his front door. Neither of us was happy, and, considering the shit we had found ourselves in, determined to get some answers.

I rapped my knuckles on the metal frame of the decorative glass door, a reverberating bam-bam-bam. The door was pulled open almost instantly by a heavyset woman we hadn't met before. She was about five-eight, with a rounded heavy figure, an African fertility goddess, although this particular fertility goddess wore jeans and a T-shirt. Her age was somewhere from late thirties to mid-fifties, her dark hair streaked with gray and pulled back in a tight, severe ponytail. Startling gray eyes met our gaze through rectangular glasses.

"Whoever you are," she said, "it's kind of early, don't you think?"

"I'm Megan Malloy and this is Jack Bear," I said with a flip of my hand. "We have to talk to Reverend—"

"Blowing up in our faces, isn't it?" she interrupted. "Come on in."

Jack nudged me, giving me a sideways look. "Is there room in the garage?" Jack said.

This formidable woman leveled a thoughtful, considering gaze on Jack. She nodded, more to herself than him, I thought. "It's like that, is it?"

Jack nodded.

"I'll move Jim's car to make room," she said.

"Just give him the keys," I said. "We need to talk—"

"Yes, of course. Come in, I'll get them."

We stepped into the foyer with its oak floor and crystal chandelier; she returned a moment later with a set of keys. "Just put the car out front in the turnaround. Nobody'll be able to see yours in the garage."

Jack and I passed each other another look, a silent comment on this woman's canniness, then he left to make the switch. The woman shot her hand toward me. "I'm Nancy Phillips, better known around here as Sister Nancy, but that makes me feel like a nun. You can call me Nancy, if you want. You want some coffee?"

"I thought you were in Sri Lanka," I said. "And yes, coffee would be good."

"Got in about three this morning." She led me into the kitchen and went about pouring a mug of coffee. "Once Matt got hold of me I was on my way. I actually chartered a private jet to London, took British Air to New York, then got another private jet to Pontiac. I have no idea what time zone I'm in."

She smiled slightly at the expression on my face. "Yes, an expense. But as I said, I'm not a nun and I never took a vow of poverty. I travel on my job, spend very little time at my home, so I just keep a small apartment in Rochester as a sort of home base. If it makes you feel better, the price of the jet will come out of my own savings. I practically raised Barbara, after all. I had to get here."

"I'm sorry. Very sorry about what happened to her," I said. I sat down at the large glass-topped kitchen table, wondering why she felt a need to justify her expenses.

Nancy Phillips nodded emphatically, her expression grim. "A shock, of course, and a tragedy. I wish I could say I was surprised, but I'm not. Barbara's been troubled for a very long time. Jim liked to think it was just ... *acting out*. I told him it wasn't just acting out, that her disappearing for days at a time since she was fifteen, what to all intents and purposes looked like rampant promiscuity ... with older men, no less ... I tried to convince him these were bigger problems. But he refused to believe what he saw in front of him. She hung out with the *wrong crowd*," she said, putting quote marks around "wrong crowd" with her fingers, "but that was the least of her problems."

"Do you know any of them?"

"No, and I don't think it matters. The crowd wasn't the bad influence, I don't think. She pursued them. And maybe led them."

When she bent toward me with the coffee mug I noticed that her earrings were little gold horseshoes. And for the first time the t-shirt registered on me, an old Led Zeppelin concert tee that had seen better days. She noticed my look and smiled again.

"Not what you were expecting?"

"No, not really."

She settled at an angle from me and sipped her own coffee. "The 'sister' always throws people, I think. I'm a missionary, a Christian, a nurse. I'm an RN with an MBA and I run all over the world managing a dozen missions in a number of developing countries. We do good things, Ms. Malloy, and I'd be lying if I didn't emphasize that what I personally think we do best is provide medicine and health care and education. The religious teaching, well, that's not really my area. I'm open-minded about other religions. I believe God is too big and complex for humans to understand, so why would I think I have a clue as to what his or her will is?"

"Does Reverend Walker agree with you?"

She smiled. "No, but we agree on many things. He's not a bad man." She leveled her gaze at me. "I had a very long and frank discussion with him on the phone just a day or so ago. He told me about the website crash and about Barbara disappearing and about him hiring you. I wondered if they were connected. They are, aren't they?"

I nodded.

Jack walked in then and I introduced the two of them.

"I'll get you coffee ..."

"I can handle it," Jack said, and did, taking his black. He sat at the kitchen table, leaning back and listening.

"Jim didn't tell me about you," Nancy said to Jack. "Are you a computer troubleshooter, too?"

"Just a troubleshooter," Jack said.

She didn't flinch. "We're in trouble then, aren't we?"

"Yes," Jack said. "We all are."

"Maybe you should tell me everything. I'm not on top of things and I'm running half a step behind."

Jack shrugged, leaving it up to me. I thought about it for a second, then started at the beginning and told her everything that had happened, everything we knew, everything we thought we knew, and much of what we wondered about.

Around eight o'clock Reverend Walker staggered into the kitchen looking very much like he was suffering from a world-class hangover. He had aged again, like some sort of biological clock locked into fast-forward. His eyes were bloodshot with their own set of luggage below, his complexion pasty, a day's growth beard scarring the patrician chin. His usually rigid posture had sagged.

"Nance!"

She jumped to her feet and wrapped her arms around him, holding him tight. He wept then, cried onto her shoulder in a moment of unalloyed grief that was painful to watch. After a few uncomfortable minutes he stopped and pulled away from her. Wiping his eyes with the back of his hand, he turned to us. "Still here?"

"Back," I said. "We've been busy. We were gone most of the night. We've found out some things that need to be talked about."

Walker stared, closed his eyes and, shoulders drooping more, said, "I'm not sure I'm up to all of this."

Nancy patted his shoulder. "Sit down, Jim. I'll get you some coffee and something to eat."

He groaned. "Lord, no food."

"Dry toast," she said. "Can I get you two anything to eat?"

We both accepted and Nancy went about putting together a breakfast of scrambled eggs and toast, juice and coffee. I was ravenous, unaware until now of just how hungry I was.

Finally, when she was back at the table and we were all eating off the fine china, I sketched out what I had told Nancy so far, then finished the story. It took an entire pot of coffee and it was closing in on nine o'clock by the time I was done. I was starting to fade. I'd been up almost twenty-four hours and those hours had not been relaxed and stress-free. The adrenaline was seeping away leaving very little energy behind.

"So," I said. "Tell us about Danny Chen."

Reverend Walker closed his eyes momentarily, as if praying. Finally he said, "About a week ago Mr. Chen visited me. I had met him a couple times in my dealings with WebSpinners. I was under the impression he was a sort of ... partner in the enterprise. Is that right?"

"Not exactly," I said. "He worked for Stephanie, but they were lovers for some time. I don't know the details of their breakup, but I doubt if it was easy to work for her after they did."

"No," Walker murmured, sipping his coffee. "I suppose not. Anyway, he came to my office at the church and told me he was concerned about our website, concerned that there were some ... well, he suspected that money was being siphoned off from the donations. He told me he had broached the subject with Stephanie and she didn't agree."

"He left WebSpinners over the issue," I said.

Walker looked troubled, contemplating the depths of his coffee mug. "I didn't know that ... then."

"What was your reaction?" Jack said.

"Concern. I wanted it checked into immediately. The public is skeptical about television ministries. There have been far too many con games and scandals involving televangelists in the last decade or two. I didn't want even a whiff of that to get out."

"So you brought the subject up with Stephanie?" I said.

He sighed. "Well, no. Not directly. I thanked Mr. Chen and told him I'd be calling Stephanie right away. She's really in the hospital? I'll have to visit her today."

"You thanked Danny and said you'd call Steph," I prompted.

"Oh, well ... yes. And he left and I was planning to call Stephanie when Barbara came into my office ..."

Jack and I exchanged yet another meaningful look, one not lost on either Reverend Walker or Nancy Phillips. Neither commented.

"And ..." I said.

"And I guess I was upset and I know that Barbara liked Stephanie and spent a fair amount of time at WebSpinners. She asked me what was going on—well, actually, she saw Mr. Chen leaving as she came in. She asked me what he was doing here ..."

"You told her," Jack said.

Reverend Walker rubbed his swollen eyelids with the palms of his hands. "Yes. I told her that Chen was worried about the site and they were going to look into it."

"What'd she do?" I said.

Walker kneaded his forehead with his fingertips. I could appreciate what he was feeling because I was culturing a headache of my own.

"She told me she'd take care of it. She'd drive over and talk to Stephanie herself. Help audit the site."

"Oh, Jim," Nancy said.

"I trusted her! She was my own daughter! I thought she was finally expressing a genuine interest in the workings of the church. She seemed so ... she seemed so *concerned*."

She was, I thought. Concerned for herself. Christ. The machinery that young lady had set in motion! But with whom?

"And then?" I said.

"And then I forgot about it. She said she'd get back with me. And then on Sunday she didn't show up for dinner and Stephanie called me in the afternoon to tell me the server had crashed and she thought the data—all the donations information—could be retrieved by someone like you. I told her I wanted someone discreet and she assured me you were, that you had dealt with government agencies, that you used to work with your ex-husband when he was a private investigator, so I told her to go ahead. I never even dreamed that Barbara might be involved."

I saw something that looked like irritation cross Nancy's wide, round face. She covered it by taking a gulp of her coffee.

"When did you hear from Danny again?" I said.

"I got a call late the night before last. He told me he was in trouble, that he thought he had some sort of idea of what was going on, but he wasn't completely sure who. He said he was trying to get in touch with you, but you'd disappeared. In fact, he was concerned that Stephanie was out of touch, too. I agreed to meet him at that motel and he laid things out for me, but he knows less than you do."

"Did he say where he was going next, or what he might try to do?" Jack said.

Reverend Walker shook his head, his white hair rumpled and stiff from sleep. "No. He ... he didn't completely trust me."

Glenn Blalock had tracked the source of the e-mail warning me off. We had not tried to track whoever had tried to break into my system but gotten snagged in the Water Pit. Maybe I should—it would be a lot harder, maybe impossible. The hacker had escaped the Water Pit, after all. Not gone through and around it like Glen, but had escaped, nonetheless. I had made an assumption, always a bad idea, that the hacker and my 'friend' had been one and the same. But ... maybe whoever was really behind all this was the hacker, not Danny.

"What ... what are you ... we ..." Reverend Walker faltered.

"Jim—" Nancy began.

"No. No, this is out of hand. Miss Malloy, perhaps you should quit now and take all of this to the police."

I saw the effort that statement required. This would be a big—maybe even huge—scandal. Embezzled funds. Porn movies. Murder. A badly damaged, disturbed young lady willfully bringing destruction down on her father and the ministry he had built.

Choices. Take a right turn instead of a left. Write a computer program to please your father. Open a company to please your boyfriend. Marry an unsuitable man. Divorce the man, divorce the company. Run away. Hide.

Turning everything over had its appeal.

How deeply in trouble were Jack and I?

Even if we coughed up everything we knew, would I be investigated by the Secret Service? Would Jack?

I wasn't sure if they went over my background looking for irregularities that something wouldn't turn up. I'm not sure anybody's life would stand up to that. Tax problems? Not quite legal access to databases and online services like America Online?

I thought of my friend at NCIC who occasionally broke rules for me.

I wondered how much scrutiny Jack could withstand?

I shook my head. "No," I said. "It's too late. I doubt we'll be able to cover this all up—even if you wanted to—but right now it's too big a mess to walk away from."

I yawned. "But we've got to get some rest. Can we sleep here for a few hours?"

Walker nodded. "What ... what do you intend to do?"

I thought about cause and effect, thoughts flashing through my head like a nuclear powered rubber ball. Barbara had known they were siphoning money off the church's website. She had probably planted the program. But had she actually written it? Did she have that kind of skill? I didn't think so. Had she had that kind of access to Chavez Tech's server? Chavez Tech was a small place. A half-dozen Dell server units, a couple cubicles, an office for Henry Chavez. Two or three employees with staggered shifts. There were time periods when the servers weren't monitored personally, but I imagined Henry or somebody checked them remotely on a regular basis when nobody was actually on-site.

How would I have done it?

Cause and effect: Danny got a hint of trouble, Barbara found out, she or whoever she was working with had pulled the plug, crashing the system to cover up. But before that, somebody tore Danny's house to pieces, scaring him into running for his life.

Who sent the porn video to Walker? And why?

But I thought I knew that one. Barbara had. *Look at me, Daddy! I'm not the sweet little girl you think I am! Ha-ha-ha!*

Cause and effect.

I'd started poking around, trying to track her down. What had I done? I'd talked to Lisa Dunn and Joe Mason. I'd talked to Brother Matthew. But my money was on Dunn and Mason. Both had known more than they were saying, both had lied to me, and both had disappeared when the shit began to fly.

Had one of them called Barbara after I talked to them?

Bet on it.

And Barbara had told whoever she was working with—the guy with the cat tattoo in the video?—that I was some sort of computer P.I. trying to track her down and figure out what was going on with the server and this guy had killed her, dumped her in my car and rigged a bomb. Then he'd also tried to kill Stephanie and tried to firebomb the offices of Chavez Tech and WebSpinners. Covering their tracks, trying to eliminate the people who knew most about what was going on.

My arms broke out in goose flesh. Danny, wherever he was, was in serious danger.

And so was I.

I reached into my backpack and yanked out my phone.

"Who're you calling?" Reverend Walker said.

I held up a hand for silence, double-checked the number, then called Lisa Dunn's cell number. A deep male voice answered, "Yeah?"

"Um ... can I speak to Lisa?"

"Who is this?"

"A ... a friend."

"She's busy. She can't come to the phone right now." The phone clicked off. I felt the blood drain from my face.

"Meg?" Jack said.

I couldn't be sure, but the voice on the phone sounded like the voice of the man on the videotape. The man with the cat tattoo on his left bicep.

24

I threw my backpack on Barbara's bed and rubbed my eyes. So tired. Jack stepped in after me and closed the door behind him.

I smiled. "I like you Jack, but I'm not ready to share a bed with you."

"Damn," he said. "I was hoping." He smiled back. "That's not why I stepped in here. I'll be across the hall in the guest room. Just holler if you need anything." In a moment of silence that I found very un-Jack-like, he frowned, then continued. "You trust them? Walker and Phillips?"

I sighed and sat on the edge of the bed and kicked off my shoes, wriggling my toes. "I think so."

He waited, not commenting, just waiting for me to clarify. I didn't want to. He wanted me to say, "Yes, I trust them," or "No, I don't really trust them, but at the moment they're all we've got," and both those answers were in the back of my mind. Slowly I said, "I think Walker is a man with good intentions—yes, I know what the Bible says about those—who was so involved with his church, his business, his congregation, his image, whatever—that he probably ignored his daughter. I doubt if it's easy growing up the daughter of a minister. Compound that with the extent of Walker's success, the kind of quasi-TV star quality—it had to be tough on her. He reminds me of Ronald Reagan—he guides the boat but lets the people under him do what they want. And sometimes those people let it go to their heads and run amuck."

Jack crossed his arms over his chest. "Phillips, she's something else, isn't she?"

"Tough," I said. "A tough broad, in the nicest sense of the phrase. Very practical. Their relationship's a little quirky—"

"They're both a little quirky," Jack said. "But you trust her."

I nodded. "I have to at the moment, but yes, I trust her, even if she is a little strange."

He nodded and reached for the door. "Just don't trust them a hundred percent, okay? Something else could be going on with Chen. The Rev's relationship with his daughter could be much more sinister than an absent-minded, distant dysfunction, and Phillips may have chartered jets at the drop of the hat to get back here for some reason other than grief and familial crisis."

"I know."

"Good. Like I said, call me if you need anything." He pointed at Barbara's computer perched like a big toad on its desk. "And leave that thing alone. Get some rest. This isn't over yet." And then he left me alone.

I rested my elbows on my knees and balanced my head on my hands, eyes closed, giving into a wave of exhaustion. This wasn't over yet. *Dear God*, I thought, almost, but not quite a prayer.

Kicking off my jeans, I slipped under the comforter on Barbara's bed, closed my eyes and tried to sleep. But I couldn't. My brain buzzed like a stirred-up hornets' nest. I looked a the computer. Despite what Jack said, I was tempted to start diggning. But I was so tired....

In the dream I didn't use the remote start on the Hummer. Carrying Glen Blalock's gift of a jar of M&M's, I climbed into the driver's seat, jabbed the key into the ignition slot and turned. There was a moment in the dream, one of those split-second schizophrenic moments when the terror of the vision fought with the rational, conscious part of my brain that said, "Where's Barbara?" and then I shuddered awake, eyes wide, struggling in panic.

There was a hand over my mouth, pinning me to the bed.

I lashed out, realized it was Jack, his hand over my mouth, his own lips close to my ear. "Sshhh," he whispered. "We've got company. Get your stuff together and prepare to bug out of here at a moment's notice."

I was on my feet, conscious I was only wearing panties and a T-shirt. I jumped into my jeans and joined Jack near the window overlooking the front of the house. It looked like it was mid-afternoon. Parked out front was a black Ford Taurus. Careful to move the drapes as little as possible, Jack pointed downward to the front door. Two men in dark suits stood on the porch, talking to someone.

I nodded and slipped into my shoes then made sure everything was in my backpack. Jack stood at the door, opened a crack, listening.

I took another peek out the window, my gaze drifting from the two men at the front door to the Taurus. Peering through the tiny slit, I squinted, not sure I was believing what I was seeing. There was a third man in the back seat of the Taurus. He was watching the two men at the door, his face in profile, then his head swung to the side, his gaze scanning across the house and up, zooming in on the windows. I froze, heart racing, blood roaring in my ears.

The rear door of the Taurus swung open and Danny Chen stepped out of the car, standing on the decorative red brick driveway of the Reverend's house. Casually he raised his arms over his head as if stretching, but he looked directly at the window where I was hiding. As he dropped his hands, his head shook slightly from side to side and he rested a finger on his lips. *Ssshhh*. With a gesture that could have been a small shrug he turned, said something to the two men at the front door, and climbed back into the car.

What was going on?

After another moment the two men—who I recognized from the Mason's house the night before—walked back toward the car, gazes shifting, heads turning, scanning the property, alert and inquisitive.

Making sure not to move the curtain I took a step back so I wouldn't be visible. I couldn't see them; I hoped they couldn't see me. Then I heard the slam of two car doors, the muffled rumble of the Taurus's engine turning over, and the car pulling away.

Jack turned to me, eyebrows raised in question. I said, "Danny Chen was in that car."

"You're sure?"

"Yes," I said. "And he saw me. He stepped out of the car, saw me, then shook his head and put his fingers on his lips as if to tell me to be quiet ... and to be careful."

"Chen's working with the Secret Service? And the FBI?"

There was a light knock at the door. Jack opened it. Sister Nancy Phillips stood in the doorway, her lips compressed into a tight white line. "They're gone," she said. "They were looking for you."

"What did you tell them?" I asked.

"I told them we hadn't heard from you and wanted to know why the Secret Service and the FBI wanted you. They wouldn't say."

To Nancy I said, "Where's the Reverend?"

"At the church. He had some things to discuss with Matt—Matt'll be taking over the services for at least this Sunday, and coordinating the funeral. Then I'll pick him up at the church and we'll drive over to the funeral home to talk to the director about ... arrangements." For the first time since we'd met tears welled up in her eyes. "Oh dear," she said. "I didn't want you to ..."

I put my arms around her and she cried onto my shoulders, deep wracking sobs. "She was such a sweet little girl," she said, voice muffled. "So lost after her mother died. We used to play with dolls, have tea parties ... I was the first person to introduce her to computers and she was so smart, she—"

Jack slipped out of the room, leaving the two of us alone. I could hear him across the hallway putting his gear together.

"—took to them right away. But ... but then the missions grew and I moved up in the organization. I began to travel. I think ... I think Barbara felt abandoned. Abandoned twice. I thought maybe this was something God wanted me to do, but I don't know, we aren't really very clear receivers of God's will."

She stepped away from me, wiping her eyes. "Thank you," she said. "I'm sorry. I've tried to keep it together ... but ... we failed her. We failed her, didn't we?"

"We can't control everything," I said. "As you said, Barbara embraced these things. Did you understand the acting?"

"Well ..." She sniffled and laughed softly. "Barbara was so smart. And talented. I think it was the TV that got her interested in acting, the services being televised. I always thought she'd end up doing something technical, she was so good at math and computers, but somewhere along the way the acting bug bit and that was it."

"Did she know Larry Clinton?"

"Larry ... oh, the director of the services. Of course she ..." Recognition marched across her face. "You think ... ?"

"I think we need to talk to him." I looked at my watch, saw it was 3:30 in the afternoon. I needed a shower. I needed another ten hours of sleep. Running a hand through my snarly hair, I said, "You know where his office is?"

25

Jack returned. "You ready?"

I shook my head and pointed at the computer. "There's something I want to check first. Something I didn't look for the first time through."

"Make it quick," he said. "It's probably not too good an idea to stay too long in one place." He looked at Nancy, who was sitting on the bed, hands folded demurely in her lap. He said, "You lied to the Feds very convincingly." There was a tone of admiration in his voice.

She smiled through her grief. "A useful talent in some parts of the world where I've been. I've lied convincingly to Tutsi rebels in Congo when they wanted to steal our medicine and sell it on the black market. I've lied successfully to Cuban police officers who don't trust Americans ... I've had quite a bit of experience with it. Why the FBI? As you've explained things to me so far, I understand the Secret Service. Why the FBI?"

I sat down at Barbara's computer and turned it on, not answering. Jack deflected Nancy's gaze by looking at me. He said, "What're you doing?"

"I'm going to do a quick and dirty forensic data recovery on Barbara's modem log. I want to know how she got into Chavez Tech's servers on Sunday to divert all the info and crash out the system, all while erasing the entry logs. It's not dramatically sophisticated, but it takes some doing. Just how good at computers was she, Nancy?"

"Good, but not brilliant," she said. "I never thought she was ... you know ... a hacker. Of course, there's a lot about her that Jim and I apparently didn't know."

"That's my impression of her, too," I said. "When I went through her computer the first time and checked out her software, the mockup of the database and other things ..." I moved into the part of the computer memory I was interested in and started reconstructing keystrokes from Sunday. "Well, she struck me as being a well-educated, experienced user. Most kids are today, some more than others. When I was eighteen I was light years ahead of the game because my dad started me on computers when barely anybody used them. Nowadays kids are as comfortable with computers as they are with TV remote controls. But that doesn't make them good programmers. Some are, but most just know how to use the things without thinking too much about it. Barbara seems somewhere in between. Am I right?"

Nancy nodded, edging closer to where I was working. "I think so, yes. She took some programming classes in school and some Web design, and she didn't seem to have any problems. She could take new software and learn it a lot faster than I could. But I never thought she was someone who was breaking into, say, her school's computer system to change her grades, or anything like that."

I grinned.

Jack said, "Let me guess ..."

"Never caught except by my dad," I said.

"You changed your grades?" Nancy said.

"Well, I was a freshman in high school. I changed everybody's grades. Everybody in my entire freshman class got straight A's first semester."

"They knew somebody did it, of course," Jack said.

"Yeah, but nobody ever found out who. It was in the newspaper. When my dad read it he marched me to his computer, did pretty much what I'm doing now and forced me to go back in and return all the grades to what they'd been before."

"And he didn't turn you in?" Nancy asked.

I shook my head, tapping keys. "No. He got my promise to never do it again, which I haven't."

"No punishment?"

"Well," I said. "Actually, returning all the grades to their original designation for five hundred people was a lot more work than turning them all to A's. Dad had to teach me how to do forensic data recovery to do it, and it was a lot of work. I was up all night. That seemed punishment enough; it was pretty tedious."

I hit return and said, "Bingo."

The computer read:

MATT21:12-13

"What's that?" Jack asked.

"I wasn't really sure how Barbara broke into Chavez Tech. She had access off and on over the last few months, I know that. And Henry Chavez let her do some programming. But I wasn't sure she'd want to be there to crash the system out on Sunday. There might have been somebody there—on the weekends people come and go. There'd be no guarantee she'd have privacy. But then I thought about how I'd have done it. And I decided, at least since this was a long-term theft, that Barbara had uploaded a small program into the server that acted as a back door. She had to have done that when Henry was letting her play around, get used to things. She slipped in her own secret access to the system. So any time she wanted to go in, she could, from here or any other computer system. And if she was careful about when she went in and made sure she doctored the error and entry logs on her way out, nobody would ever know. So what I just did here was go into the modem log and find what she typed to get in."

"So anybody who knew the password could move in and out," Jack said.

"Exactly." I pointed to the monitor. "If I'm right, that was her password to get into Chavez Tech."

I punched more keys, the modem buzzed, I typed MATT21:12-13, and in seconds I was inside Chavez Tech's control protocols. "See? Nancy, what's wrong?"

The woman's face had gone white, her hand to her mouth. "It's a Bible verse," she said. "Matthew 21: 12-13." Tears began to roll down her plump cheeks and she shook her head.

"And Jesus went into the temple of God, and cast out all them that sold and bought in the temple, and overthrew the tables of the moneychangers, and the seats of them that sold doves.

"And said unto them, It is written. My house shall be called the house of prayer: but ye have made it a den of thieves."

As we were leaving, Nancy said, "Do you think she meant that Jim had turned the church into a moneymaker, that she was angry about that?"

I turned to face her directly. Jack was anxious to leave, his face impassive, but his posture tense and impatient. "I think it was a black joke," I said. "You call it a house of prayer, but I'll make it a den of thieves. Or the victim of thieves."

Nancy looked doubtful. "She was very angry at Jim. He showed me that video. She sent it, didn't she?"

"Pretty sure."

"'Look at me,' she was saying. '*Look at me!*'"

That was exactly what I thought, but I wasn't certain Nancy needed to hear my confirmation. I said, "It may have been a cry for help, too. She may have realized she was getting in too deep. It may have been, '*Daddy, see what's happened to me. Help me!*'"

Nancy mulled that over for a second. "Perhaps both." She fired her intense, penetrating gaze on me again. "But I'll give that to Jim, for some reassurance. I don't know if he'll take it. Now ... before you go ... why the FBI?"

Jack looked at me, one eyebrow cocked, flashing me a question. I nodded. He said, "The M.O.—you know what I mean by that?"

She nodded.

"There's something about the bombings and the shootings and the porn video that screams organized crime. The Secret Service doesn't do that stuff, but the FBI does. That would explain the FBI." He hesitated. "But, the

FBI cleaned house in Detroit a few years ago, took down the top guy and most of his underlings. The Bureau publically claimed that to all intents and purposes the mafia—La Cosa Nostra—doesn't exist in any legitimate way in Detroit. Some low-level guys, not much to worry about."

"You know a lot about it," Nancy said.

Jack didn't respond.

"Jack thinks that whoever's been doing this—the person behind Barbara—might be a mafia wannabe, or some low-level, mildly incompetent mafioso leftover."

"But the computer crimes have been sophisticated, don't you think?"

I hesitated, then nodded. "Yes. Reasonably."

"So it's possible there's more than one person involved?"

"Maybe," I said.

"Be careful," she said.

"We will," I said. "We'll be in touch." I hesitated. "If we're not in touch by ... noon tomorrow, I suggest you turn everything we know over to the police. Talk to Lieutenant Eli Rosenbaum with the Sheriff's Department."

Nancy's jaw hardened and she nodded. "Godspeed, then. And thank you."

26

I have a theory. On any given day—today, for instance—there are hundreds of thousands of scientists generating new information on a seemingly unlimited number of topics. Thousands of scientific papers are published every year on almost every subject, ranging from the sex lives of fruit flies to how breast cancer cells respond to electrical current to the TV habits of 79-year-old Scandinavian women who married Yugoslavian men in the year 1947. Computer chips and semiconductors are designed and discarded and postulated and discarded and articles are published and published and published and published.

The top, top, top minds in any given field—let's say cancer research—understand their subject better than the rest. But, even though they read hundreds of articles a year from three or four journals on their given specialty, and attend conferences and lectures, they can't possibly keep up. Most people in any technical field run years behind on their reading. When I ran CyberConduits I tried to keep my nose above the waves, but it was impossible. Nobody can read all that material, let alone assimilate it.

My theory is that the answers are out there already. Answers to the cure for cancer or the common cold, the formula for a workable superconductor, cold fusion and quantum processors. In this day and age knowledge is like a jigsaw puzzle scattered around a large house by a hyperactive seven-year-old: one piece in a technical journal here, another in one there; one piece in a journal that was published six years ago in Hungary that nobody but Hungarian scientists reads; another vital piece that is needed to make sense of a theory is in a journal published in Uzbekhistan for which there are only three translators in the world.

Sometimes it seems to me that all the scientists and researchers on the planet should call a halt to all original research for a five-year period so everybody can just catch up on their reading.

I was sitting in the passenger seat of Jack's Corvette, reading the pages of printouts I had made at my parents' house. Background checks on Joey and Linda Mason and Lisa Dunn. I felt overwhelmed with information.

Forty-two single-spaced pages of credit records, employment histories, academic files and insurance profiles. Everything I had been able to pull off the Net and from restricted databases in a three-hour period.

It wasn't interesting reading. And I didn't know what I was looking for anyway. We were driving east on M-59 toward Utica, where the offices, and presumably the studio, of LTC Video were. LTC was the company owned by Larry Clinton, the one that provided television production services for the Missionary Church of Jesus Christ Evangelical.

"Find anything?" Jack said.

"I don't know."

"Masons have vacation property anywhere?"

"Not that I can tell."

"There's probably something in there but we don't know what it is."

"No shit," I said.

"Testy."

"Shut up and drive, Jack."

M-59, as usual, was under construction, and we were slogging along at about twenty-five miles per hour, bumper to bumper with harried commuters. I was morbidly convinced we'd get to LTC Video so late that the place would be closed, everybody gone for the night.

"Why don't you start on the top page and read out loud to me," he said. "Two heads are better than one."

"A two-headed animal is a mutant," I said.

"You're in a fine mood."

"No I'm not, and you damn well know it." I scowled at him, glared out at the river of automotive steel we were afloat in, glared at the suburban sprawl of eastern Oakland County that always seemed to be in an uncontrolled state of development. Strip malls sprouting like mushrooms, woods, forest and farms plowed under to make way for the next Wendy's, Office Max, Home Depot and Farmer Jack's. It was ugly and so was my mood. We were trapped behind a truck for a road construction crew that stunk of tar and a poorly maintained exhaust system. The foul odors made my stomach churn.

"I've got an alternate theory," I said after a moment.

"Go ahead."

"Matthew DuPuis is behind all this."

"Mmm," Jack said.

"Insightful, Jack."

"Tell me more."

"He was bopping Barbara. Together they're behind ripping off the church. MATT21:12-13 actually refers to DuPuis."

"The numbers, too?"

"Hell if I know."

"I haven't met him. Could he be the guy in the video?"

"No."

"Maybe he was holding the camera," Jack said.

"I doubt it. That was semi-pro, according to Glen. Maybe even pro. I think that movie was done by a professional, not some horny guy with a video camera."

"Okay. Tell me more."

"I don't have any more. It's just a theory."

"Okay. File it under UNLIKELY."

I held out the printout of the enhanced photograph from the videotape that Glen Blalock had e-mailed me. Most of it was a blurry mess. Glen had isolated a tiny segment of the videotape, then blown it up and used some very sophisticated software to enhance it. The problem with these types of enhancement programs is that they can sometimes make things up. It all depends on the type of data and parameters you feed it. If you have, for instance, a photograph you want to enhance taken at the Detroit Zoo of a vaguely humanoid head, you need to have some idea of what was photographed for it to work. If you feed the computer information that this is a human being when it is actually a close-up of an orangutan, the software is going to make it look like your brother Bill instead of Lancelot Link, Secret Chimp.

What Glen had gone after had taken place in a split second. There had been a cut from Barbara splayed spread-eagled on the bed to a static shot of the bedroom door. The door had opened and the masked rapist had entered. For just a moment there had been background visible through the doorway. What appeared to be a large room and a lighter area Glen suspected was a picture window.

Glen had isolated the picture window, which was mostly glare from sunlight, and tried to enhance the background. What he was after was what appeared to be a street sign, as if the building or house the video had been made in was on or near a street corner. The computer did pretty good work, but the light cascading off the glass had caused a lot of distortion and "bleed" into the rest of the image. What he had come up with was a close-up of part of the street sign, white on green, most of it gone, with the letters ARPE visible. I explained all this to Jack.

"So read all the names and addresses in there, maybe we'll get lucky."

"I don't feel lucky," I said.

"Just read."

I picked up the first page. It was a financial aid statement for Joseph Anthony Mason I had purloined from the Oakland University computer system. "Try not to fall asleep," I said, and began to read.

My voice droned on. Traffic congealed. There must have been an accident somewhere up ahead. I was glad I didn't have to commute. How did commuters keep from turning into homicidal maniacs? I read. The phone book would have been more interesting. I read Joey's address, his birthday, his mother's name and age and employment status. The social security benefits he received after the death of his step-father.

"His mom's only thirty-eight," I said. "She had him young. When I met her I'd have put her in her mid-forties to mid-fifties. Life hasn't been easy for Linda Mason."

"Uh-huh," Jack said, eyes shifting constantly to the rearview mirror. "We being followed?"

"I don't think so."

"You sure?"

"Pretty sure. Keep reading."

"Her income as a nurse at Crittenton Hospital is, hmmm . . ."

"Whatever it is, it's not enough," Jack said. "Think about what she does."

"Good point."

"Let's see, no income from the father and ex-husband, no child support, but, let's see ..." I flipped through the second page, sure there had been something about Joey Mason's birth father on one of the sheets of paper. "Okay, here, Joey's father's name is Joseph Catalano. Joey's a junior, then, isn't he? Joe Catalano, Jr. He mentioned he took his step-father's name."

Jack startled, jerking on the steering wheel, heading us toward traffic for a heart-stopping moment before returning to his lane.

"What?" I said.

"Joseph Catalano."

"Yeah. That name ring a bell?"

Jack's jaw was clenched, his knuckles white on the steering wheel. "Think about it. Joe Catalano. Joe Cat. The cat tattoo."

"Oh."

"Oh," he said. "Got an age?"

"No."

Jack's expression was grim, concentrating.

"That's not all, is it?" I said.

"No—"

My cell phone chirped. I looked at Jack. I'd had the phone off most of the day and night, conserving batteries, reluctant to have the world get in touch with me. I had checked my voicemail before we left and there had been a half-dozen messages, all having to do with proposed work. I hoped I'd be able to get back to them soon. The phone rang, loud, electronic and insistent.

"Jack?"

"Answer it," he said, edging over to the right-hand lane. I didn't know where he was going. Utica was still a good ten miles away.

I answered it, handling the phone like it was a scorpion, cautiously tapping the TALK button and pressing it to my ear. "Yes?"

"Where the hell are you, Malloy? Do you know what's going on?"

Lieutenant Eli Rosenbaum.

"Hello, Lieutenant."

"Oh, act so nice and innocent. What the hell is going on with you? Where are you?"

"I'm a little busy right now. What can I do for you?"

"A little busy? A little busy? Hey, Malloy? You want to tell me why in hell the FBI and the Secret Service want you? You know I got several calls wanting to know where you were, that they'd like to talk to you and your pal, Bear?"

"No, Lieutenant. I didn't know that. What's that mean?"

"It means *everybody's trying to find you!*"

"Is this my fifteen minutes of fame?"

I had to hold the phone away from my ear as Rosenbaum shrieked at me. When the volume faded a bit I returned to the phone. I said, "I'm just fine, Lieutenant. Nothing to worry about. I'm safe—"

"I want you to turn yourself in right now, Malloy! I want to put you in protective custody for your own damned good! Now tell me where you are! Right now!"

I turned off the phone and dropped it back into my backpack.

"He excited about something?" Jack said, as he steered the Corvette off M-59 and onto a four-lane divided highway ripe with fast food restaurants and chain stores.

"Where are we?"

"Just inside Oakland County."

"What're we doing?"

"We need to find someplace where you can go online. Can you do it from a phone booth?"

"No, I don't think so. Why?"

"We need information. More than you can get from your PDA, from what you've said. Maybe there's a cybercafe around here or ..."

"Why? What's going on? Besides Catalano and a cat tattoo. Who's Joe Catalano?"

"That's what I want you to go online and find out," he said, hands drumming nervously on the steering wheel. I had yet to see him this agitated.

"*Stop being so damned cryptic!*" I shouted, feeling heat suffuse my face. "Tell me who the hell you think Joe Catalano is."

"You're cute when you're mad, you know that?"

I almost hit him. It would have given me a lot of satisfaction. Instead I clenched my teeth like the onset of lockjaw, and said, "Just. Tell. Me."

He sighed with a small shake of his head. "Anthony Catalano went to prison a few years ago on racketeering charges, among others. May have been conspiracy and fraud charges, too, I don't know, I didn't follow it that close."

"Anthony Catalano."

"Yeah, like Joseph *Anthony Catalano* Mason."

"Okay," I said. "I don't need a roadmap, I can see where you're going."

"Tony 'The Cat' Catalano—"

"That's what they called him?"

"Yeah. Anyway, Tony was the head of the Detroit mob. The FBI'd been building their case against him for years, finally put it together and locked up eighteen or twenty of the very top guys. Tony was the grand prize."

"You think Joseph Catalano—Joey Mason's *dad*?—is this guy's son?"

Jack frowned, shaking his head again. "I don't think so. I didn't think Tony had a wife and kids. So it might be a nephew or somebody, I'm not sure."

"So you want to dig up as much info as we can find on Joseph Catalano and Tony Catalano."

"That's where I'd lay my money."

Me, too. But I didn't want to give up on Larry Clinton. Not yet. "Let's go talk to Clinton first. The Net never sleeps, but Clinton might."

Jack pulled back onto M-59. "You're the boss."

"Shut up."

He smiled, the confidence back. But Jack had been worried. Not scared. I'm not sure Jack scared very easily, if at all. But it had been more than casual concern.

Traffic was still slow, but we made it to LTC Video before 5:30 and there were still lights on in the low-slung office building. As we got out of the car I said, "Tony the Cat. He a real bad guy, Jack?"

Looking at the entrance to LTC Video, Jack nodded. "Real bad."

27

I remembered Larry Clinton from Reverend Walker's rehearsal. He also remembered me, especially the fact that he had walked into Reverend Walker's office while the Rev and I had been viewing a pornographic video-tape. Larry was tall, maybe six-two, and thin, his face shaped like a horse's, bald on top, a square but narrow jaw. He wore jeans and a red and green plaid shirt open at the neck and he rubbed his hands together all the time as if warming them over a fire. When his secretary, who was leaving for the day, ushered us in, he'd replied graciously enough, but his face had turned a pleasant shade of pink. He had waved at two chairs in front of his desk and told us to sit.

"We'd like to talk to you about Barbara Walker," I said.

Clinton's eyes darted like dragonflies, not meeting our gaze. "Barbara? What about her?"

"She worked for you, right?" I said.

"I don't really understand what you want," he said from behind his cluttered maple desk. It was big and square and battered, a high-quality piece that had seen a lot of hard use over the years, awash in stacks of scripts, memos, Post-It notes and half-filled coffee mugs. There were three coffee mugs, two blue with LTC VIDEO in white, one yellow with a not-smiley face that said, HAVE A DAY on it. I couldn't quite figure that out. Why did Clinton have three used coffee mugs on his desk? Did he forget and just grab a new cup of coffee each time he passed the kitchenette?

"You know Barbara Walker was murdered," I said.

He nodded, his expression completely neutral, as if glued in place. Not unlike the face on the yellow mug. *I don't want to talk about it, go away, have a day.* "A tragedy," he said.

One more time with feeling, I thought, my gaze drifting to the book-case behind him. It was filled with bound scripts. Pretty boring ones, I imagined. Industrial films. Advertisements. Instructional videos. I could just imagine one:

RELAXATION TECHNIQUES BEFORE SURGERY

EXT: HOSPITAL PORTAL — DAY

Doctors and Nurses pass before the hospital entrance

VOICE-OVER:

You are about to undergo major surgery. Most people are understandably nervous before major surgery. But our professionals rarely make mistakes, and when they do, your family can sue them for huge sums of money. Sure, you'll be dead, but your children will be much better off.

And then there were rows and rows of videotapes. I assumed they had a library or archive somewhere, but Larry Clinton kept a few hundred of his favorites in his office on a special maple bookcase on one wall just behind three comfortable-looking chairs and a round maple table. We weren't sitting in them. We were sitting in front of his desk while he stalled us. But why, I couldn't figure out. It made me antsy. I wondered if he was waiting for someone or something. I wondered if he'd had his secretary call the cops as soon as we walked through the door. I wondered if those cops were even now on their way to arrest us.

"Yes," I said. "It is a tragedy. I'm still looking into some things for Reverend Walker. I understand Barbara worked for you."

Clinton shrugged. "Couple of weeks. She wanted to be an actress. Thought she could learn the basics of film from me. She could have, but she wanted to act, not direct. She wasn't really that interested in what I had to offer."

"You couldn't use her in any of your commercials?"

He shrugged again, the hands still in motion. "It doesn't really work that way, though sometimes it does. I do work for ad agencies, companies that need instructional video, that sort of thing. I mean, we hire actresses, sure, but I work hand-in-hand with the ad people or the PR department of these companies. A lot of them come in with ideas or people they want. I mean, I could introduce her to them, but it was up to them."

"Did you?" Jack said.

"Did I what?"

"Introduce her to any people in the business."

Larry Clinton seemed distracted. Nervous. "Well, yeah, a couple of people. They didn't have a need for her talents."

"What talents were those?" I asked.

He froze, even his hands not moving. After an awkward moment he said, "Acting talents. Isn't that what we're talking about here?"

"I'm not sure what we're talking about here," I said. "Have the police talked to you about Barbara's murder yet?"

"Police? No. No, they haven't. Why would they?"

I stared at him, gave Jack a sideways glance, kneaded my forehead with my fingertips for a moment, then said, "Let's back up, Larry. You mind if I call you Larry?"

"No, go ahead. Whatever." He shrugged.

"Barbara worked for you, right?"

"Not really worked, but was ... she kind of hung around. Just a couple of weeks."

"Why'd she leave?"

He shrugged, turning to look out at a window overlooking a small patio: three picnic tables and a couple lawn chairs.

"You make porn movies here?" I said.

He jerked back to look at me. "What? Porn? No way. None of that. None of that at all. I'm a successful commercial and industrial film maker. We do mostly industrial films, some TV commercials—"

"The Missionary Church of Jesus Christ Evangelical's services," I said.

"Right. No porn. None whatsoever."

Jack and I contemplated Larry for a few seconds. I said, "What did you see when you interrupted Reverend Walker and me?"

"Hey, nothing. That's between—"

"What you saw," I said, "was a clip of a videotape somebody sent the Reverend of Barbara being raped."

Clinton's jaw dropped and he met my gaze this time. He was confused and possibly frightened. "I don't ... she was ... ?"

"It wasn't a rape," I said. "It was a loop from a porn video that Barbara was in. Do you know anything about that?"

"What? No! Absolutely ... No! And now she's ..."

"What did she do when she was here?" Jack said.

Clinton swallowed hard, his Adam's apple bobbing. He leaned back in the chair and pressed his hands against his eyes as if in pain. With a groan he sat up and said, "The cops are going to want to talk to me, aren't they?"

"Yes," I said.

"Look. I don't know anything about her ... death. You want to know about Barbara? Here's my experience. She asked me if she could come here, learn how things are done, maybe get some acting jobs. I didn't want her to, but my wife's a big fan of Reverend Walker and they're a significant client for us. We do the whole thing for him: production and feed, all of it. We don't do much of that, so it's kind of nice, might lead to other things besides films. Might be able to go in business with a station or something.

"Anyway, because of her dad, I said, okay. She showed up and was hanging around in the studio mostly, watching us do shoots. Went out when we did commercials on location. The first couple of days it was okay—all she did was watch—then she started nagging for acting parts. I told her it wasn't my decision, she needed representation, you know the drill. Then she really started bugging the ad reps and the actors and actresses. I got complaints. She came on too heavy ..." He hesitated. "Look, she propositioned a couple of the ad guys. They came to me, uncomfortable with it. She came on ... really strong."

"Uh-huh," Jack said. "Who's your biggest client, anyway?" He gestured at the wall of tapes.

"General Motors," he said. "Industrial films. After that, one of the big ad agencies here, Mantrell. Mostly car ads."

"No work for attractive young women in car ads?"

"Not thin enough," Clinton said bluntly. He eyed me nervously, his watery blues shifting from Jack to me, his face taking on a deeper rosy hue. "Hey, sorry. She wasn't a model. You stick some woman ... you see that ad for the Focus? Tiny little thing, looks like the old Chevette or the early Honda Civics? I mean, it's a damn ... excuse me. It's a roller skate. But they shoot it at jivy angles, never let the viewer really get a look at the thing, pretend this is how the young get to their night life. It's got this cut, I mean it's about one second of tape, three women climbing into the thing. They're all young, thin, beautiful. One of them, the one the men all notice, she's wearing this shiny black leather outfit, spike heels, it's backless. They can call themselves actresses, fine, but they're not. They're models, and Barbara Walker didn't have the look or the build for it. She might have done okay in industrial films if she were a little older, or we could dress her up a little older, but she was too ..." He trailed off, looking at me.

"Look," he said. "I don't really know why you're here, okay?"

"We're trying to help her father," I said.

"But the cops are the ones, right? The ones, you know, investigating her death?"

"Of course, but Reverend Walker wants us to ..." and I trailed off.

Jack said, "Provide closure. Assist the police. We're trying to assist, to keep things from blowing up at the church ... No pun intended."

"What'd you do," I said, getting back on task, "about the accusations?"

Clinton blinked. "Do?"

I sighed. "Larry, just tell us. We're all adults here."

He looked down at his hands. "I asked her into my office and told her she had to leave. We were getting complaints. I run a professional shop here, okay? Sure, that sort of stuff goes on, but I didn't want to have anything to do with it. I'm happily married, two daughters. I'm around beautiful actresses and models all day long. Some of them would gladly do me for future work. But that's a slippery slope and I don't want to get on it."

"What'd she do?" Jack said.

Clinton's face grew redder. "Look ..."

We didn't say anything.

He said, "She was wearing a T-shirt and a mini-skirt. She took them off. She wasn't wearing anything underneath. She said she'd ... said she'd— you know—anytime I wanted if I'd just get her some acting work."

Silence.

"And?" I said.

"*And? And* I told her to get dressed and go home or I'd tell her father what she was doing."

"What'd she say?"

"She said if I didn't go along with her she'd tell her father I—took advantage of her."

"Ah," I said. "And ... ?"

"*And* I told her to put her clothes back on, *and* she did. I don't need that kind of trouble. She wasn't eighteen. Nobody's going to take my word for it, that I didn't take advantage of her. My bread and butter is industrial films. You might be able to keep making feature films, even ads, if you get a rep for doing that to underage teenage girls. You're likely to go out of business in my particular niche. So I gave her the name of a guy, Don Tittaglia, who runs a digital graphics company down in the city. In the New Center Area, by the Fisher Building. We work with him sometimes and Don knows everybody. I mean absolutely everybody. I told her to talk to him, maybe he could find something out. I also gave her the name of a talent agency, The Weyer Agency in Southfield. Talk to Richard, maybe he could help her out."

"He involved in porn?" Jack said.

Clinton snorted. "Weyer? Not one little bit. Totally mainstream talent: actors and models. On the other hand, Tittaglia's involved in everything. Very cutting edge stuff at 24/7. That's his company, 24/7 Communications, Inc. They do computer graphics for all the sporting events, the news production, local programming, national stuff, even some Hollywood work."

"Is Tittaglia involved in porn?" Jack repeated.

Clinton sighed. "Maybe. Probably. I wouldn't be surprised."

I stared at him, then turned my gaze to Jack, who raised his eyebrows. I said, "Did she go talk to him? Either of them?"

"I don't know. She just left here, and that was fine by me. And you know what? You guys can leave, too." He was shaking as he stood up. "If the cops come, I'll tell them the same thing. I don't know what she did or where she went. She was bad news. Real bad news, and though I'm not glad she's dead, I'm not surprised, either. Girls like her, they're looking for trouble. When you're like her, and look and act like her, you're only going to find trouble. Or it's going to find you."

Jack and I walked back out to the car. I said, "What would you have done if she'd come on to you like that?"

Jack grinned, pulling onto M-59 and heading west. "In his shoes, probably the same thing."

"In yours?"

"Hard call. Barbara wasn't without her charms." Jack shrugged. "I get the feeling that when Barbara turned on the ... *charm*, a lot of men found her kind of hard to resist."

I thought about the video. I wasn't engineered to appreciate the nuances of her sexuality, but I suspected Jack was right.

"You think he actually knew about the porn video?"

"Hey, we got the man to admit that he was propositioned by his minister's daughter. Getting him to admit he got her a job in a porn video is a little tougher."

"Nasty business."

Jack shrugged. "If you're going to dig into people's lives, you're going to find some pretty unpleasant things. If you dig, you find dirt."

"What do you think of 24/7 Communications?" I said.

"The computer angle's interesting. They might be worth checking out. Too late tonight. And trying to find out who the local porn merchants are might be worthwhile, too. You have a plan?"

"We need to find a cheap motel."

Jack nodded. "With a phone line, right?"

"Right."

Independent motels are getting harder and harder to find these days, almost as tough as finding an independent bookstore or grocery store. The chains are here, the Holiday Inns, the Fairfield Inns, the Marriotts. But the chains are very reluctant to accept cash. We checked into the Welcome Inn in Pontiac on the Dixie Highway, a one-story place with twelve units that offered Air, Cable and Hourly Rats. I hoped it was just a misspelling. I was happy about it having air, though. I asked if there was a phone in the room, and the clerk at the desk, who eyed us with a completely unsurprised expression on his face, nodded. "Local or credit card calls only," he said.

The Welcome Inn was in one long row, twelve units with cheap windows, old green paint and a parking lot so potholed it looked as if it had been bombed during the last war. Jack parked with the license plate facing the door. We checked in, paid our thirty-five bucks cash—five hours, he must have figured us to be optimists—and inspected the room. A queen-sized bed with clean sheets that appeared to be laid over plastic wrap, the way the bed crinkled and crackled when I carefully sat on it. A dresser/desk combo with a heavy black phone. A 20-inch TV with cable offering three free porn stations.

"This has been such an enlightening week," I said, inspecting the shower. Rusty and old, but clean. "I'd have expected this to be dirtier than it is."

"Be grateful."

"I am, I am." I took out my laptop, unplugged the phone jack and plugged in my modem. Wi-fi was the Next Big Thing (Mitch would have been on it like a pike on a minnow), but the wireless connection wasn't consistent and although I'd fooled with it, I found it frustrating. It was about as fast a connection as you'd want, but it was currently only available in certain zones. I had hopes, but for now it was just an unreliable toy. Besides, my wi-fi card was back at the house, not one of my better moves. When I headed for Webspinners, I'd left it at home. I hadn't, after all, known I would be on the run from the mob. Short of a shopping trip, I would have to settle for dial-up.

As my link with Chavez Tech went through, I turned on my cell phone to check my voicemail. There were three calls.

The first was from Lieutenant Rosenbaum to turn myself in at once. Yeah, yeah, yeah.

The second was from Henry Chavez, telling me that Chavez Tech was up and running, and did I have any idea what was going on.

The third was from Danny Chen. He was speaking in a hushed, hurried voice, barely audible:

"Meg, it's Danny. I know you're looking into this shit with the church. I can't talk, these two Feds'll be back any minute. This is serious, serious shit you're into. Mafia shit. That's why the FBI's involved. I'm consulting with them, but ... I ... they're coming. Stay away from it. Get out of town. The guy we think is behind it is a stone killer. Shit, gotta go. Just stay out of it."

And he clicked off.

28

I let Jack listen to the message. He nodded. "Pretty good advice."

"Goddamnit, Jack! First you tell me to run and hide, then you tell me to fight, then you tell me to run and hide. Make up your mind!"

He shrugged. "I know what I would do. I can't be sure what you would do. You seem like a woman who can make up her mind, but this has got to be new territory for you. I'll do whatever you want."

"Why?" I said. "Maybe you can tell me why you're doing this. I'm not paying you. And no bullshit about, '*This is what I do. Help people.*'"

"You didn't like that? I was thinking of putting it on my business card."

"Can I believe a word you say?"

"Sure."

"If I ask you questions right now, you'll tell me the truth, the whole truth and nothing but the truth?"

He raised his right hand. "So help me God. There must be a Gideon's in here somewhere."

I stared at him. "Honestly."

"Is this what you need right now?"

I sighed, turned to look at the computer, then back to Jack. "I don't have time right now to ... one question. Total honesty."

"Total honesty," he said, jaw set. He looked like he was preparing to play chicken with a locomotive.

So many questions I wanted to ask. I peeked at the computer screen, then looked back at Jack. One question. Which one did I want to know most? "Are you still in love with Mattie?"

Jack closed his eyes and hung his head, shoulders slumped. He looked back at me, brushing his long hair away from his face. "Let me get this straight, Malloy. We're short on time, we have possible mobsters, the Secret Service, and the FBI on our ass, you need an honest answer to one question—just one because we're short on time—to help you make up your mind, and *that's* the question?"

"Um ... well ..." I hadn't thought that through, it was true. I sighed. "Okay, I'll ask you that one later. What I want to know, *need* to know, is:

What do you honestly think we should do? The best course of action?"

"Find out what's going on and turn everything over to the cops and let them sort it out. We're almost there. If we can put a couple of names and motives together, it'll be enough for the cops . Then I can go back up to TC and you can go back to your house in Lake Orion or your place in Maui, whatever."

"Okay," I said, turning back to the laptop. I hit *Google!* and cast the widest net, typing in "Detroit" and "mafia" into the search window.

The Detroit News
March 15
**ALLEGED MAFIA BOSS ANTHONY CATALANO, 17 LEADERS
INDICTED BY GRAND JURY FOR
EXTORTION, OBSTRUCTION OF JUSTICE**
by Steve Franklin and Gene Bulow/ The Detroit News

Calling it their biggest case since New York crime boss John Gotti, Federal authorities on Thursday swept up 18 alleged Metro Detroit Mafia leaders, including reputed crime boss Anthony "The Cat" Catalano and most of his lieutenants.

"We believe we've driven a stake through the heart of La Costa Nostra," said FBI agent Jerome Fitzgibbons, of the crackdown on organized crime.

The indictment is a Who's Who list of alleged organized crime figures in Michigan. ...

Jack, reading over my shoulder, said, "A stake through the heart?"

"You're skeptical?"

"A bit. It neatly forgets that if you put so many guys out of business you create a vacuum. Farther on, the FBI say they think the lower-end guys aren't bright enough to take over. It's true for some of them. But figure some guys, LCN or not, are pretty damned bright. They'll do just fine. They may have been waiting for a chance to take over, and the FBI's given them that chance."

I skipped down to another article.

**DETROIT MOB BOSS ANTHONY CATALANO
SENTENCED TO TWO YEARS**

Anthony "The Cat" Catalano, considered to be the boss of Metro Detroit's Mafia was sentenced to two years in prison for charges of racketeering by Judge William Schales, Jr., U.S. 6th District Court. Along with 17 others ...

"Huh," I said. "He should be out by now."

Jack tapped the screen.

DETROIT MOB BOSS ANTHONY CATALANO
DIES IN PRISON

Anthony "The Cat" Catalano, 69, died in Milan Federal Correctional Institution from a knife wound. Catalano was indicted March 27 on eight counts of racketeering and conspiracy. Halfway through his two-year sentence, which was being appealed by the Federal Government because of the unusual leniency of the sentence, Catalano was stabbed to death by an unknown assailant.

"Only two years for a mob boss? That's a travesty," said Assistant U.S. Attorney Steve Talbot, head of the Organized Crime Strike Force.

When questioned as to his opinion regarding Catalano's death, Talbot refused to comment.

"This wasn't an accidental death," says Catalano attorney Blake Schaffrin. "This was an assassination. I demand a full investigation. The U.S. government does not have clean hands in this."

Warden Julian Gillman says the circumstances surrounding the death of Anthony Catalano "are being fully investigated."

"What do you think?" I asked Jack.

"I think he was assassinated." Jack sat back and looked off into space. "Let's see if we can find something about Catalano's kids or relatives."

What I found was an obituary:

Anthony Catalano, 69, was stabbed to death while serving a two-year sentence at Milan Federal Correctional Institution. The alleged head of the Metro Detroit organized crime family, Catalano was a long-time resident of West Bloomfield. The owner of Catalano Development, Inc., and several other businesses, he was survived by two sisters, Francine Catalano Tittaglia and Laura Catalano Torreano. Two of Catalano's brothers, Vincent and Leon, died in 1982, both victims of apparent gangland style slayings. Anthony Catalano's wife, Meredith, died in 1988. They had no children.

"No kids," Jack said. "Let's look for Joe Catalano then."

I typed in "Joe Catalano"—no hits. I tried "Joseph Catalano." One hit, a tiny blurb in the *Observer-Eccentric*'s website about a nuisance lawsuit involving the "Tomcat Theater" on Woodward Boulevard, Detroit. Residents complained of a graphic movie ad in the front door. The proprietor, Joseph Catalano, insisted it should stay up, but was forced to remove it. .

"Right occupation," Jack said. "Though I wonder if he's still open. Porn theaters are a dying breed, what with cable and video."

"And the Internet."

I typed in "Joseph Catalano" and "porn" and received exactly what I was afraid I'd hit: over one hundred and ten thousand available sites. The word "porn" had done the trick. I mulled that over for a moment while Jack paced the room, peeking out the single window, glaring at the framed landscape painting on the wall, running the water in the bathroom sink and splashing it on his face.

I tried "Joseph Catalano" and "Tomcat" and was rewarded with five hits, all reviews of porn movies produced by Tomcat Studios, whose director was Joseph Catalano.

"He's a porn movie director and producer now," I said.

"In Detroit?" Jack leaned over my shoulder.

"I'm looking in the yellow pages."

A moment later we had it. Tomcat Studios, Adult Movie Production Company with the address 17653 Carpenter Street, Detroit, Michigan.

"Carpenter Street," Jack said.

I rummaged in my backpack and came up with the enhanced photograph Glen Blalock had created for me. ARPE on the street sign. *CARPE*NTER.

"We got him," Jack said as I went into Google's map section and brought up a map of Detroit, locating Carpenter Street. I downloaded it to my hard drive so we'd be able to find Tomcat Studios. Was it enough of a connection? It certainly was good circumstantial evidence. If we could find evidence that Barbara had actually been there ...

Jack was leaning over my shoulder, tapping the BACK button on the browser. "Wait a minute," he said, voice suddenly tense.

"What?"

"A 100-watt-er just flashed over my head," he said, and brought up the obituary for Anthony Catalano. His finger came to rest on a name. "Right there," he said.

One of Anthony Catalano's sister. Francine Catalano Tittaglia.

"Why's that familiar?" I said.

"Larry Clinton told us he sent Barbara to two people. Richard Weyer, the talent agent, and Don Tittaglia with 24/7 Communications, Inc. There's a Tittaglia." His finger jabbed at the screen. "Joe Catalano's a porn director and producer, a former owner of a porn theater. What's he know about hacking? But here ... here," he said, voice excited. "We've got a guy running a computer graphics company. A guy who not only might know Joe Catalano because of a business connection, but might be related to him."

"Brothers?"

"Only if half-brothers. Cousins, maybe. Maybe Joe Catalano's one of the deceased brothers' kids, Vincent's or Leon's." He shrugged, sitting back down on the bed, which crinkled loudly under his weight.

"The porn connection and the computer connection." I said. "Is it enough to go to Rosenbaum with?"

Jack thought for a minute, staring down at the cheap blue carpet. "Maybe. It'd be a lot better if we could get a look at Joe Catalano, see if we think he's the guy in the video."

"The guy in the video had a ski mask over his head," I said.

"Yeah. A problem." He tapped his chin with his index finger. "I wonder if Tony the Cat was a murder for hire."

"Let's not get sidetracked."

"Hear me through," Jack said. "The FBI takes down Detroit's entire upper echelon, eighteen guys out of about a hundred. Some of those guys got a lot of years. Didn't that one guy in the first article—"

"Martin Vincenzo," I said.

"Yeah, he got nineteen years. Some of those guys are getting up in age, sixties, seventies. But the top guy, Tony the Cat, he was 68 when he went away, and only for two years. He could probably run the operation from inside prison if he trusted whoever was left outside. But he got killed. Let's assume the power structure didn't really get destroyed when they went to prison, it just got moved to Milan, the Fed prison. It's a power shift, and a big one, but depending on who's still outside running what's left, there might be some problems."

"So someone outside gets somebody inside to kill Anthony Catalano."

"Right. The people left inside, probably scattered all over the country in Federal C.I.'s, have no central control. They may not have any control."

"This is guesswork," I said.

"Totally," Jack agreed. "But ride along. Let's say the son of one of Tony's brothers-in-law, possibly a legitimate businessman, maybe not, decides to update and modernize, turn to computer crime."

"Don Tittaglia," I said. "This is a big guess."

"Sure. But does it seem likely?"

"It seems possible," I said. I turned back to the screen and typed in "24/7 Communications, Inc." and found that their headquarters was on the Lodge Service Drive near West Grand Boulevard in Detroit.

"Which do you want to visit first?" I said. "Tomcat Video or 24/7 Communications?"

Jack reached into his pocket and retrieved a quarter. "Flip you for it?"

29

We didn't go with a coin toss. I argued we should check out 24/7 Communications first primarily because I'm more comfortable with digital imaging than porn movies. Jack's stand was that Tomcat Studios was less likely to have a security guard or possibly an alarm system.

"We're going to *break* in?"

He shrugged. "I don't know what we're going to do. We're making this up as we go along. Let's just go check them out, starting with Joe Catalano's place of business."

I sighed. Maybe we should've gone with the coin toss.

We left the Welcome Inn—Air, Cable, Hourly Rats—by 10:30, half-way through our pre-paid five hours. If the clerk saw us, I wondered what he thought. *Guy couldn't do it that long*?

I wondered who he thought we were. *Cheating spouses*? I didn't think I came off as a ho, but maybe I was fooling myself.

Jack ignited the engine of the Corvette and said, "I still love her, but we're not *in love*, you know what I mean?"

I glanced over at him, puzzled. What was he talking about?

"Mattie," he said. "We're friends. Good friends, but just friends."

Oh. My one question. The honest answer.

"Such good friends she took off to a job in Europe like she was being chased by Huns?" I immediately regretted saying it.

His face settled into a deliberately neutral expression, shadowed eyes, closed mouth, shut jaw. He cocked his head. "You think she wanted to ... what, get as far away from me as possible?"

Why in hell did I ever ask that question? "You said it. Not me."

Jack swung the car out onto the Dixie Highway and aimed the bullet nose south, angling over onto Telegraph Road. Telegraph—like the Dixie—was lit up like Christmas, a blur of incandescent, fluorescent and neon lights: restaurants, fast food, bars, motels, office buildings, malls and chain stores ...

Jack was quiet until he merged onto the Lodge Freeway, arrowing straight through the middle of Detroit.

"Mattie never told you why she left?" Jack said.

"No. I was in Maui." Running away. Did Mattie run away too? All I'd heard was an e-mail saying she'd be living in London, the Tampa Tribune's European correspondent. New job, she was so excited, hoped I'd come visit her after she got settled. It hadn't made a lot of sense to me—Mattie was, through and through, an investigative reporter, a crime reporter. I couldn't imagine why she had wanted to spend a chunk of her career covering Euro Disney, Mad Cow Disease and the exchange rate. I'd e-mailed her back, wrapped up in my hedonistic frenzy, telling her I would visit, just say when.

I hadn't called and neither had she.

"Yeah," Jack said, breaking into my thoughts. "We're just friends now."

I looked at him, at his profile. Wondered what went on behind the mask he wore so well. A good looking man. A good man. A lot of mysteries to him, though; a lot of shadows; a lot of puzzles.

I like puzzles.

Tomcat Studios was in a two-story house in a nondescript neighborhood on the middle-east side of Detroit. Like almost every other neighborhood in Detroit, the street it was on—Carpenter—had a number of burned-out houses, charred and skeletal remains abandoned by the owners, abandoned by the neighborhood, abandoned, finally, by the city. Left as homes for vagrants and rats.

Hourly rats.

We drove in widening circles around the house, getting a feel for the neighborhood. It was dark. Jack commented on it.

"City forget to pay the electric bill?" he said as we passed through yet another streetcorner whose streetlight had been shot or burned out.

"It's in the news all the time," I said. "City services aren't too hot."

"I thought it was on the rebound."

"It is," I said, not entirely confident of that statement. "But Mayor Young dug a very deep hole for a very long time."

"Well, it'll probably be to our advantage. That and the weather."

It had been overcast all day, threatening rain, only spitting from time to time. Once we were five or six blocks away, Jack began spiraling inward toward the darkened house. The lots were small, some with fences around the back and in between. Most were narrow two-stories with generous front porches. A sidewalk but no driveway. I guessed most had been built in the city's prime, sometime between the 1930s and the 60s.

"Traverse City's kind of the same," Jack said. "There's an alley between streets, runs behind the houses. People park back there. Some, I've noticed, have garages on the back of the property. Tomcat doesn't."

Tomcat was identified only by its street number next to the front door. Like a lot of the houses in the neighborhood, the windows on the main floor had wrought-iron bars or grating over them. I wondered if the neighbors knew what went on in this house. I wondered how—or if—Joe Catalano was licensed for business in this neighborhood.

Jack parked the Corvette behind a rusty hulk of a Toyota Celica about two blocks west of Tomcat Studios. "Car kind of stands out around here," he said. The houses we were parked in front of were all dark except one, a dim light burning on the second floor and on the front porch. Probably a night light upstairs, a psychological warning beacon on the porch.

We climbed out of the Vette, trying to make as little noise as possible. Jack opened the trunk of the car and scrounged around in the canvas duffel bag. He pulled out what looked like half of a binocular.

"What's that?"

He twisted a knob on it and handed it to me. "Take a look," he said.

I did, holding it up to one eye. Through the monocular the world was lit up in a ghostly green. Details were fuzzy, but it was a shock. I pulled it away from my eye, looked at one of the darkened houses, then put it back to my eye and examined the house through the scope. In eerie jade light I could see the house numbers canting diagonally—35879—next to the screen door, a small plaque beneath the numbers that said Washington's and the details of the peeling paint on the sagging porch steps. In one corner of the door was a sticker proclaiming that this house was protected by Guardian Alarm. Scanning, I picked out tree branches moving in the brisk wind, the diamond-hatch pattern of the chain-link fence that divided the two properties, and more. It wasn't like seeing in daylight, but it was seeing, and seeing well.

"Cool," I said.

"Night scope. You've never seen one before?"

I shook my head. "You ever a Boy Scout, Jack? Always prepared?"

"Never," he said. "Just well equipped with the basics for P.I. work."

"Except a license."

He shrugged. "Ready?"

Was I? I nodded and we headed down the street, trying to look casual, like we belonged on the sidewalk of an empty neighborhood of sleeping households in the middle of Detroit.

Tomcat Studios was framed by two large trees, an ancient oak that loomed over the house, and a towering evergreen, possibly a blue spruce. We stopped and studied the house. No garage in back. Rusty chain-link fence. The grass seemed recently mowed, the house itself in decent shape with painted asbestos siding, reasonably new tar shingles and no broken windows or sagging wood.

Jack examined the house through the nightscope, then we walked closer. Again Jack swept the house with the night scope. He held up a finger for me to wait and crept up onto the porch. I wondered if it was my imagination but I thought I could hear the old wood creak under his weight. The wind rustled in the trees. At the nearby street corner I thought I saw headlights coming and I instinctively moved into the cover of the evergreen. The car turned right, away from us.

When I turned back to the house it took me a moment to find Jack. He was crouched down, peering into a window with the night scope. There were wrought-iron bars on the bedroom windows, but not on the picture window in front. That was the window we had glimpsed for just a second on the videotape as the door opened and Joe Catalano had entered, a ski mask over his head. All the windows had drapes, but the drapes weren't completely pulled, leaving Jack an inch or so to peer through.

Jack soft-shoed down to the yard and waved me over. I followed as he led me around to the backyard, checking windows with the nightscope as we went. A dog barked. We froze. My heart raced. Did Catalano have a dog?

But it sounded further away, and after a minute the dog shut up.

Stretching to reach the window, Jack tried to look in the room, but he shook his head and handed me the night scope. Lips almost touching my ears, he whispered, "I'll lift you on my shoulders so you can look in."

Okay. Whatever.

He crouched down and I climbed aboard. He stood without a wobble and I could easily peek in with the night scope. Shifting around, I realized this was the room where the video of Barbara's "rape" had taken place. A closed door directly across from the window, a step ladder in one corner, a big brass bed.

There was someone sprawled on the bed.

Beneath me Jack shifted position. I tapped his shoulder, gesturing for him to move over to the left a little bit so I could get a better angle. It wasn't easy scanning an entire room through a two-inch slit in the curtains.

I focused on the person in the bed. A woman. Long hair hanging in a waterfall, probably light in color, but hard to tell because of the distortion of the night scope. Familiar.

Lisa Dunn.

That made sense. When I called Lisa's cell number the second time I was pretty sure Joe Catalano—if it was Joe Catalano—had answered. The guy in the video, the one with the cat tattoo on his bicep. Joey Mason's biological father. What came first, I wondered? Did Barbara go to Joe Catalano first because of something Joey Mason had said? Or did she go to Don Tittaglia first?

She rolled in her sleep and I thought the way she moved was a little strange.

Jack made an impatient gesture and I held my hand low and out flat. *Give me a few seconds here.*

I focused the nightscope, looking for details, frustrated with what the scope did to resolution, making everything fuzzy around the edges, rimmed with emerald hoarfrost.

But I saw it.

Her left arm was held above her head. On her left wrist was what looked like a bracelet. But it wasn't a bracelet. It was a handcuff and a short chain connected to the other handcuff which was attached to one of the brass rails of the headboard.

I gestured down and Jack knelt and I stepped off. He shot me a question and I waved him to follow me away from the house. Lurking in the cover of the evergreen at the front of the house, Jack whispered, "What'd you see?"

I told him.

He turned to look at the house. "I want a look at the second floor."

"Why? We've got to get her out of there."

"Yeah, but what if he lives on the second floor?"

"Oh. But ..."

"Stay here."

He melted into the darkness, moving across the yard, sticking to the shadows, headed for the oak tree. He disappeared from my sight onto the far side of the oak. I waited. And waited. A car drove down the street and my heart thudded against my chest. The car kept on going, slowing at the corner, then turning right.

I closed my eyes, willed my heart to return to normal.

I caught movement out of the corner of my eye. Jack. Climbing in the oak, moving out onto a branch that reached out over the porch roof. As gracefully as a cougar Jack stepped onto the roof and moved silently to the upstairs windows. After a moment he shifted to the right to check the other window. Then he was back to the tree and down, standing by my side.

"Storage and what's probably another room for filming. A set, I suppose. Nobody else is here. You ready?"

I nodded. I followed Jack up the front porch. There was no little sticker indicating the house was being protected by Guardian Alarm or anybody else. I didn't know if that was true, but hoped Jack was prepared for it. He worked on the lock for about two minutes with his picks, two minutes that seemed like two hours. Then he turned the doorknob and we went in.

In the darkness I could see that the living room was probably a movie set, too. Half the room held a Jacuzzi. The other half looked like a bar. But they didn't seem quite right, as if they were props of some sort, a feeling reinforced by the large professional-style videocameras, one mounted on a tripod, another riding a curved section of what looked like small-scale train track.

Jack took my hand and, holding the nightscope to his eye, picked his way through the room, around the cameras and light equipment, over the track, to one of the two doors on the opposite side. My eyes were fairly adjusted to the darkness, but all I could really see were the outlines of all this equipment. Then Jack cautiously opened the door and led me in.

He scanned the room through the scope, then closed the door behind us. He let go of my hand and stealthily crept across the room to the bed. I felt lost. This room was as black as a cave, a slanting bit of gray light angling in through the one window.

Jack, voice soft, said, "Don't scream. We're here to take you out of ..." Silence. I heard rustling sounds, a low moan, the clank of the handcuff chain, then Jack saying, "What the hell?"

He returned to my side, whispered, "Close your eyes," then flicked on the room light. A lamp off to one side came on, bathing the room in harsh yellow light.

It was Lisa Dunn, but she wasn't moving.

"Is she ... ?"

"Drugged, I think," Jack said.

"Can you pick the handcuffs?"

Jack reached into his pocket and pulled out a ring of keys. He picked out one of them. "Handcuff key. Should do the—"

There was a thud of footsteps from the front of the house, following by a key grating in the lock of a door that was already unlocked.

Jack grabbed me, and practically threw me across the room, stuffing me under the bed. He was headed back toward the door when it flung open. Joe Catalano exploded into the room, a shotgun held at waist-height.

"*Freeze*, asshole!"

From my vantage beneath the bed I could see him raise the shotgun to shoulder height. "Freeze or you're dead!"

30

Jack said, "Hey, take it easy."

"Who the hell are you? Hands on the top of your head. Do it! Now!"

Jack's hands disappeared from view.

"Who are you?"

"I'm a P.I. Lisa's parents hired to find her. Uncuff her and I'll take her home. No cops. We'll keep you out of it. Call it a big misunderstanding."

"Yeah, right. I don't think so, Tonto. She's not goin' anywhere. And you do what I tell you or I'll paint the wall with your guts. Down on your knees."

"Come on, man—"

"Do it!" The menace ... and promise ... in Catalano's voice was instantly recognizable and instantly believable.

Slowly, Jack dropped to his knees, hands still clasped behind his neck.

"Now, face down on the floor."

"Give me a—"

Catalano jabbed at Jack with the shotgun, nailing him in the back of the skull with the barrel. "Down!"

Jack sprawled on the floor near where I was hiding, arms spread wide so they were only inches from me.

I could see Catalano's black leather boots and faded blue jeans loom over Jack, the shiny black barrel of the shotgun angled toward his head.

"Hands behind your back, Tonto."

Dark eyes steady on me, Jack withdrew his hands and swung them into the small of his back.

My gaze rested on the set of keys Jack had left on the blue shag carpet right in front of me. He'd palmed them right under Catalano's nose.

Metal rattled on metal as Catalano leaned over Jack. I froze, afraid to breathe, afraid Catalano'd hear my heart racing. If he moved back or looked under the bed, he'd see me.

Catalano snapped cuffs on Jack's wrists and backed away. "Get up"

I heard a click and an electronic tone. Jack awkwardly rolled to his side, then rotated to his knees.

Catalano said, "It's me. More shit. The alarm went off at the Studio and I caught some P.I. in the room with Lisa, says he was hired by her parents ... Yeah. I know it's turning to shit ... It's not my fucking fault, Donny. You started all this fucking mess with Barbara ... No, we finish it up tonight, we finish it all up ... No living witnesses ... It's not my fault ... I'm bringing them both over ... Yes, now, so you get over there now ... I don't care."

There was another click as he shut off the phone, a loud snap as he closed it, then Catalano said, "Out. Don't try anything funny or you're a dead man. Got me?"

"Where're we going?"

Bless you, Jack! I bit my lip, hoping Catalano would actually say.

"Shut up. Move it."

I watched as their feet moved away through the door and disappeared.

Whump.

I jumped, head smacking into the bedframe, my blood turning to ice. What was that sound? A sharp, hollow sound from outside.

Had it been a shotgun blast muffled by the walls? Had Catalano marched Jack out to the porch and shot him?

I heard footsteps and Catalano came back into the room, the shotgun aimed at the floor. He walked right up to the bed. He set something down, probably the shotgun. He grunted and the bed creaked. He shifted, grunted again, then I saw his feet move away. Just as the lights flicked out I saw that Catalano had slung Lisa—still unconscious—over his shoulder.

Then he was gone.

I snatched up the keys, counting silently to ten, straining my ears.

One-one thousand ...

Two-one thousand ...

Three-one thousand ...

Nothing.

I didn't want to wait too long, but I sure as hell didn't want to leave too early and run into Catalano still outside with the shotgun.

Four-one thousand ...

Then I heard the roar of a car engine. I slithered out from beneath the bed and sprinted for the door, tripping through the living room debris to peer out the front window just in time to see a Ford Mustang pull away from the curb.

I burst out the front door expecting to see Jack dead on the front lawn.

Nothing. I wished I had the nightscope, but either Jack had it or it was in the house. Straining my eyes in the dark, wind ruffling my hair, I looked for him.

No. He must be in the Mustang. In the trunk? Was that the whumping sound I had heard, Catalano slamming the trunk?

I sprinted in the opposite direction, toward the Corvette.

Frantic, gasping for breath, I fumbled the keys, unlocked the door and tumbled behind the wheel, igniting the engine and peeling down Carpenter Street, headlights off, hoping to catch up to Joe Catalano and the Mustang.

Hoping I'd catch up to Jack.

I rocketed down Carpenter after the Mustang, already out of sight, praying I'd catch up. As I flew through each intersection I slowed just enough to scan the offshoots, looking for receding taillights.

The Motor City was dead. Unlike the City That Never Sleeps, Detroit had its eyes closed, the covers pulled up to its neck and was snoring away.

It wasn't until I crossed over the Lodge Freeway, nestled in its below-ground-level concrete canyon that I realized I had lost them totally. Pounding the steering wheel, I shrieked in frustration. I was losing it, my breathing accelerating to panicked gulps, pressure building behind my ears.

Get it together, Malloy!

I took a deep breath, forcing myself to think. My brain latched onto Catalano's phone call.

"Look, Donny, it's not my fault ..."

Donny?

Donny Tittaglia?

"I'm bringing them over to your place. We've got to end this."

Your place.

Tittaglia's place? His home? Or his place of business? 24/7 Communications?

24/7 Communications was near the Fisher Building in the New Center Area. I knew where that was, not far from where I idled in the Corvette. In fact, I could see the granite tower of the Fisher off to my left, its pointed green-copper pinnacle capped in gold, lit up with buttery yellow light.

What if I got to 24/7 and the Mustang wasn't there?

"Stop it," I said out loud, not liking the strident quavers of panic in my voice. "Just stop it."

I put the transmission into first and aimed the 'Vette in the direction of the Fisher Building and the nearby tower of Henry Ford Hospital. The name of the facility shone in elegant blue script across the upper lip of the building.

I'm coming, Jack. Hang on.

24/7 Communications was in a low-slung, one-story poured concrete office building the color of desert sand. In the shadow of the Fisher and Ford high rises, it was an easy place to ignore, surrounded by newer condos and older, historical homes.

There were two cars in the parking lot. A black Porsche Boxter and a British racing green Ford Mustang.

I controlled the urge to rush in the front door.

I circled the block and came to a halt in the back of a darkened McDonald's parking lot on West Grand Boulevard. I took a deep breath, wondering if I had a plan, decided I really didn't.

I could call the cops but an explanation would take forever, and if they did go tactical—meaning they actually believed my tale—the whole thing would turn into a hostage situation.

I snatched up the ring of keys, sorted out the cuff key and took it off the ring, tucked it into the tight inner pocket of my jeans. The rest of the ring went under the driver's seat. I opened the trunk and checked out Jack's duffel bag, hoping it might hold something useful.

It did.

A sawed-off shotgun and a box of shells.

Shit. A gun wasn't exactly what I'd been hoping for. I didn't know what I'd been hoping for, but a gun wasn't it. I don't like guns.

Shit.

Bracing myself, I jammed shells into the breach of the sawed-off.

I strode off in the direction of 24/7 Communications, jaw clenched. I had nothing anybody with any sense would call a plan, but I was armed and pissed off. That would have to do.

Standing behind a sycamore tree on the edge of the 24/7 parking lot, I realized that a plan would be better. I wondered if it would be possible to get into the building without them knowing about it. There were half-a-dozen darkened windows on my side of the building. Maybe I could get in that way.

Steeling myself, I ran in a crouch across the lot, staying well away from the two cones of illumination cast by a street light and a security light high up on the building. I stood stock still for a few seconds, calming myself, peeking into the window. In the dim light it looked like an office. A modular desk, a mammoth computer, filing cabinets, scanner and printer. The window was closed and locked. Of course. But the office door was closed, too. If I was careful, maybe I could break the glass, reach through and unlock the window, then crawl through without their hearing me. I pressed the butt of the shotgun against the glass, applying pressure, slowly leaning against it, not needing to shatter the window, just needing to put a large enough hole to fit my hand through, not wanting to splatter glass all over the room and onto the floor, make a loud noise and bring Catalano and Tittaglia running, guns drawn.

"I really wish you wouldn't do that."

I spun, heart triphammering.

A slim, average-height man with a shaved head stood a dozen feet away. He seemed completely innocuous in jeans and a sweatshirt except for the shiny blue-steel semi-automatic he held in his fist and was aiming at me.

"Come on, Ms. Malloy. Let's go inside."

31

He adjusted the aim of the handgun, a small smile on his face. "Come on, Meg," he said. "Drop the shotgun. Let's keep this clean and simple."

My heart was pounding so hard I thought I could hear it against my ribs. If I raised the shotgun and pulled the trigger ...

"Now!" he said, no longer friendly. "I'm counting to three and then I'm firing and I'm a fucking good shot. Drop it now!"

I did.

The smile was back and he walked toward me. "Kick it away," he said.

I did.

He bent down, eyes never leaving me, and retrieved the shotgun. He stood up, gun never wavering, and said, "Okay, hands behind your head. Let's go inside. It's nice to meet you again. Sorry about the circumstances."

"Again?" I said, lacing my fingers behind my neck and starting toward the front of the building.

"We met five or six years ago at Def Con. In fact, I voted for you for Hot Babes of Def Con."

"I'm flattered," I said. Def Con was a yearly computer hackers convention in Las Vegas held in July. It was where people involved in hacking, computer security and computer theft went to mingle, learn and act like normal conventioneers, drinking, doing drugs and getting laid. It was where hackers with names like Trogdyke met members of the National Security Agency or the FBI's Internet Crime Squad over drinks in the bar. Def Con was weird. Think of any other convention that would have a Hot Babes contest and not end up in court over it.

"Your talk on infrastructure was fascinating."

"I thought it was probably boring," I said.

"No, it wasn't. I really liked it. Go on in."

I leaned against the glass doors of 24/7 and walked into the entryway, done in spotless white tile, chrome and steel finish, high-tech and cutting edge all the way.

"Turn right," he said. "I'm impressed with Water Pit. You patent it yet?"

"It's for personal use."

"Well, when you're dead I think I might try to market it."

Like ramming an icicle down my spine. *When you're dead ...* He marched me down a hallway done in cold white tile, bone white walls and dropped acoustical-tiled ceilings to what must have been a digital studio. There was a raised platform, really a low stage backed by a blue screen. There were half-a-dozen digital video and movie cameras on dollies scattered around the room, and desks dominated by the biggest, most powerful computers available.

Jack and Lisa sat on the stage, Jack's hands behind his back, his expression watchful. Lisa was awake now, a slightly frightened look on her face. That was probably good. Frightened, right at the moment, meant she was awake enough to have some idea of what was going on.

Joe Catalano was pacing frenetically around the room, keeping a cautious distance from the two of them—especially Jack—his own shotgun still clutched in his right hand, Jack's Beretta tucked into the back of his jeans.

"What the fuck're you two chatting about?" Catalano said. "Shit, Donny, we're not having a fucking cocktail party here."

Donny. Donny Tittaglia. He gave me a small shove. "Go join your friends," he said. To Joe he said, "This is Meg Malloy, that computer geek that got all this shit going."

"You got all this shit going," Catalano said, "when you brought Barbara on board. Going after a fucking church." His voice seemed higher pitched than it had before and he was talking faster.

I stood next to Jack, watching the two of them. Donny Tittaglia narrowed his eyes and glared at Catalano. "You take a hit while I was out?"

"Hey, just a couple grains, my attention was starting to wander."

Tittaglia shook his head. "No more. No more fuckin' meth. Let's get this done, get rid of them." He grinned now, suddenly merry. He crossed over to a computer console and tapped a few keys. Suddenly, behind me on the blue screen, was a view of the parking lot. "See, Meg," he said. "You're a star."

The view was remarkably similar to that seen through the nightscope, but in hues of varying shades of black and red. Infrared, I thought, then stiffened as I saw myself approach the treeline, glowing brilliantly on the screen.

"Our intrepid heroine recons the site," Tittaglia said. "Who do you see playing you, Meg? Sandra Bullock? Gwyneth Paltrow? Helen Hunt?"

My image on the screen crouched, waited, then:

"Said heroine makes a dash for the building, carefully keeping to the shadows." I ran across the parking lot, looking ridiculous.

"Little did she know that the diabolical director of 24/7 Communications had his security system installed with infrared and motion sensor viewing and alarm systems."

Then I was out of sight on the screen. There was a sudden cut and pan, then there I was looking through the windows.

"We don't have time for this shit," Catalano said. "How do you want to do these guys? Why don't we just take them out and blow them away, get on with our lives."

Irritation flashing across the perfect oval of his face, Tittaglia said, "Oh, that would be good. How many people do you think are looking for her?" He pointed at Lisa, who I now realized had bruises on one side of her face, as if she had been hit repeatedly. "And you think that Papa Walker doesn't know they're checking into things? And the cops? They've got to *disappear*, not end up dead somewhere."

"What then?"

"Shoot them, then we'll use the chain saw to dismember the bodies, put the parts in a bunch of trash bags and dump them all over the city."

"Fuck," Catalano said. "You know how much work that is?"

"Well we're not going to leave them on somebody's front lawn! We're not going to put them in a car and blow up the fucking car, but not blow up the intended target, you moron!"

"Hey! Fuck you!"

"Yeah, well fuck you right back! So far you're 0 and 3, buddy. Malloy's alive, Chen's alive and Jones is alive. You'd fuck up a wet dream. We're doing this one my way! Did you bring the chain saw and the tarp?"

Catalano looked ready to jump out of his skin. His eyes were like staring into the empty black barrels of a shotgun. "It's back at my goddamned house! I went straight from the house when the alarm went off, straight to the Studio and found this guy here!" He pointed at Jack.

"And you missed her, I'll bet." Tittaglia pointed his gun at me. "And the tarp and garbage bags."

"The tarp's at home. I don't got any garbage bags. I'm out. They're on my shopping list."

"*Do I have to do everything?!*" Tittaglia screamed.

"Let's just do them here," Catalano said, raising the shotgun. "Then I'll get the saw and bags and shit, come back and we'll take care of the bodies."

"We're not having blood and guts blown all over the floor here. I don't want to clean it up. Eventually the cops are going to come talk to us. No way. We need the tarp."

"You don't have any of that—"

"No." Tittaglia thought for a minute. "Okay," he said. "Here's the plan. We're going to lock these three in one of the inner offices. I'll run out and get the garbage bags, you go back to your house and get the chain saw and the tarp. Come back here and we'll do it."

Catalano looked uneasy, dark eyes darting around the room. "That's your idea? You call that a fucking idea?"

"Yeah, that's my idea. Go. Now."

"Not till we get them locked away. I want to see this office you're talking about. This guy here's tricky." He pointed at Jack. "Picked the lock on the Studio, man. I found the picks. And a night scope."

"Well, you've already searched him and you can tell Lisa doesn't have anything on her, so search Meg."

Lisa's eyes widened at the sound of her name. She was wearing an Oakland University T-shirt and a pair of white nylon panties, nothing else. Catalano walked over to me. "Stand up," he said.

I looked up at him. "Fuck you," I said.

His hand lashed out, catching me on the right side of my face, knocking me into Jack, whose hands were still cuffed behind his back. He almost fell over from the impact, but shouldered me back to a sitting position. "Cooperate," he said softly.

I reluctantly stood up, thinking of the handcuff key in my pocket.

"Turn around," Catalano said, handing his shotgun to Tittaglia.

I turned around, found myself facing the blue screen now showing me walking toward a camera, hands laced behind my neck.

Catalano reached around me and began a slow frisk, starting with my shoulders and slowly running them over my breasts and down my stomach. I wanted to scream, his hands like snakes on my body. He reached my hips and began a slow crawl inward, very near the pocket with the little handcuff key.

"Enjoying yourself, dirtbag?" I said and snapped my head back so it connected with his chin. There was a hard *crack!* Catalano shouted in rage and lashed out. His fist caught my shoulder and I staggered. He came around swinging, caught me on my upper arm, which went numb. Another swing caught me squarely on the side of my head. It knocked me off my feet. The entire world became the 4th of July, pain exploded in my head. I covered my head, curled into a ball on the stage, hoping it would end soon, hoping ...

"Ah, cut the shit," Tittaglia said. "Come on, let's get going or it'll be daylight. Let's get this taken care of. Come on, Meg. On your feet. All three of you. Let's go."

I wasn't sure I'd be able to stand, and when I did the room seemed to waver. Did that punch do permanent damage? My entire head throbbed where he had hit me. Good, I thought. Irony. Worried about brain damage when they intended to dismember me with a chainsaw.

But the key was still in my pocket.

At gunpoint they made us leave the studio, turn right down the main hallway, then stop at a doorway on the left. Tittaglia told Lisa to open it. Meekly, she did. It was a small storage room, long and narrow with metal shelves stacked with computer disks, printer paper and other office supplies. Catalano satisfied himself that it would be secure, then we walked inside and the door was closed and locked behind us.

We waited until we could no longer hear them talking. Jack said, "You okay? That was a hell of a hit."

"I think I'll get over it. How about you?"

"I don't think we've got a lot of time. It only took him five minutes to get here from the Studio. Before you showed up they said he lives a couple of blocks from the Tomcat. I think Tittaglia's in one of the condos a block or two away."

I reached into my pocket and hauled out the handcuff key. "I hope this works, Jack, or that slam upside the head was a total waste."

His eyes sparkled. "I think I love you."

"Save it for later. Turn around."

The handcuff key slid into the keyhole, turned, and Jack's hands were free. First thing he did was check the door to make sure it was solidly locked. He examined the keyhole and shook his head, glancing around the room.

"Anything you see you could pick the lock with?" I asked.

"In the movies they pick locks with damned near anything—bobby pins, toothpicks, paperclips, eyeglass stems. Sorry, in my case it's lock picks, a jimmy or nothing."

He surveyed the room. His eyes narrowed. Pressing his ear to the door, he listened.

"Hear anything?"

"No."

He climbed onto one of the shelves and cautiously pushed up on one of the acoustical tiles in the dropped ceiling. It lifted up and he slid it aside, climbing further and peering overhead. A moment later he was down. He looked at Lisa. "You okay?"

Her voice a whisper, she said, "They're going to kill us."

"They're going to try," he said. "But we won't be here." He looked at her bare feet. "This is going to be really hard on you. We've got to climb up there and sort of edge along on the metal rails that support these tiles. They're kind of flimsy and they're metal. They're bolted into the ceiling and walls. They should support our weight if we stay spread out. But it's gonna cut into your legs and feet. You're going to have to do it. Ready?"

"I'll go first," I said. "You help her up, then follow."

"Works for me."

I climbed up, swaying slightly as a wave of dizziness washed over me. I took a deep breath, climbed to the top of the shelf and angled my upper body through the opening in the ceiling. There was a space of about three feet between the upper ceiling, of concrete and insulation, and the acoustical tiles. It was dark, the only light seeping from the fluorescents up through cracks between tiles. It was rich with dust, mildew and something that smelled faintly electrical. I squirmed onto the supports, which vibrated beneath the weight.

Which direction to go?

Once my eyes adjusted, I could see that there were wires—electrical and fiber optic—running everywhere, and the basic plumbing, PVC and copper and galvanized pipes. Most of the walls didn't extend above the tiles except for the weight-bearing walls, which typically ran north and south in this building. Those ran all the way to the ceiling, and as far as I could tell there wouldn't be any way around them. It didn't look like we could just drop into the hallway and run. We were going to have to zigzag around support walls to find a room with an open door or a window.

I moved a couple feet away, the metal supports biting into my knees. I reached, grabbed a pipe and held on, then stretched out to help Lisa climb up while Jack pushed her from below. She balanced next to me on her hands and knees, biting her lips, her eyes wide.

"Let's get out of here, okay? We're going to be fine."

She nodded and didn't say anything. I moved further away like a spider, moving a hand, then a foot, then another hand, then another foot, picking my way across the squares of metal bracing.

When I was about eight feet away, I pointed for the direction I thought Lisa should go. Following my lead, she spidered her way in that direction. Jack popped up into the hole, crouching like a frog on the supports. He looked around, said, "Is that an I-beam over that way?"

I looked.

"Yes."

"Let's go," he said. "Once you two get over there I'll close the hatch. We're going to lose most of our light, though."

I went first, tottering for a moment, scrabbling for a hold. I caught onto a hot water pipe, burning my hands, and I let go instantly, pinwheeling. Lisa, behind me, caught my arm and gave me a little push.

"Thanks," I said.

"You're welcome."

I made it to the I-beam. We would be able to walk crouched over on the I-beam all the way to an outer wall. With any luck the room on either side of the I-beam would have a window—or even better, an emergency exit—that we could make our escape through.

"Set?" Jack said, his voice as harsh as mica on chalkboard.

"You?" I asked Lisa.

"Yes."

In the light flowing up from the hatch I could see that her knees and feet were bleeding. Her face was pale, strained, determined.

"All set, Jack."

"Lights out," he said, and replaced the acoustical tile.

I realized with a sinking feeling that this was going to be an entirely different ballgame. If moving like a daddy longlegs with Parkinson's Disease had seemed slow and awkward before, it was nothing compared to what we would be doing for the next fifty or sixty feet along the I-beam in the dark, hands groping for purchase on whatever we could find.

We could feel vibration moving along the steel structure as Jack picked his way over to us. It seemed to take forever. My eyes grew accustomed to the little bit of light filtering upwards and I was able to see forms better, but still, this was going to be hairy.

Jack said, "About two feet to your left, running parallel to the beam is a pipe. I think it's a natural gas line. If you start to lose your balance, grab for it. There's some PVC up here, too, but I'm not so sure how strong that would be. Ready?"

"Ready," I said, and began what felt like a tightrope walk in the dark. I was able to shuffle along in an awkward half crouch, one knee down on the I-beam, the other foot directly ahead of it, foot flat on the I-beam, back curled over almost pressed to the rough concrete of the roof, hands raised to the ceiling for balance. Inch by inch by inch by inch, shuffling forward. I felt sympathy for Lisa who was doing this in bare feet and no pants. My knees were already sore through my jeans, my back and neck cramping as we moved.

We were about a dozen feet from the storage room when I heard a noise.

It was someone entering the building. I strained my eyes to see ahead, to gauge how close we were to the wall, wondering if it would be worthwhile to just drop where we were and make a run for it.

The sound of footsteps below us. Then another sound. The door opening again.

They were both back!

"You ready?" Tittaglia said.

"Let the good times roll," Catalano said. "Maybe we should tape this. Bet I could find a buyer. Snuff films sell for big bucks, fifty G's and up."

"No evidence. We're not leaving any goddamned evidence. Even the chain saw's going in the river."

"Hey, this thing's expensive."

"I don't give a—"

They discovered we weren't there. I shifted out of my crouch and began a much faster, far more dangerous bent-over shuffle. Lisa and Jack followed suit.

"Where the fuck are they?"

"The goddamned door was locked. Where they ..."

Shit, I thought, trying to move faster. I heard a cry behind me and turned to see Lisa tottering, arms pinwheeling. I was too far away.

Jack hissed, "Keep going," and in a fluid movement that would have made the Wallendas proud, covered a half-dozen feet in a second, caught

Lisa around the waist and began to whisper in her ear. When I glanced back, I saw that Jack had moved around her and she was behind him, clinging to his belt as he moved.

Then the space was flooded with light as an acoustical tile was raised. "They're up here!" Catalano yelled.

There was a harsh roar and the place seemed filled with sparks and smoke and flying objects.

"Are you out of your mind?" Tittaglia screamed. "We'll get them from below!"

And the shaft of light disappeared. Suddenly, moving like a whirlwind, Jack was at my back, hand pressed against my spine. "Go, go, go, go, go," he said. "Move it!"

I moved it, breath shallow and ragged, pulse pounding, cramps racing like electrical shocks through my muscles. I moved it.

Below us we could hear them slamming into individual offices, a head poking up, then disappearing, shafts of light blasting into our crawlspace.

Then Jack kicked down and an acoustical tile shattered beneath him. Below us we could see a dark office—one with a window. Grabbing my wrists, Jack abruptly lowered me down. "Lock the door," he hissed, then turned to Lisa.

I scrambled to the door, punched the lock, then flicked on the light, blinking in the sudden harsh illumination. We had a window. Then they were at the door, pounding on it. Lisa was beside me now.

Jack peered down. "Where's the car?"

"McDonald's. Come on."

"Go," he said. "If I'm not there in five minutes, I'll see you later." He disappeared from view.

I looked up, frozen. "Jack?"

He was gone.

"Help me!" Lisa was struggling with a four-drawer filing cabinet. On the other side of the door we could hear someone trying to get the key in the lock. I threw all my weight against the filing cabinet, levering it over sideways. It crashed to the floor in front of the door, making enough noise to be heard in Toledo. Together Lisa and I shoved it tight against the door.

Lisa, frantic, picked up one of the office chairs, groaning under its weight, and slammed it against the window, which shattered out onto the parking lot.

I jumped up on the desk to look for Jack. He was crouched on the wire supports a couple feet away, struggling with something, I wasn't sure what.

"Come on, Jack," I said.

"Go, goddamnit! Go!"

"Jack!"

"Go!"

Shotgun fire blasted into the upper space.

"Go!" Jack yelled. "There's not much time!"

He had the gas pipe in his hands, wrapped around a connector bolt, twisting with all his strength.

I dropped back into the office just as the cheap blueboard wall disintegrated inward in a rain of buckshot, wood, fiberglass and dust.

Lisa was on the ledge, ready to leap. I gave her a shove and followed headfirst, shards of glass snagging at my arms.

We landed hard on the pavement, Lisa whimpering, blood running down her legs, staggering away from the building. Then I was next to her, her elbow caught in a pincer grip, running as fast as I could, running ...

The explosion caught us when we were almost out of the parking lot, fifty yards away. A jagged, ripping crunch that reverberated off the surrounding buildings and lit up the night with a golden fireball.

The force of it knocked Lisa and me to the ground as if someone had taken a giant paddle to our behinds. Debris, mostly smaller chunks of concrete and wood, fell down around us, the bigger chunks landing closer to the building.

I peered back to see half the building in pieces, the rest on fire.

"Jack," I whispered. "Jack."

32

I pulled Lisa to her feet and we set off toward the Corvette. "Where's Jack?" she asked me. It was the only thing she asked me, and I didn't answer. I didn't look back. I just got to my feet and started to move. Away.

By the time we made it to the car we could hear sirens, dozens of them, and it was obvious that traffic had increased in the surrounding neighborhoods. I got Lisa into the passenger seat, found the keys under the driver's seat, then scrounged in Jack's duffel bag. I found a pair of black sweatpants and a couple T-shirts. She used one of the T-shirts to wipe at the blood, then, shivering, pulled on the sweatpants, which were way too big for her.

I fired up the engine, glanced at my watch. The Timex was dead, dead, dead.

We waited for what must have been ten minutes.

"I'm sorry," Lisa whispered.

Without replying I slammed the car into first and got onto the Boulevard, making an almost immediate right onto the Lodge Service Drive and caught the first exit onto the northbound Lodge. Above I could see a billowing cloud of black smoke lit by pulsating red, blue and white lights, like neon lightning. There was a sensation of activity, voices, and, in the distance, a helicopter.

I drove north, not too fast. I did not need to get caught by the police for speeding. I felt numb. My ears rang, everything muffled, like having cotton stuffed in your ears. My head still hurt from where Joe Catalano had punched me. My arms and my sides were cut, my knees and ankles scraped raw.

And there was a raw ache inside me, an emotional wound.

I slammed on the brakes, slewing to the shoulder of the road, staring in the rearview mirror.

"What? *What?*" Lisa said. "Why'd you stop? Let's get *out* of here!"

I dropped the shift into neutral, set the brake and climbed out of the car, peering through the pre-dawn darkness. Had I ... ?

A man appeared, walking down the shoulder of the Lodge Freeway. Long legged in jeans, white shoes and a red sweatshirt.

I ran forward and threw my arms around him. "You bastard," I said.

He grinned. "Glad to see you, too."

His face was red as if sunburned, his clothes mildy charred and dirty. The knees of the jeans were torn, his shoes blackened from grime. He held me back at arm's length. "You mind driving?" he said. "I'm a little shaky right now."

I grabbed him again, tight, then we walked back to the Corvette.

Jack hadn't thought he'd be able to unscrew the pipe connector. It was stuck on hard, corroded into one solid piece. Then, just when he thought he'd better bail out, it moved.

"Then they fired a load through the wall," he said. "Time was about up."

He spun the connector, yanking hard to pull the pipe ends away from each other. A piece of tile rose and Catalano peeked through. Jack grabbed onto the pipe end with both hands and jumped. The pipe bent away from the connection under his weight, the smell of natural gas filling the space.

Dangling, Jack arched over, dropped through an acoustic tile and slammed onto the desk in the office Lisa and I had just vacated. Rocketing through the window, he landed on his feet in the parking lot.

"I saw you halfway across the lot," he said.

But he took a hard right instead, running toward the front of 24/7, sprinting as fast as he could toward the Lodge Service Drive.

Catalano fired the shotgun from the crawlspace just as Jack was landing in the parking lot. Jack made it to the front of the building when the gunfire ignited the natural gas.

"Two steps into the street, then bang!" he said. "I was airborne."

As I'd seen, the explosion was directed north and upward. Jack had been on the very northwest corner of the building heading west. He found himself in the middle of the street with burning wood and chunks of concrete raining down around him. He jumped to his feet, scaled the chain-link fence dividing the Service Drive from the concrete slope that led downward to the freeway.

And down he went.

Lisa said, "Are they both dead, do you think?"

She and Jack were sharing the passenger seat. It looked cramped and uncomfortable, and I would have traded Lisa for it in an eyeblink.

"Does that bother you?" Jack asked.

Lisa closed her eyes then opened them, looking right at me. "He raped me," she said. "I called Barb after we talked at Mr. B's and told her you'd come by. She told Joe—she was in love with him, I think. Or thought she was." She visibly shuddered. "When she told him, he killed her then planted the bomb in your car. That's what he told me ... later."

"How'd he get you?" Jack asked.

"I was stupid. I'm sorry," she said, voice small and soft, but not breaking. Flatline.

I drove the Corvette onto Rochester Road and rolled into the empty parking lot of a Century 21 office. It was Saturday morning. Dawn was less than an hour away. "Go on," I said, my tone rough.

Jack raised an eyebrow at me, but didn't comment. Yes, I thought, Lisa had been a victim. And yes, she had been stupid. Her stupidity had cost Barbara's life and very nearly my own. The well of my sympathy was only so deep.

"He called me back, saying he wanted to talk to me about you. I drove to his studio after I got out of work. He was being charming. He really could be, you know. He brought me to that house and left me there. He ..." She shook her head and didn't look upset, she looked embarrassed.

"All of it," I said.

"He offered me booze and coke and, uh, grass. Speed if I wanted it. Ecstasy. He was fully stocked. I spent the rest of the night and most of the next day buzzed."

"That's when I called you," I said.

"Yeah."

Catalano had been out shooting Stephanie and firebombing WebSpinners. She hadn't known about Barbara.

"Did you wonder where Barbara was?" My words were clipped. She had sat in that house, stoned on her ass, her friend already murdered. She blithely waited to become the next victim.

Her lower lip trembled. "I didn't think Barb was in any trouble. Joe ... Joe Catalano said he wanted to keep me safe and out of sight while he and Barbara got things straightened out with her dad."

"But you didn't actually talk to Barb."

"No. She was ... she was already dead." Her voice was as bleak as the dark side of the moon.

"How long had Barbara and Catalano been together?" Jack asked.

"Couple months. Joey told Barb his dad was in movies to impress her. That's why Barb tracked him down and introduced herself. She wanted to act in one of his porn movies, but he wouldn't let her until she was eighteen. Said it was too risky. She was pissed. So she tried to get a job with that guy, Larry Clinton. But Clinton told her to talk to Tittaglia, who it turns out was Joe C's cousin. Barbara figured it was, like, a sign from God. Everything led to Joe. It all came back to Joe Catalano."

And Tittaglia figured out a way to use her to steal money from the church's website. The New Mafia. Cyber crime and credit card fraud. And Tittaglia fed her back to Catalano.

And Linda Mason, Joey Mason's mom, probably nagged Joey to tell her why I was there, and where he thought Barbara was. He'd told her she was with Joe Catalano and Linda Mason had bugged out. Did she call the FBI? Was that why they had gone to her house? Or had she gone to them to hide her? If that was the case it would make a lot of sense. It would explain why they saw someone in her house and went in without warning, expecting Catalano and maybe Tittaglia, not Jack and me.

With prompting, Jack and I got Lisa to talk about what happened when Joe Catalano returned to Tomcat Studios. When he discovered the cell phone, and found that she had made a couple calls, he flew into a rage, hit her, handcuffed her to the bed, and raped her.

For two days.

We tried to get our minds around it all. Finally I said, "The cops are going to want to talk to us eventually. What we say, though—"

"I'm not talking to the cops about this," Lisa said vehemently. "No way. They're dead. I'm done. Over. All I want is to forget about it all."

She would need counseling, I thought. Eventually she would have to talk to someone. But the cops? Tittaglia and Catalano were dead. Jack had seen that those particular loose ends were taken care of. As far as I was concerned, the money stolen from the church was lost forever, resting and gaining interest in some numbered account in a Panamanian or Bahamian or Grand Cayman bank. The money might be tracked, but stealing it back was beyond my hacking skills or inclination. If Reverend Walker wanted to pursue it, he'd have to be much more forthcoming with the Feds than I thought he was likely to be. Or more than willing to risk possible imprisonment for robbing a foreign bank.

Let it go. Move on.

We dropped Lisa off at her dorm. Her roommate met us at the car with a pair of jeans and shoes. While Lisa got dressed in the car I took Cindy Simmons aside and urged her to convince Lisa to seek counseling.

Without a backward glance, Lisa disappeared into the dorm.

Jack drove to Reverend Walker's house and we laid out the entire story, every last detail, to Reverend Walker and Nancy Phillips.

"But what about Lieutenant Rosenbaum and the FBI and the Secret Service?" he asked.

I looked at Jack, who said, "We'll just deny everything. We were holed up in Meg's parents' house waiting for things to blow over."

"But ..."

"It's over," I said, reaching out to take his hand in mine. "I'm so sorry about Barbara. She was a very troubled young woman."

Sister Nancy put her arm around the Reverend's shoulders and thanked us for everything.

It was over.

<Epilogue>

The other shoe dropped. It was only a matter of time. Jack and I had discussed it, made plans, constructed scenarios, but it didn't work. We weren't prepared. Tuesday afternoon, two o'clock, Jack and I were hanging around the house doing nothing. Jack hadn't left and I hadn't asked why. We circled each other in nervous patterns like vultures deciding whether their dinner was dead yet. I think he was waiting for something, a resolution neither of us felt. Closure.

Jack was listening to a Muddy Waters disk on the stereo and I was putting together notes for my meeting at Solar MicroSystems in October, when the doorbell rang. Jack glanced at me and I shrugged. Together we went downstairs to see who it was. Was it Rosenbaum paying yet another visit?

Agent Bradley Meyer with the FBI, and Agent Michael X. Zilway with the Secret Service shouldered their way in. Meyer was taller, older and blonder. His complexion was ruddy, deep lines cut into his face near his eyes and along the lines of his jaw. His eyes were a pale blue, like washed-out denim. Zilway was younger, maybe in his mid-thirties, and dark. His brown hair cut short, almost military. His eyes were the color of fresh mud, almost black, his skin smooth and tanned, like he spent a lot of time at a spa. Both men wore navy blue three-piece suits, Meyer's with a faint chalk pinstripe. Both wore tan trench coats that hung open. Both held up their IDs and said they wanted to talk to us.

"You got a warrant?" Jack asked.

Meyer pushed past Jack, his blue eyes flinty and cold. "Shut up, Bear. I really don't have patience for you." They shut the door and crossed to the piano. Meyer placed his briefcase on the closed top of the Steinway and opened it to reveal a laptop, which he opened and booted up.

"We're here to discuss your little adventures the last couple of days," Zilway said.

"We don't know who blew up my car," I said.

"Yes," he said. "You do. You know damned well that it was Joe Catalano who bombed your Hummer and you know why."

"We were at her parents' house the last few days, holing up," Jack said.

Zilway smiled. "Bullshit. You've been playing amateur detective, getting into a lot of trouble and generally doing what you do best, Bear."

Neither man seemed angry. In fact, they seemed rather smug. Meyer removed a disk from his pocket, opened the jewel case and slipped it into the laptop. A second later the screen showed images from 24/7 Communication's security cameras. In eerie reds and blacks we watched a Ford Mustang pull into the parking lot. Joe Catalano climbed out, a gun in his hand, and pulled Lisa from the driver's seat, pushing her in front of him. She stumbled, groggy, but stayed on her feet. Catalano opened the trunk and reached in to pull Jack out. Catalano forced them toward the entrance of 24/7. There was a cut, then I got to see myself skulking across the parking lot.

"You need more?" Meyer said. "You want to see you and this woman, who we haven't actually IDed yet, running across the lot just moments before the whole thing goes ka-bam?"

"No thanks," I said, almost relieved I didn't have to lie any more. "Nice data recovery. I would have thought the fire got it."

"Coming from you, that's a compliment. The Bureau does, in fact, have good forensic people."

I hesitated. "I want to call my lawyer—"

Zilway waved me to calm down. "Let's sit, shall we? We've got some questions to ask, lots of them, and we want honest answers."

"Or?" Jack said.

Meyer turned a stony eye toward him. "Or we turn it over to prosecutors and let them take a whack at the two of you."

"And if we cooperate?"

"We'll see."

I looked at Jack. He shrugged. "Your call."

"If you guys answer some questions we'll tell you everything," I said.

A nod passed between the two agents. Zilway said, "We'll answer a few."

I said, "Why were you staking out Danny Chen's house?"

"We weren't," Zilway said. "We didn't pick you up at Chen's house, we picked you up at your house. We had WebSpinners' offices tapped."

"*What?*"

"Ms. Jones's phones and office were bugged. Chen kept insisting she didn't know anything about the fraud, but we went ahead and bugged her office. So we got you and the Reverend's conversation. Very screwy. We ran a background check on you and were on our way to talk to you, but when we got here you were leaving with Bear and the cops were all over your place. We followed. That was just dumb luck."

I glanced at Jack, who shrugged ruefully. He hadn't caught the tail until after we left Danny's house.

Jack said, "Why were you at the Masons' house?"

Both men looked unhappy. "After we lost you," Meyer said, "we spent some time looking, then decided to check out the Masons' house again in case Catalano was there. God knows he was going after everybody else."

"Where were the Masons?" I asked.

"Hiding out. We've talked to Mrs. Mason over the years, but she refuses to help us. That night, after her son told her what you were there for, she called us, said Catalano was probably involved with Ms. Walker's disappearance and she was taking off. Mrs. Mason has good survival instincts. Now," he said, leaning against my piano. "I think it's time you answer our questions."

We did. We told the two Feds almost everything we knew. They asked questions, then more questions, then asked them all over again. If they were wired or had a recording device on them, I never found out. Finally, by almost 5:00, we wrapped it up. We told them everything but Lisa Dunn's name. They didn't need to know. They asked us over and over, even threatened us, but we didn't tell them. An innocent bystander, we said, which was bullshit. She wasn't innocent, but she was definitely a victim and being mauled by the Feds wouldn't help her any.

Meyer shut down the laptop and closed the case. "Thank you."

"What now?"

He grinned. "There are times when the Federal government could make use of someone with your and Mr. Bear's talents. We'll get in touch with you."

"Talents," I said.

"You're very resourceful. I've read your file, Ms. Malloy."

Jack raised his eyebrows. To Jack I said, "I did government work, Internet infrastructure, that sort of thing. My security clearance is—"

"High enough," Zilway said.

"What if we don't want to work for you?" Jack said.

Meyer pulled a jewel case out of his trenchcoat pocket and held it up, waggling it so it flashed in the light. "You will anyway."

"I'm not a snitch," Jack said.

"You're whatever we want you to be, Mr. Bear. Don't worry, we'll only call on you when we need you. But do count on it. We'll be in touch."

"I'm a very expensive consultant," I said.

Meyer shook his head and flashed the jewel case again. "No you aren't, Ms. Malloy. No you aren't." And then they were gone, back in their black Ford Taurus and disappearing around the bend in Heights Road.

I stared at Jack. He rubbed his jaw. "Well shit," he said.

"Yeah," I said.

He looked at me. "Want to go running?"

I closed my eyes. "Life goes on?"

"I guess. Till our pals give us a call."

My eyes opened. "You think they will?"

Jack nodded. "Yeah. They probably will."

Jack and I went for a long run, pounding the pavement in silence. I took a shower and then waited for Jack to take one. When he got out, he began packing things away in his duffel bag.

He said, "Time to go. It's all over now."

"Thanks," I said. "I don't ... I don't want you to go."

"Job's done," he said, voice casual. Too casual. There was always a strain of emotion between us now. Chemistry, real chemistry. And Mattie, my best friend and cousin. She was between us, too.

He looked up at me now and our eyes met. We had not slept together. I wanted to. I wanted him to stay. I wanted to go back to his boat, the *Canowakeed*, and take a long trip on Lake Michigan and get to know him.

But he was going back home and I was staying here.

"You've got my number," he said.

"And you've got mine."

He nodded. "If you get in trouble again, call me."

"I will," I said. "But answer a question for me. Truthfully."

He sighed and rolled his eyes. "Just one."

I steeled myself. "You came and went through all this, almost got killed ... Lost both your guns, didn't you? They didn't recover them?"

"Weren't registered."

"Oh. Anyway, you said it's what you do, help people, and I figure that's got to do with your brother and your friend dying, but—"

"Is there a question in here, Malloy?"

"Shut up, Jack," I said. "I'm being serious."

"Ask your question then."

"You helped me out because of Mattie, right? You did all this, even when you could have gone back home and minded your own business ... you did it for Mattie."

He stepped close to me, inches apart. I could smell the soap he used, and an individual scent that was just Jack. His voice low, he said, "Yes. I did it for Mattie." And then he pulled me to him. Our lips met and I fell against him, kissing him back in a swirl of sensations that I had not felt in a very long time.

When he broke the kiss, he smiled and said, "But next time—I come back for you."

He turned, picked up the duffel bag and crossed the street to the Corvette. He revved the engine and waved as he drove away.

"Next time, Jack," I said. "Next time."

\<The End>

Mark Terry works in the field of genetics and is a freelance writer and editor. The author of one previous book, *Catfish Guru*, he has also published several short stories. His nonfiction regularly appears in trade journals and magazines such as Mystery Scene Magazine and ADVANCE for Medical Laboratory Professionals. He is currently the mystery reviewer for The Oakland Press. He lives with his wife and sons in Michigan.

Visit his website at www.mark-terry.com.

High Country Publishers, Ltd

invites you to our website to learn more about Mark Terry and his work. Read reviews and readers' comments. Link to Mark Terry's site and find out about his other works and upcoming Meg Malloy mysteries. Learn what's new at High Country Publishers. Link to other authors' sites, preview upcoming titles, and find out how you can order books at a discount for your group or organization.

www.highcountrypublishers.com

High Country Publishers, Ltd

Boone, NC
2004